CARLISLE DIVIDED

Stories of Justus and Mercy Part 1

RE Russell

D1248463

ISBN: 978-1-953114-65-5
LCCN: 2022904346

Published by EA Books Publishing, a division of
Living Parables of Central Florida, Inc. a 501c3

EABooksPublishing.com

To Janie

PROLOGUE

"Go to Carlisle." I heard the Master say. "Your mission is there."

He didn't always speak audibly. Most of the time I just heard his quiet voice when I calmed my mind and meditated on his word. These words came with a vision I found confusing.

I saw a dark-haired lady, three partial men all of a different color, a well-dressed black man, strangers in the land, blood, a river, rain and hills. At the end a verse repeated like a welcome song, 'I know the plans I have for you ... plans to give you a hope and a future.'

He often showed me visions before a new mission, especially one so far away. They became signs of affirmation as the mission un-folded before me. Parts of this one disturbed me.

What did he see in us that he keeps us around. I've seen such cru-elty. I've been a part of it. Why does he keep me around? But we are also capable of such loving kindness just like he is.

After leaving the mission in Ecuador in the hands of the local lead-ers I'd trained for a few years, the Master was sending me far away. Would I ever return here? I hoped to. I enjoyed these people and the simple way of life. He seldom sent me back to the same place. When I did return to a mission after many years, they were never the same. Just like children grow up and move away so to do these churches change into something new by the power of the spirit and the opposi-tion of the enemy.

I traveled alone in a group of other migrants. The money he pro-vided paid the way into America using people smugglers better known as coyotes. The journey took weeks.

Now I stand on Interstate Ten in New Mexico. I'll continue the journey east from here. The coyotes took most of my money. What was left I gave to those migrants with small children.

I have good shoes, a nice hat and work gloves. That seemed like enough for me. I had all of this and America too.

I'll pay my way to Carlisle picking the crops that come in this time of year all along the route. Good thing about picking fruits and vegetables, there was always something to eat.

The migrants in the farm camps are nervous around new people. I'll keep moving toward the goal. I hope they'll let me cook for them. It is easier work for me than the fields and I can make the food taste wonderful. Plus, the food never seems to run out when he blesses me along the way.

I must go to Carlisle. My mission is there.

CHAPTER 1

"This is Jacqueline Hyatt WWNS News, on the scene at Hart Park. Demonstrators have been gathering all afternoon. They're here to protest the shooting of Lamont Wilson, by white Carlisle police officer, Henry Byrum. People are increasingly agitated after speeches by Jalen Timmins and Tonya Harrison of the local chapter of Black Lives Matter. People are frustrated over the shooting of an unarmed man by police and the ensuing video that hit social media.

"Earlier today I spoke with Sheriff Roman Ward for clarity on what happened and what the department is going to do about it." A video feed began of the interview with Sheriff Ward.

Jackie lowered the mic and went to the van.

I wish I had more comfortable shoes.

On the monitor, she watched Sheriff Ward, "Three of our officers responded to a domestic disturbance at the Knollwood Apartments on 14th street at 10:43 PM. When we arrived, there appeared to be a dispute between Lamont Drew Wilson and a woman we later determined to be his wife, Demaria Wilson. They were both in the front parking area of the apartments. Mr. Wilson was yelling obscenities at his wife when we arrived. We tried to calm the situation, but you know domestic disputes can be very dangerous for anyone on the scene. Mr. Wilson had a long criminal record. His prior offenses included drug charges, spousal abuse, and robbery.

"He refused to listen to the officers, who instructed him to be silent and lay face down on the ground. In his statement this morning, you know that Officer Byrum believed he saw a gun. He did what any reasonable person would in those circumstances. He ordered Mr. Wilson to drop the weapon and lie face down on the ground. Procedure dictates that we carefully try to disarm an enraged suspect with a weapon in a domestic dispute.

"Mr. Wilson refused and began yelling at the officers who fanned out around him. He said he didn't have a weapon and he was only having a fight with his wife. He told us to go away. He didn't raise his hands nor show us what he had in them.

"After repeated warnings to get on the ground, one of my officers moved in-between Mr. Wilson and Mrs. Wilson, to protect her. For an unknown reason, she assaulted the officer and began shouting. The officer turned to protect himself, Mr. Wilson charged at the officer. At that point, Officer Byrum fired twice in the direction of Mr. Wilson. One shot hit him in the upper leg, the other in the torso." He paused and looked down, then he continued.

"Immediately officers began life saving procedures on Mr. Wilson. He was pronounced dead at the scene. We detained Mrs. Wilson due to the assault on the officer. She has since been released. That officer sustained minor injuries. No gun was found on or near the suspect. The officer who shot Mr. Wilson was white.

"This is a tragic development and we will do all we can to be certain that justice gets served. In the meantime, I urge the citizens of Carlisle to please keep calm and don't compound this situation. The Wilson's are grieving a loss, we encourage the community to support them in their grief. We will continue our internal investigation into the death of Mr. Wilson."

Jackie heard her voice off camera ask, "Will you release the body camera footage to complement the amateur footage shot by the neighbor already out there on social media?"

"We're reviewing the footage for the investigation. Due to its graphic content, we do not plan to release the body camera video."

"Will the department reconsider this position?"

"Not at this time."

"What happened to Officer Byrum?"

"He is on administrative duty until the investigation concludes. That's SOP for any shooting involving an officer."

As she was watching the feed, her phone rang. Caller ID said Mitch Baxter, her producer.

She signaled her cameraman Leonard, and they were back on the air in a moment.

"Jacqueline Hyatt, WWNS News back live reporting from Hart Park. I've just received word that all downtown businesses are encouraged to close early today, to avoid any confrontation with the growing demonstration. All businesses in the main business district between River Street, near Broker's Wharf and Commonwealth Avenue, from First to Twelfth Street are affected. The Mayor and the police appreciate your cooperation. For your own safety, please vacate the downtown business district by 4 PM this afternoon which is only about an hour from now."

The demonstrators seemed to enjoy having the media so close, and some began yelling obscenities at the camera, along with the requisite hand gestures. Jackie got nervous and decided to relocate further from the action, at a different vantage point. They could still zoom in on the speakers if needed. She felt a safer distance would keep her from becoming a rescue mission for the CPD.

We're here to report the news not become the news.

She agreed with the Mayor and Police that this crowd would grow as the day progressed. After they moved, she decided to stay in the van and watch things simmer.

The phone startled her as it jumped to life again.

"You should get far away from the crowd." Mitch said on the other end.

"Way ahead of you boss, but we won't get too far away. We need to be able to move as this gets interesting. It's a dynamic situation, we'll stay put where we are now. We're safe enough and you want someone here. Hey, get someone to send us some dinner . . . Chinese. Tell them to bring my walking shoes from under my desk. Don't worry about us. We'll be fine."

She stepped out and did some additional On the Scene shots and reports for teaser footage, in advance of the nightly news at six.

This story was special since it was certain to make the national news. Jackie always wanted to be sure she projected an appealing professional image but never more than when she got a national spotlight. She checked her appearance on the monitor. Her light brown hair properly parted just off center. Tucked behind her left ear. Light pink lipstick, not drawing too much attention to her mouth. *I wish my lips were fuller.* Teeth showing all the money spent with orthodontists and dental specialists. Cheekbones high, but not over emphasized by her makeup. Round, hazel eyes highlighted just the way she liked. Makeup covering the chicken pox scars on her forehead and left cheek. Her royal blue V-neck blouse highlighted by a small gold pendant necklace. All this worked well with her olive skin tone. The black slacks, though not on screen, were just the right complement. It was the high-heeled shoes that were the problem. Flats were imperative for navigating the soft ground at Hart Park. *I could run in those shoes if things get bad over here. I work out. I run. I'll be fine. Yoga body brought to you by cardio dancing and some surgery. Not as thin as I would like, but not bad for a girl in her thirties.*

Leonard noticed her. "You're stunning. No need for more primping."

"Thank you, Leonard," she said in a flirty tone and batted her eyes, half-joking. It was a brief bit of levity to relieve some stress from the situation. She smiled.

"That's the smile that keeps the ratings up," he smiled back and pointed his camera her way.

⁂ ⁂ ⁂

By the six o'clock news slot, civility deteriorated markedly. She stepped out and did her On the Scene report keeping the news van in the background for the free publicity, but also to cut down on the people performing behind her.

The rhetoric preached from the speakers was venomous against the police, against businesses, and against oppression. She could hear their frustration with the government, the police, the schools, their opportunities, and their lives. She saw signs that said Defund the Police, No Justice No Peace, and Stop Killing Our Fathers.

This may become a difficult place for a white reporter to be after a while. You've been in tougher spots, Jackie. Besides, this is why you got in the business in the first place. Keep your head, lady. It's only the Wharf, you've been here many times, and no one has come after you yet. They know me. I'm a local personality.

After the six o'clock feed, Mitch told her to pull back further since the demonstration was growing more violent.

"No sir," she said, "This is ground zero. These people won't hurt the media. We're the ones getting their message out." *I hope.*

"Leonard is a cameraman not a bouncer," Mitch responded.

As darkness set in, trashcans in Hart Park were set aflame. The crowd swelled to a few hundred. Black teens and many students of Carlisle State filled the park. She saw older activists there too. *Professors and old hippies.* The demonstrators had signs with slogans she couldn't put on air. The BLM leaders continued to take the stage, proclaiming they were fed up with black men being murdered by the police. "Something must be done!"

A runner from the station arrived with dinner and her shoes. They went inside the van again to eat. The passing demonstrators knocked into the van from time to time. They felt it rock back and forth. Leonard had a nervous grin. Jackie remained steadfast. They finished the Chinese food and she put on her flats. *They don't match the outfit, but I have to be ready to move.* "No shots of my feet please," she told Leonard.

Now that the sun was gone, the trashcans, still burning in spots, gave off an eerie glow and the shadows played like a bizarre campfire gathering. The police stayed nearby but didn't confront. The crowd began to move toward the central business district up Commonwealth. They walked by shouting slogans.

"Black Lives Matter!"

"We Want Justice for Lamont!"

"Say the name—Lamont Wilson!"

The crowd, though furious, stayed nonviolent for the moment.

"Let's go now. The bulk of the crowd has passed by." He moved to start the van and she said, "No! I mean out there. We need to see where this is going."

They trailed the crowd at a safe distance. In the streetlights, she could see the crowd stretched for several blocks. Glass broke in the distance. *Must be a storefront on Fifth Street.* People carried large sticks and rocks. They got closer and she could see the looted drug store on Commonwealth. *Going after the pharmacy.* Now they fashioned Molotov cocktails from liquor bottles. Cars were on fire. "Are you getting this, Leonard? The fury of the crowd is two blocks ahead of us. We'll be safe from here." She clicked on the mic.

"As you can see the demonstration has moved out of the park and is now moving toward city hall. I suspect they're marching on the sheriff's office. I hear a bullhorn from the police warning people to stop and disperse. Also telling them, "Looting and fires won't be tolerated." I can't see the police line from here, but I can hear them. It's hard to hear over the shouting and chanting." She passed a flaming car feeling the heat and smelling the burning tires. She heard more breaking glass and saw another car up the street, burning.

"We're moving up Commonwealth now and there are more fires. Lots of broken storefronts, the windows of the lobby in the Hart Building are broken out. Lobby furniture in the street is on fire. The police appear to be in front of the Whittaker House Hotel near Ninth Street."

Police in riot gear began beating the street with their batons in unison. The noise added both a small tremor on the ground and a distant thunder. The crowd continued to advance on their position, although they hesitated at the noise.

There was a blinding light and loud boom. "Wow! That's a flash bang. Tear gas will be next. We'll stay on air while we can. The crowd paused, but now continues to advance. I see some police in riot gear a couple of blocks ahead. Now they have fired tear gas as well. Hard to see with the fires and the tear gas. Oh no. Gunshots! Shots have been fired. I repeat shots fired. I don't know if the protestors or the police fired the shots. The advance stopped. Another firebomb thrown at the police. More shots fired. I can see the muzzle flashes from the police now. We need to get back, Leonard."

The crowd turned back toward Jackie and Leonard and began to retreat. Tear gas and flash bangs continued to detonate, more gunshots fired.

The panicked crowd moved quicker than she thought possible. All of a sudden, they were in the midst of the mob. Jackie desperately tried to keep her head. "We're going to get trampled." She and Leonard moved inside the Hart building lobby, through the broken glass. They went to a bathroom down a flight of stairs off the main lobby. She knew the building well since she had done many interviews there. *Surely the rioters won't linger here. We'll be safe in a hard to find restroom.*

Her phone rang and she quickly silenced it. In a whisper she said, "What is it Mitch?"

"You and Leonard OK? That footage was incredible. Your comments were spot on. Please stay safe. It's very bad. Our chopper shows a few on the street with faces covered. There must be at least a half dozen killed. Not sure if it's the cops or the rioters or both. This is bad Jackie, but you're one crazy lady. Great report. Where are you?"

"We're in the Hart Building, in the men's room on the floor just below the lobby level. We'll wait until you give us an all clear sign."

"Stay put until I say it's OK. I'll let the cops know where you are."

After what seemed like an hour, a knock came at the door. "Jacqueline Hyatt, this is the Carlisle Police. Are you in there?"

She opened the door slowly and raised her hands with palms open. "It's just me and my cameraman. May we survey the scene?" She looked at his nametag. "Officer Lemoyne."

"No ma'am. I'm here to retrieve you and get you to safety. This is still a very volatile situation. We need your complete cooperation."

As they exited onto the street, she saw the destruction. The chopper overhead still beat out the rhythm of the night. She could feel it in her chest, like the loud bass on a passing gangbanger's car. Fires still burned, and sirens screamed. There were people in triage and some covered bodies. She counted at least three covered corpses. Ambulances took the injured to University Hospital. Meat wagons took the dead to the morgue. Jackie's mind raced, she needed to know more. Officer Lemoyne said in a very deliberate cadence, "Ma'am, I need you to get into my vehicle now. It's not safe here."

She got in, knowing she'd pushed her luck far enough for now. Leonard didn't have to be told twice. They drove to Fourth Street and headed back to the station. The van remained at the park.

After a debrief at the station, she turned in her News at Eleven report, then went home to bed. All the adrenaline draining at last, she laid in bed and trembled. She cried for the people of Carlisle and those killed and injured tonight.

CHAPTER 2

Paul Stanley invited a group of neighbors and clients to his home up the hill in Carlisle. He loved to have dinner parties with a twist. He arranged a local wine storeowner to come and give a tasting. They invited three couples, but he enjoyed the Harts and the Reynolds the most.

Paul and his wife, Alexandra. were gracious hosts. "What a great night for a party," he said to Ally. He took in a deep breath to enjoy the floral scent of the gardens nearby. *Ally, my bride of 20 years still looks good for a woman her age. A bit of middle-age spread but still a beautiful lady.*

"Our guests will join us on the deck overlooking the pool. The weather is just right, not too hot. The sun setting in the distance and the gentle breeze. It'll be just perfect." She brushed her long blonde hair out of her face. "We'll have to be on good behavior since Pastor Rich is coming as well."

The guest sommelier this evening, Quentin Randal, the owner of a local wine shop and bar set up the tasting area near the pool. Quentin had a ruddy complexion and was balding with a bad comb over. *You can tell Quentin enjoys his wine and food pairings,* Paul thought.

The Harts and Reynolds arrived within minutes of each other. *The Pastor must be running late.*

"I think you'll enjoy tonight. Quentin brought wines from California. There's *hors d'oeuvres* to pair with the whites and the reds. He's proud of his selections." Paul said to Remy Hart. He motioned in the direction of the outdoor bar. "Cabernet and pinot noir for the red wine lovers, and Riesling and sauvignon blanc for white wine fans."

Remy Hart was the oldest of the Hart children and now helped run the department store chain his dad had founded 50 years earlier. Remy was slim, with black hair slicked back over a small bald spot. His mustache was thin and well groomed. Paul noticed such things in men since his own fading red hair was proudly still full. Remy was always dressed well and tonight was no exception. A blue striped oxford shirt with black jeans. He sported a lot of bands and such on his wrists. *I need to ask him about that someday,*

"Paul, I really admire what you've done here. You have the pool with trees in the distance and then the river further on to watch the sunsets. I can tell you're in real estate, you know how to build for stunning views." Remy said while he waved his right hand in a slow arc in front of him.

"You have a good eye, Remy. I tried to plan the angle of the house just right to catch the sunrises from the master bedroom to the sunsets on the patio. In addition, Ally has done a great job with the decorating." Paul smiled at Ally.

Ally feigned modesty by nodding her head. "It was my decorators. I just had to say yes and then stay on them to be sure they followed through. You know how hard it is to find good workers."

"The gardens are beautiful this time of year with late blooming flowers. Our gardener is great," Paul said. He pointed to the pansies and late blooming azaleas. "The fall colors start soon too. This is quite a view when all the trees down toward the river turn color."

"Who is your gardener, Paul? Mine needs help, and I like what I see here," said Eric Reynolds, one of the senior vice presidents at the Bank of the New South. Eric was heavyset from all those years behind a desk. Clean-shaven with a male-pattern baldness he didn't try to hide. He dressed like the banker at the dinner party in his khakis and Carlisle Country Club golf shirt.

"It's José or Jesus. Oh, what's his name, sweetheart?" He looked at Ally.

"You're way off, dear. It's Raul. We had Jesus a couple years ago, but I think he got deported. Anyway, you can't have him, he's occupied with our property and the Whittakers' house up the street." Ally had a way to say such things while being both polite, but convincing.

"That's a shame; I need some help. Let me know if you hear of any others that could use some extra money," Eric said.

Pastor Richard Taylor and his wife, Maryanne, arrived just as the *hors d'oeuvres* were ready.

"Sorry we're late, but it was hard getting the kids sorted out for dinner tonight before we left. We hoped the two older ones would be more cooperative with the two young ones but teenagers have minds of their own," Maryanne said as she shook Paul's hand.

"Nonsense, not a problem at all. We are all gathering by the pool just now. The food is just now coming out of the kitchen."

Pastor Rich also apologized for being tardy, and then his eyes got wide as he looked at the house and gardens. "Wow, Paul. The Lord has blessed you with many things." Looking at Ally, he continued, "Your home is beautiful, almost breathtaking."

"You're too kind, Pastor. It keeps the rain off our heads," Paul said.

Pastor Rich was lean with dark hair and average build. He sported a green-striped, short sleeved shirt and jeans. Maryanne wore a modest black polka dot dress with flats and a small white sweater.

After the tasting and the *hors d'oeuvres,* dinner was served. There was a dull hum of various conversations by all those seated near each other. Remy had a loud voice that carried, which is why Paul seated him far away near the pastor and his wife. Hard to hold a conversation near him.

"The Cab goes great with the beef bourguignon. You got the sauce just right too." Jenny was dressed even better than Remy in a blue print sundress with a small jacket. Paul always thought she was the prettiest lady at his parties. He couldn't help but notice Maryanne as well; she was striking in a downhome way.

Others heaped complements on the chef and sommelier, and Paul took it all in like he had done it himself.

Eric leaned over while buttering his roll, "How is the Hilltop development going?" He took a bite, so Paul had plenty of time to answer.

"We won't call it that when we begin construction, but the plans are about ready to go to the city planners for review. If all goes well, people'll be living there this time next year." He took a long sip of cabernet.

"Is that IRS audit still going on?"

"Yes, it's been quite a while already. I plan to keep them spinning until they give up or propose a reasonable resolution. These things can go on for months . . . years even. But that's not my problem. That's why I have Mike Winter, my finance guy. What else would he do?"

Eric chuckled and nodded. "Yes, always good to keep the tax boys at bay."

Paul looked at all his guests enjoying their meal and the company and smiled, satisfied. He watched the moonlight bounce off the pool surface.

After dinner and desert, Paul asked, "Who wants a cigar and a brandy?"

The men all accepted Paul's offer. The ladies moved indoors where the smoke wouldn't get in their hair. They'd have brandy too.

He passed around a box of select cigars with a punch cutter nearby.

As everyone lit up, Paul joked with a fake British accent, "I wonder what the poor people are doing tonight."

The guests laughed politely and puffed on the cigars to get them lit well.

Pastor Rich was clearly uncomfortable in the setting as he fidgeted in his chair and toyed with his cigar, trying to keep it lit.

"Are you OK, Rich?" Paul asked.

"Not used to this kind of thing, Paul. I appreciate the invitation but think it may be best if we go. I suspect the evening will be more relaxed without a man of the cloth nearby.

"Nonsense. We love having you here. No need to rush off." Paul wondered, *Is my speech slurring?*

"We do need to check on the kids; they weren't behaving well when we left and really should be going. It's been a lovely evening."

"Are you sure?" Paul said, nervous about the slur. *I need to stay away from "s" words.*

"Yes, I'll speak with Ally as we go. Thank you again. See you Wednesday at the elders' meeting."

I'm going to get the third degree from Ally because the pastor left early. It'll seem more relaxed with him gone now. I hate to say it.

With that Paul went and sat back down at the table by the pool with the others. "It's wonderful out here in the evening . . . so peaceful and removed from the hectic pace at the office," Paul took a long draw on his stogie, not speaking to anyone in particular.

Eric said, "I agree, but you do get a lot of helicopter traffic, don't you?"

"That's just tonight. They must be having training or something," Paul said, looking up into the evening sky.

Paul noticed that Jenny Hart was distracted by her phone. *Must be a text message.* She motioned to Remy to come to her.

Annoyed, he got up and went to the door. Paul couldn't tell what was happening but could see Remy and Jenny having words. He didn't want anything to upset the evening. He could see Remy pull his phone and begin tapping away.

The wine, brandy, and ambience overtook Paul. He was mellow but could sense concern. He decided to investigate after one last long draw on his Arturo Fuente Opus. He exhaled, extracted himself from his chair, and ambled over to see the Harts.

"What's up, my friends," he said, a little irritated but trying not to show it.

"There's a riot happening downtown. There've been shootings, lots of property damage. The police are breaking it up now," Remy boomed. He was flushed and concern showed on his face.

Paul grabbed the remote and turned on the TV near the pool. There was footage of the riot from WWNS TV. Jackie's report sobered them fast.

"That's my dad's building they're showing!" Remy said.

"I told you to sell all those downtown properties and move to the burbs," Paul said.

"What's the cause of all this?" Diane Reynolds asked. "Get away from here with that cigar, dear," she said to her husband, Eric. She waved the smoke away.

Eric put it out.

"It has something to do with that black guy who got shot by the police last night, I think. I don't know the whole story," Ally said.

Paul could no longer mask his irritation, "Quiet! Let's hear what the reporter says." He directed it toward Ally. *I'll hear about that later.*

"They have agitators from out of town, I'm sure," Eric said, "No one in the Wharf would make such a mess of our city. Has anyone been killed?"

The somber TV news anchor said, "There are at least two officers killed tonight and one of the demonstrators. We don't have an accurate count on the injured."

"There's going to be hell to pay after this. More businesses will leave downtown. The city's getting a real black eye over this crook that got killed last night. Now, two of Carlisle's finest are down. This is horrible," said Jenny, fear and concern in her voice. She moved closer to Remy and took his hand.

"What do you think they want?" asked Diane. "Why tear up your own neighborhood? What's to be gained? You're right; they have to be from elsewhere. Probably out of state. They had all day to get here."

The party atmosphere passed. Couple by couple the guests headed home.

Paul and Ally stood in the doorway, waving goodbye to the Harts, the last couple to go. "We hate that the party ended this way."

Ally turned and looked at him. "Don't you ever tell me to be quiet in front of guests again. It's very insulting. Don't treat me like your employees. Boy, did I get the looks from the wives nearby." Her face was beet red with anger. "I don't like to be embarrassed! People got to see the real you there. How could you treat me that way in front of our guests?

And what did you say to Pastor Rich to make him leave early like that?" She turned and headed upstairs, not waiting for any answers.

Paul opened his mouth to respond, but decided it wasn't worth the effort. He settled into the living room for another brandy, intending to watch the news but fell asleep before it started.

Someone needs to clean this mess up. The maid'll do it in the morning.

ENJOY THE INVENTIONS OF MAN

High buildings that cast great shadows
Lights to dazzle the darkness
Law and order imposed on life
The reordering of nature

Warm in winter
Cool in summer
The comfort of hot showers, frozen food
So many ways to control our world

And yet nothing
Compared to the creation
Our bodies that heal themselves
The great canyons carved in the earth
The clouds above us
The rain that comes in season
The refreshing of our spirits
The way God's world controls us

Listen or don't

CHAPTER 3

Jackie jolted awake at six the next morning. She stubbed her toe on the foyer stair as she went to the front door to grab her paper. The headline of the *Carlisle Guardian* shouted, "Riot Downtown." She scoured the front page for details about last night's troubles.

Did I miss anything while I was holed up in the men's room? That big toe is going to bother me all day. I need caffeine to go.

She popped a pod in her Keurig while she dialed Karl, the Carlisle city manager. "Karl dear, I need an exclusive interview with Ward before the news conference. Yes, I know it's early and you were up late last night, but can you arrange it? Thanks, you're a star, sweetheart. I owe you one." *Best if I don't give him room to say no.*

"You owe me a lot, and I'll collect someday soon," Karl said. Jackie heard the innuendo in his voice.

On her way out the door, she took one last look in the mirror to make sure the image was intact. She wore the standard-TV-news-lady-issue, fitted, sleeveless, solid-color dress. Today it was light blue with a black jacket and black heels. *Won't wear the jacket on air, but I'll freeze this morning without it.* She tried to project a confident and appealing image to her viewing public. Her morning ritual included a "Looking Good, Jackie" whispered to the mirror as she headed out the door. Sometimes she believed it.

Waiting for Sheriff Ward, she flipped through the Guardian app on her phone. Pictures in the article told remarkable stories about yesterday's riot. *Didn't realize the photographers at the Guardian were so good under pressure. I didn't even see them last night.*

Jackie wondered what the diverse groups of Carlisle thought about last night's events. She looked at stories from multiple perspectives. *What did the black people think? How did the cops react? What was the view up the hill? No doubt, they saw rioters as hoodlums, malcontents, and paid demonstrators . . . troublemakers who should work harder to get ahead. They always ask, "Why are they breaking windows and setting fires? If they had jobs like us, they wouldn't have time for this kind of thing. How can the police allow this?"*

They won't ask why they don't have jobs like us and no one asks why none of these alleged professional demonstrators ever get arrested.

Are we going to deal with it or sweep it aside?

The room was a normal, municipal small-conference room. Pale paint, old gray Steelcase table, and only somewhat newer rolling chairs. Typical florescent lighting above, one had a hum in it. She clicked on her recorder app and put it in plain sight when Sheriff Roman Wade entered the room. *Now I can get some facts. Hope he'll be open and honest. We need that. He thinks he has a future in politics but not if this keeps up.*

The sheriff came in with a wrinkled newspaper under his arm. His neatly tucked uniform shirt contrasted with his tie, which was askew. His red-rimmed eyes told her he had too much coffee and not enough sleep. At over six-feet tall, he looked like a law enforcer. Strong chin, barrel chest, and big hands, but a bit of a paunch. Over 40, he still had all his hair, thick and black.

"Sheriff, thanks for agreeing to see me ahead of the news conference. I know you have a lot going on. Just a few questions please."

Sheriff Wade put the paper on the table. "I know you have ways of getting your exclusives Ms. Hyatt. I can only say the facts. No conjecture."

"Sheriff, what are the facts about last night??"

"We have twenty-five people hospitalized. Eight are my officers. Most with broken bones, burns, and other serious injuries. Five are in the morgue. Three were my officers. We haven't had this much trouble in our town since the civil rights movement decades ago."

She could see a *why now* look on his face she noticed with most politicians in crisis.

Jackie waited a moment to give him time to breathe. *He must be replaying episodes of last night's tragedy in his mind.* Then she pressed. "Was the trouble contained between Fifth Street and Ninth Street or did it spread up the hill?"

"Yes. My officers contained it there. It cost us, though. Those officers all have families. Some are single moms. What will happen to them? The protestors have families too, I suppose." The last sentence trailed off. He stared at his newspaper. Then his words seemed to gain strength, and he went on.

"Anyway. Yes, we kept it to a five-block area. Too many broken storefronts. Office buildings will have to be shut down for a time. At least a dozen cars vandalized and set aflame. Trash can fires were all over the area."

He relaxed taking about property damage.

Jackie pressed on. "What about the victims of last night's violence? Why did your officers open fire? What type of munitions were they using?"

She could see him struggling with emotions.

He took a deep breath and said, "The crowd of about 300 began moving from the rally at Hart Park toward the government center, toward the population centers. They'd already set trashcan fires. We heard some windows breaking but the smoke obscured the damage. We set a line about a block in front and warned them to disperse. We warned them about the tear gas, pepper balls, flash grenades, and rubber bullets. We warned them about our resolve." His voice was now getting louder with each statement. "We warned them. We couldn't let this violence escalate.

"Then people in the crowd threw rocks and bottles. We had to respond. Three officers were already down. We were out-numbered. We launched tear gas and flash bombs and the mob came faster. Some ran away but several came right at us. Several officers fired. Our riot team shot rubber bullets. Apparently, several of the uniformed officers shot live rounds. People went down. You saw the footage. Too much smoke to see who did what on video. The crowd fell back to regroup. It appears they had some weapons also. Not sure if my officers were the only ones firing. Several rocks and bottles came at us and we fired again. This time the crowd panicked. I suspect we must've hit some of the leaders with that salvo. That means they're either in the hospital or in the morgue with many of my team. We'll get to the bottom of this.

"If my guys did the wrong thing, we'll deal with that. If this criminal element is responsible, they'll be brought to justice. We live in a town of law and order. We have to make this right. You can print that!"

"I'm not with the *Guardian,* Sheriff," Jackie corrected him without aggression.

He flashed an agitated smile, embarrassed.

"The crowd was incensed by the time it got to that point. They saw a white officer shoot an unarmed black man," she leaned forward and said. "A familiar story that has played out in many places now. Your team must've known better than to incense them further."

"Are you going to sit there and lecture me on my tactics? Who do you think you are, news lady? Have you been there? Have you been in such a situation? They feared for their lives!"

"What mobilized the crowd last night?" she asked.

"There was a group of agitators maybe from out of town, maybe not. I heard conflicting reports. The demonstration stayed non-violent until it got dark. Trashcans were already ablaze. Then someone set a car on fire at Fifth and Commonwealth. The fire department responded and the stones started flying. When the riot police arrived, the crowd moved down Commonwealth Ave. They set another car aflame. They got to a drugstore and smashed windows. Broke into the pharmacy and took drugs. They moved down the road, broke into a liquor store and started hurling bottles back at my officers. Anyone in the crowd close to my team got hit with bottles and rocks from behind. Then the alcohol hit some of the burning cars and burst into flame. Fire began moving up the sides of buildings also going inside of the broken storefronts. People were lighting more trashcans too. Smoke from burning debris clouded the area.

"We set a perimeter along Tenth street and would not move. There are high buildings along Commonwealth from Ninth to Tenth so we could contain them there. The crowd trapped itself between the burning area and my team." He took a deep breath.

Jackie pressed on. "They had nowhere to go, did they? Where were they supposed to go?"

"They should've stopped and put the rocks and weapons down like they were told," he replied.

"How do you stop a riot?" she asked.

"They should've laid things down and stopped. They were warned multiple times."

"But they couldn't go backward or forward. They were enraged!" she said.

"We were not going to let them go forward and they knew it. They attacked us and we responded. Not our proudest moment but we did break it up. Once the gas, flashes and pepper did their work and several of the instigators went down, the crowd panicked. Some just fled back through the narrow openings on the road toward the park or disappeared down alleys. Others stopped to help the wounded. We were happy to see it break up. Then I sent one of my men to come and save your bacon."

"Thank you for that by the way. I appreciate it very much."

"At that point, we allowed the EMTs to respond and they came to help both sides. Our officers also helped with triage. We used the light from the fires to assist us. It took quite a while to get everyone to University Hospital. Some couldn't be saved. Twenty-seven went to the hospital. Two died in the emergency department. Six are in critical condition. Three were dead at the scene."

"Who got killed last night?"

He recited the names, "Officer Desiree Houston separated from the riot squad was found beaten to death. Officer Wayne McCaskill was shot in the throat during the confrontation on Commonwealth. Officer Craig Forsythe was also burned badly by some sort of Molotov cocktail. He died at the hospital. All were young officers. They never dealt with this type of thing. Tragic.

"The other victims were Rodney Clark, age 35, died at the scene from gunshot wounds and burns. William Putnam, age 23, died at the hospital from significant burns and internal injuries caused by the stampede, I suspect.

"We're still gathering information on the twenty-five others hospitalized. Like I said six are critical. I'll release more information to the press soon, after we make sure all their families are notified."

Jackie tapped her phone and stopped the recorder. "Thanks for your time. I know this is hard for you. You know there'll be a lot more reporters and networks here today. I'll get something up on our website today and get a report on the morning news to help give you some room. It's going to get fierce now. There'll have to be arrests and prosecutions."

She got up to go. "You may want to fix your tie," making a hand motion around her neck.

He just looked at the paper and muttered, "Why now? Why on my watch?"

Jackie headed straight to the newsroom. She wanted to get a cameraman with her and head to the scene now that the sun was up. *Not going to let those network people outshine the locals.*

CHAPTER 4

José traveled in the passenger seat in the cab of a tractor-trailer. He'd gotten picked up about forty miles earlier and agreed to buy the driver breakfast for a ride into Carlisle. The cab, cluttered with paper wrappings and old plastic Diet Coke bottles, reeked of cigar smoke.

"Jake Baucom's the name. Driving trucks and running around's what I do. Citizen of the US of A. Headin' home to Carlisle. Where can I drop ya?"

José recalled from when Jake picked him up. They dined at a Flying J before getting back in the truck for the last leg. *Probably be another hour or two.*

Jake loved to talk and José just let him. He gave a detailed history of Carlisle, which José found useful but later determined wasn't always accurate. "Carlisle was founded back in the 1800s . . . "

While Jake droned on, José recalled the route he'd taken to get here. *Hard to believe it's almost time to begin anew. Am I ready? Am I worthy?*

The Master has used me for many years to minister to the poor, the sick, the forgotten, but also to correct misconceptions about his ministry when the church grows too attached to the ways of the world. I've been to many places over what seems like lifetimes. Each place has such amazing creations. Those who seek his will and those who follow their own or worse. Learned over time that the things of the world get broken, die, or just grow old and useless. Don't care much for things anymore. But the souls of the people are so precious to him and to me now.

He remembered the beatings and persecutions he'd endured or was forced to watch. *I wish to be a source of comfort not the cause of pain. I've stumbled in my calling too often. Forgive me my many shortcomings. Lord, make me worthy of the time you are calling me to now. I don't know what to do or who to approach. I'm totally reliant on you at this point. Thank you for making me a part of your ministry again in a new place. Be glorified in what I say and do.*

"Yo friend, you awake?" Jake jolted him back to reality. "You shoulda finished your coffee back at the J. We're about to cross the Lumber River Dam. It got built in the late 50s and created Bass Lake. It's one of the biggest lakes in the state. May be the biggest. I used to fish it with my dad when he was around. The dam gave electricity for the area but also stopped the floods that came sometimes. We had some doozies, back in the day. Since we got the dam though, no more floods."

José looked at it in awe. It was an impressive monument to the men who designed and built it. A beautiful, concrete dam that straddled the two tall hills. The exposed spillway down one side must be used to control high water levels, he guessed. It had a road across the top that led to an area with a parking lot and boat slips for occasional boaters. There were high-tension power lines stringing their way toward civilization below.

Jake continued, "The National Park Service created a park on the far side . . . ."

José remembered the faces of those he had left. He was haunted by the ones who wouldn't listen to the Master's message. The demons of the mind would taunt him about how inadequate he must be. *I've not had an episode of long despair in years now. I think I'm stronger than I really am. Pride creeps in at times. I want to do it my way. Sometimes I'm impatient with the Master but usually with the people. Why don't they get it? Why won't they listen?*

José came back to the reality of the truck cab as Jake finished a draw on his crinkling plastic bottle of Diet Coke. He said, "The rich folks began moving up the hill away from the river due to the noise and the smell over the past few years, such that now all the money in Carlisle ain't downtown but in the burbs."

"That happens a lot in America I hear," José responded, only half listening.

Jake never missed a beat. "When they moved, they left the stores, schools and houses. Those got old and rundown . . . "

He could feel the Enemy now making him doubt himself. Bringing back past failures. His enjoyment of the company of women. *I vowed long ago not to go down that path again.* He watched as the tree-lined road gave way to a cityscape. The vision came back to him and he knew the Master prepared this place for him and him for this place.

"You ain't much of a talker are ya bud?" Jake brought him back to reality once more. "I never asked. What do you do?"

"Been a lot of things over the years. Farm hand, priest, cobbler, but these days I like to cook. Never drove a truck though."

There ain't nothin' to it. Just learn to sit all day and look from side to side. Hey, this here area's once named Brokers' Wharf, 'cause all the lumber money-changing hands down there back in the day. Now it's called Broken Wharf. Most folks just call it the Wharf.

"Over the years, the blacks ruled The Wharf. They had crime lords and gangs who took different parts and warred amongst theirselves until one bad dude showed up. I guess he knew his business but they don't come no meaner than him. He got named Da Wyz. Not sure why. They mostly just fight with the Latino gangs in Villa Maya these days."

"What's Villa Maya?"

"You don't want to go there 'less'n you speak Spanish. They all moved here when the construction boomed in the '90s. Now we can't get rid of 'em. Bad hombres, I hear."

José noticed the plywood on the storefronts as they drove down Commonwealth Avenue but decided not to mention them.

They wound their way through the city toward the riverfront. José prayed for the city and for himself as they traveled. *I thank you Lord that you don't require me to be perfect just willing to serve. It's not my strength I need but yours. You've endowed me with many gifts and talents over these years of service. You are good. Help me to bring you glory in this place. May I bring your comfort to those in need and make uncomfortable those that need that too.*

"Well José, this is my stop. You need to get out before I go in the terminal so they don't see me takin' riders. Thanks for the breakfast and for the company. You don't say much but that's OK, I make up for both of us." He smiled his charming grin with a few missing teeth.

As José climbed out of the cab with his duffle bag, he said, "Jake I enjoyed our talk, even if it was a bit one sided. I learned from a great teacher. Thank you for the ride and the information. One last favor, can you point me toward Villa Maya? I want to stay there."

"I didn't take you for a Latino. Go back toward the big white bank building we passed. When you hit Commonwealth, turn right. When everything changes to Spanish, you're there. Vaya con dios, amigo!" he said and drove toward the truck yard across the street.

José walked along Commonwealth. The river on one side, the wealthy were up the hill. The poor squeezed into the waterfront. The University and big business in the middle of it all. Carlisle had so much money, so much intellect and so many needy people.

The Master brought him to the right place.

CHAPTER 5

Now, only a couple of days from the riot came the unpleasant task of funerals.

Reverend Tony shook some dirt from his shoes and he looked at the fresh grave of Rodney Clark. He had officiated the service for William Putnam earlier in the morning. William had been cremated so no need for a graveside service. He stood in a gentle breeze that caused the canvas awning over the gravesite to shutter. The crowd dispersed with heavy hearts.

Da Wyz attended both services. Tony saw him. The chief gang lord in the Wharf was hard to miss. He stopped by to pay his respects to the two dead men.

Da Wyz, Jeremiah Michaels, was always dressed well, not just for funerals. He was about five feet five inches tall. He was lean and wore his usual designer sunglasses. Tony guessed it was so no one could see where he was looking. Da Wyz had a mustache and goatee always trimmed well, just like his short hair. He reeked of confidence and wealth even if he didn't appear too menacing at first glance. He was a street thug all grown up, now in his forties. Da Wyz was the real law in the Wharf. None had challenged him for years. Any who did, disappeared. Calls his organization the Business to make it sound more legitimate. Recruited members into it using the gangs in the Wharf. They were like his farm team. All he touched turned to gold, at least for him. Some rapper called him Da Wyz in a song years ago and it stuck. No one called him Jeremiah anymore. Tony didn't like what he did but couldn't do anything about it.

"Reverend Tony, this was sad and so unnecessary."

"I don't agree with you often, but I agree with that statement. Rodney was a long-time member of our church. He grew up in it. You know he had some trouble with the law when he was young, but he'd settled down to be a great member of the church and our community. He leaves a wife and two teenage boys. What's gonna happen to them now?"

"You know I can always give those boys somethin' to do," he lit a Black and Mild Royale. "Want one?" he offered Reverend Tony.

Tony shook his head, "No sir, that can't be the way. We have to see these boys get a proper education and stay out of trouble."

"That's your department Rev. I know you don't like what I do, but you know it's necessary in our world. We have to protect ourselves from those up the hill. This shows that more than anything. The Biz is a way for the kids in our community to get ahead. It also helps keep the Man and the Mayans out of here. No one looks after our own like we do."

"You make the Biz sound like a charity out for the betterment of the community. We both know better. By the name you gave it, it's a business out to help those inside. But, this isn't a day to argue. Counting Lamont and Officer Houston, we buried four of our own within the last week. They didn't all attend Commonwealth but they were all from the Wharf."

The Reverend Anthony Hibbert was a man with a bright smile and a firm handshake, who had enjoyed leading the flock at the Commonwealth Ave AME Zion church for many years now. He had a strong voice that went along with his six-foot three-inch frame. He towered over Da Wyz. In high school he'd been a defensive lineman and had won a college scholarship to a prominent, historically black university. An unfortunate knee and ankle injury cut his football plans short. As he got older, he'd gone soft but still was an impressive man to meet for the first time. Tony knew Da Wyz wouldn't confront him in this setting. Maybe it was the circumstances or maybe it was the location but Tony felt emboldened to speak with candor to Da Wyz. *I'm one of the few to dare confront him.*

"Like I said, a sad time for us. You know they ain't gonna do anything about this. There'll be a lot of talk. Some police may even get fired, but nothin's gonna happen. It never does. No one's goin' to jail. The white folks don't understand how life is in the Wharf. How could they? They keep us down. They been doing that since they brought us here, since they red lined our neighborhoods years ago. You know we're in the south Rev. They keep us in the ghettos. We're less of a threat. They just stay away. They move to the burbs and try to keep us out. Make sure we got bad schools. Arrest and imprison the black men and then get high and mighty about how our women sleep around. Boys without fathers are easy to recruit into crime. That's nothing new. The ones up the hill don't want to give any money to help. They say we got to earn it. 'Make your own opportunity.' How you gonna do that with no education and no businesses that'll hire you? All the jobs go to the white kids. Then my favorite is they just pass more laws to make it harder for us to get out of the hole. I love it when they get surprised that poor people steal and provide necessary services. Whether its whores or drugs or whatever. It's what we have to sell. They buyin' too. They say how lily white they are, but we know better. Some of my best customers are up the hill.

"Sorry Rev, but that's the way it is. I don't feel bad selling my stuff to them. I'm in the customer satisfaction business," he drew out the syllables of the last few words.

"It's not the way it should be. 'There is a way that seems right to man . . . ' My God has a better way, if we'll listen. What's happening is wrong up there and down here. We have to find another way. We can all be better. Even the Mayans and the police. We have to talk to each other . . . understand how we're all the same."

Da Wyz chuckled at that. "Rev, you keep dreamin' and preachin'. I'm gonna do it my way. My way works better. Brings money from up the hill down here. Puts money in my Biz and allows me to do what I need to. We're on the same team Rev, tryin' to get the black man out of the ghetto. We just have different ways of doin' it. Whitey's got plenty of money to share. He won't give it away. He has the police to stop us from takin' it. We got to find him something to spend it on. That's what they understand and appreciate."

"We're not on the same team brother. I don't want your poison and corruption up there or down here. There's another way. God will find it."

"Well, 'till he does, I gonna keep doin' what I do. Rev, you need to be careful and more respectful. I came to you today. I'm a member of your church, you know. One day you gonna need something and you'll come to me. Let's both agree we need to make life better for the people of your flock here on the Wharf."

With that, Da Wyz crushed out his smoke on the ground and walked toward his driver.

Tony thought he'd overstepped. Da Wyz didn't let him get away with it. Tony couldn't agree with all his points, but he was troubled by what the folks up the hill would do after the riot. Would they be helpful or roll up the ladder even more?

⚜ ⚜ ⚜

Da Wyz didn't show it, but when he got back to the car, he thought about what Tony said. Tony hit too close to home and had to be put in his place. *There is a way that seems right to a man.* He knew the rest, *but in the end leads to death.* Such thoughts began to haunt him like never before in his life.

He was getting tired. Age and fatherhood matured him in ways he hadn't expected. But he'd made too many enemies over the years. He took in a deep cleansing breath as reality kicked in. *Wake up Wyz, Tony's got you dreamin'. Something has to be done about these black men dying. I know just the thing.*

CHAPTER 6

José arrived in Villa Maya after his long walk from the Wharf. He went to the local Catholic church, Saint Francis of Assisi, to meet the priests and sisters, to see how they could help each other.

He introduced himself to the priest, Father Victor Menendez, "They call me José Sabio."

He and the Father bonded fast.

"You're Dominican not Franciscan," José said.

"And you must've served in an order yourself at some point, señor," Father Menendez said.

"Si, I was a Jesuit Priest a few lifetimes ago. I didn't follow all the demands so I left the order. Not to worry Father, no scandal; just a difference of approach. I still believe in the power of the church to help struggling people. I've come here to show the Master's love in this place. I need a place to stay and a church to help. The Master has led me here.

"Do you know of a place I can rent a small furnished room and perhaps a restaurant I can work for? Best if no one asks for papers."

"Go see Señora Maria Araya." He wrote down an address and handed it to him. "She needs the money and runs a clean house. Ramone Hernandez has a place called Restaurant Tapas. He hires people new in town without many questions. It's a good place to start although it's hard work. Pay is OK. Most don't stay too long. He's always looking for dishwashers, busboys. It's a good walk from Maria's but there're buses too." He looked at José with concern. "Do you need money?"

"Not now, but I need a job soon. Once I get settled, I'll come by and we can speak more of the church's ministry in Villa Maya. I look forward to helping, however I can."

"Si, get settled and come see me in a couple of days. I'll see how we can use your gifts. I'm curious about this call of yours from *the Master* as you call him." José could hear the skepticism in his voice. "The needs are many the money is few," he smiled.

✠ ✠ ✠

Señora Maria was a large rotund Latina with a firm disposition and a tender heart. Sitting in the kitchen, she began the interview.

"Father Menendez knows me well. I take his references very seriously, but I need to know about you. Are you a criminal?"

"No, señora. I don't get drunk and cause trouble. I keep to myself at home and look for ways to help others around me. I spend a lot of time in prayer and meditation. Is it quiet here?"

She looked him straight in the eye and said, "I don't tolerate loud parties or strangers in the house. I know you live here but ask that you respect others and their property. Mostly I require you respect me and my property. If you can do that, we'll get along. Otherwise, you need to find someplace else. I don't have time for thieves and troublemakers. Many of my boarders have been here a long time."

All she is missing is the wagging finger, José thought, but he said, "I understand and agree. What are the rules for kitchen and toilet privileges?"

After they both agreed to terms, including how much and when the rent was due, she gave him a key and one other firm warning. "No cooking in your room. You have to use the kitchen during the times agreed."

José gave her the last of his money for two weeks of rent. He knew he better find some income soon. Maria directed him to Restaurant Tapas.

"It's about eight blocks that way." She pointed east along the river.

After a quick shower and fresh t-shirt and jeans, José walked toward the restaurant. Along the way, he decided to tour Villa Maya. As he walked along, he could see it stretched for several blocks and was longer than it was wide. Limited on one side by the river. He walked along the riverfront and noticed an old man fishing. In the distance up river, he could see a barge dock. *Must be Broken Wharf that Jake was talking about.* As the river ran out of the city José got the vision that the riches of the city draining away. The prophet in him could see the area up the hill like a big dam holding all the gold back and what little got out was absorbed first by the Wharf and then by those further downstream.

Many of the people he encountered were from Mexico and El Salvador. He could tell by the soccer team logos on shirts and in windows. He could see the Mayan influence but he also noticed that VM had peoples from many countries in the Latino world. Like other places he lived in Latin America, soccer passions ran high. *I can only imagine the fights among the fans when the many national teams represented here played each other.*

Like all the Latino communities where he'd been an expatriate, it was close knit within and standoffish to those outside. Most of the signs were in Spanish. *It must be foreboding to those who ventured in from up the hill or the Wharf. Even the police will feel like this is foreign soil, I suspect. I'm sure that's fine with the locals who are illegal. Part of the reason to settle here is to stay out of official view. What was it my truck-driving friend Jake said? "They let the gangs impose rules and enforce them in there." They only want the police here when the gangs get out of hand. Just like the favelas in Brazil.*

José prayed for those he encountered as he went along. He asked the Master's blessing on the families as he passed by homes and on businesses as well.

José always enjoyed the fragrances around a new place and Villa Maya was no exception. At lunchtime, the smell of cooking pervaded the entire area and reminded him of his hunger. The air filled with the scent of onions, chilies and peppers, making the world smell better.

He could see trash piled up along with many other poor hygiene practices he knew from the Latin ghettos he worked in before. He wandered the back streets away from the cooking and covered his face at times to filter the smells.

One of the things he enjoyed most about the Latino culture was the use of vivid color. He could see it on old dilapidated buildings now made into dwellings. There were makeshift repairs all down the streets, but with many different vibrant colors.

Saint Francis was the center of activity in Villa Maya. José knew that Latinos and Catholicism went together like beautiful dresses at a fiesta de quinceañera. Much of the churches' practices turned superstitious over time with the implied bargain being, "If I do my part, God will bless me and keep me from suffering." He was convinced that the devout could still find the relationship with the Father, through His Son, and live a life of blessing and peace just like he'd known on both sides of the Catholic church. It does take effort that is sometimes exhausting.

But the one who endures to the end will be saved. . . .

He traveled on and noticed some Protestant churches made inroads here too. *They'll have fundamentalist congregations and amazing outreach. I enjoy the energy of their worship and the depth of their passion for the Master. I'll visit them in the coming weeks.* He prayed for the priests, nuns and protestant church pastors.

His thoughts traveled back to the great schism of the church while he walked along. He recalled the Protestant Reformation too. *The Catholic Church seems to promote salvation through works rather than grace while the Protestants seem to promote a cheap grace. Grace is free but it is not cheap. The changed life after requires labor toward holiness. Both sides can find a central ground of joy, peace and loving relationship. We all struggle to stay in that spot.*

After his tour and time in prayer for VM, he arrived at Restaurant Tapas.

As he entered, he asked for Ramone. Based on the number of tickets at the cash register, the restaurant had been busy today. He learned later that it sat at the intersection of gang territories. It was more than a diner, but not upscale. If it were his restaurant he would serve plenty of corn flour and vegetables to keep it priced so locals could afford it. A quick glance around the dining room at the remaining patrons' plates convinced him Ramone felt the same way.

A man with a wide smile and crisp light blue shirt came out of the kitchen. He extended his hand and greeted José like an honored guest. "Buenos dias! You must be José. Father Menendez said you may be coming by. He came for lunch earlier today."

"It's kind of him to mention me. I've worked in many kitchens over the years. I can do anything you need," José said.

"Your English is very good; would you like to be out front or in the back?"

"Put me where you need me, but I'm best in the kitchen."

"I don't need any cooks right now, but can always use a dishwasher or busboy. Hard to keep kids interested in those jobs around here."

"When do you need me?"

"Work the dinner rush tonight for free. Call it an audition. If you're good enough, I'll hire you for a few hours a day. Tonight, I'll pay you with leftover food. If you make it through the audition, we'll talk about money."

"Si, señor. Who can show me the way things work around here?" José said.

"Today you'll set up tables and clean up tables. If you've done this like you said, you won't need much training." He motioned to someone coming out of the kitchen, "Jesus, show our new table man, José, where the aprons and tubs are. Take him on a short tour of the dishwasher." With that Ramone turned his attention to the businessmen who just came in the front door.

Ramone turned away and José heard, "Buenos dias, señors ..."

After his audition, Ramone and José agreed on his pay and hours. It would be enough to cover his rent plus a little more. He could eat at the restaurant most of the time and his other needs were small. There were no benefits other than free leftovers.

José continued to impress his new boss and his coworkers over the next many days. He was much more than a dishwasher.

※ ※ ※

After a few days, Ramone pulled José aside, "You're interfering with my cook, I hear. I see you giving him advice. He thinks you're a big mouth. Let him do it the way he knows. How would you know better than him, anyway?"

"I picked a lot of produce along the way, señor. I learned that cooking with it meant I didn't have to pick it. Better use of my skills. Los amigos liked what I did so they just put me to cooking instead of picking. I try to make it taste good without costing much."

Ramone smiled his welcome grin at the last comment. "You know, I've heard more compliments on the food these days. Okay, you can suggest; just don't make Juan mad. He's the best cook I got."

As September turned into October, traffic picked up. The lunch and dinner crowds almost filled to capacity and Ramone was pleased. And then Juan got arrested for beating his wife.

"He was arrested and will be deported if he gets out. He is lost to us. Juan beat his wife too often and this time she was in the hospital with a broken jaw, broken ribs among other injuries." Ramone told the team that afternoon. "Amigos, I can cook but you know it's not my thing. Who of you can step up with Juan gone?"

"I can do it; what does it pay?" Jesus said.

José said nothing. He didn't want to jump in front of those who'd been here longer.

"Jesus, you're okay at this, but I need someone who knows what he's doing. José, you're promoted to chief cook. We'll talk about money once you get the job done over the next few days. Now everyone, get to work," Ramone said.

"No, señor, if you don't want me to cook, I'm out of here. I've been here longer than this guy. You owe me a chance," Jesus said. He said a few other things too, but that was the gist of it. He pulled off his apron, threw it on the table, slamming the back door as he left.

Lucinda, a waitress who had been with Ramone the longest, whispered to José, "I'm sure you can handle this." Then to everyone else she said, "C'mon amigos we got customers and jobs to do."

José appreciated the words of encouragement.

"Vamanos!" Ramone said.

José enjoyed cooking. He'd done it in many places over the years. He cooked with a flair much appreciated by the others on staff, but also by the boss since he was very frugal with the ingredients, especially the meat. The sauces and spices he used made the food taste and smell wonderful. José knew that more happy customers meant better tips.

Restaurant Tapas prospered even more now that José cooked full time. He and Ramone did come to an arrangement. He got a fair wage and could experiment after the doors closed at night. He also insisted on bringing in some of the local gang members to teach them to cook during the afternoon slow down. They learned a trade and José got some back up. Ramone was apprehensive but allowed it.

He settled in well enough now, even if it took more time than he hoped.

There is just one more group to come then it will be time to get about the Master's plan.

CHAPTER 7

Pastor Richard Taylor was new to Carlisle. Maryanne, his wife, two adopted children and he had arrived two years ago. They had two older teenage children but felt led to adopt also and have enjoyed the blessing both of being able to give life and to testify to the sanctity of life.

While new to Carlisle he wasn't new to the ministry. A senior pastor at several nondenominational congregations across the south. The Church of Carlisle called him when their senior pastor had retired after fifteen years. As large church pastors go, he was the new kid on the block. He came with fresh vision and a different outlook.

He remembered his first meeting with Reverend Tony of the large local AME Zion congregation.

"I've ministered in large cities for years and found that church cooperation was much more powerful than competition," Pastor Rich said.

"That message will be seen with suspicion in Carlisle, especially from the new guy. Our faith lines are decades old and hard to cross. The various Protestant churches didn't embrace the Catholic minority well. They didn't embrace each other's ministries either. We all have our biases and tend to mistrust each other based on long standing differences. We have many of the long-term members who will remind us of those if we start getting too cozy," Tony responded.

"So how did the ministries develop in Carlisle?" Rich asked.

"Since we weren't united, God used us the best way he could, I guess. He gifted different congregations to have different passions and thus ministries. The Episcopalians focused on feeding the hungry; the Presbyterians on caring for the sick; the Baptists on evangelizing newcomers; the AME Zion church on prison ministry, and so on."

"We have to do better than that now," Pastor Rich told him. "It's time to unite; the church with a capital 'C' could be stronger and more focused together."

The one thing he'd accomplished so far on this goal was getting some of the senior pastors to meet him for lunch once a month to pray for the city.

This month's lunch was at Restaurant Tapas in Villa Maya. He'd heard good things about it. Ramone squeezed them into the private dining area after the lunch rush. Pastor Rich liked going to the different areas of the city, but he did feel out of place here, like he was on a mission trip to Latin America.

After the riot, the lunch meeting received increased focus. It gave hope for change among the clergy. Since he started the luncheons, Rich invited the pastors of churches all over the city that included the black churches. In addition, he made sure to reach out to the priests and pastors of the Latino congregations too. Attendance though inconsistent, developed a small core of regulars. The group started a dialog about increased cooperation but it was just polite with no conviction to this point.

Today, Rich decided it had to be different. After the usual small talk about the Red Eagle's football team and the upcoming basketball season, he decided it was time for the Bride of Christ, the Church, to lead.

"Ladies and gentlemen, I suggest we let Carlisle see God moving to heal our city. We should create a community-building event to focus on our commonalities. It should be a city-wide outreach."

"It should be a celebration. Perhaps on the very streets where the riot occurred," Pastor Lucy Saunders of St. Mark's Methodist said.

"I like the idea of redeeming the streets where all the violence took place. But will people feel safe? Will they come?" St John's Baptist Senior Pastor, Brother Bruce Cochrane, said.

"We should do it in the daytime to address the safety concern. But what should it be?" Reverend Tony asked.

"How about a street fair, maybe an arts celebration. Yeah, with music and local artists . . . " Pastor Lucy said.

"But it's October now, it'll take a few weeks to organize. We'll be at Thanksgiving before you know it. The weather'll be suspect. Should we wait until spring?" Pastor Joan Clark of the St Luke's Episcopal asked.

"Joan, you have a point, but we can't wait. How about a Thanksgiving event? They have parades all over the country. Why not here?" said Pastor Harry Morrison of First Presbyterian.

"A parade could showcase our high school bands, give the kids something constructive to do and we could get some local businesses to sponsor some displays too. Time is short though. We need to get some people working on it now. A group of pastors can have an idea but lots of planning needs to go into it," Reverend Tony said.

"We need to get a group of government and business folks involved too," said Father Menendez. "Perhaps we can get some of the civic groups in as well. There's plenty of interest in trying to do something positive. People are just waiting to be led."

"Wow, you folks don't disappoint. I'm thrilled to see the different congregations pulling together. We need more than just talk. Who'll head this up for us? We need to do this across the city to show the city council and the business leaders we're united and serious," Rich said.

Several raised their hands.

He looked around excited by the enthusiasm, but nervous because Senior Pastors have a lot on their plates. He asked, "Do you have the time to focus on this or will you get someone on your staff to run it?"

"I'll have one of the young priests drive it for our church. He needs the experience and has a good connection with the young in the Latino sector," Father Menendez said.

"I'll get my Associate to work on it also. But I'll take the lead to talk it up with the leaders in my community," said Reverend Tony.

"I'll chair the committee if I can get at least five church commitments," said Pastor Morrison.

"Carlisle is in," said Rich.

"Commonwealth AME too," said Tony.

"I can't pledge any money, but we'll supply lots of labor. I'm sure the church leadership will support it," said Father Menendez.

"That's four," said Pastor Morrison.

Pastor Joan and Pastor Lucy said, "We're in!" at the same time.

"We'll put time and money in, too. Let me make sure the board goes along, but I feel sure it'll be a great event for us to be a part of," said Joan.

"Great! That makes six. Mayor Hamilton is a member, I'll speak with him to get the appropriate permits and municipal support," said Pastor Morrison.

"The Senior VP of the bank is a member. So's the owner of Stanley Builders. I'll speak with them to see if they'll sponsor it." Rich said sitting up with his chest out.

"Many of the Harts have been members for years, I'll get them in on this too," said Joan.

Others mentioned civic leaders they would speak with.

"As Tony said, time's short, we need to get this together and meet again in two weeks. Shall we schedule another lunch or just a phone call?" asked Rich.

A teleconference was scheduled in two weeks to see if this was viable.

Father Menendez closed them in prayer, "God, please heal and unite this city that is still hurting and bleeding from its wounds. Send special grace to us at this time of very difficult needs. Give your blessings on the parade idea. May your church embrace the idea and seek to make this a blessed event indeed."

Rich watched his fellow pastors as the meeting broke up and they began to leave. He was pleased at what might be, but cautious knowing there could be more talk than action going forward. He was concerned about how much follow-up would happen and how genuine the commitment from the churches really was. *Can't believe I was part of the name-dropping a few minute ago. What gets into me? Sad that not everyone wanted to be a part of the parade idea. The pastors of two of the largest congregations didn't say a word. What're they afraid of? We have to focus on those that are on the team for now.*

He said a silent prayer for the team.

The meeting room was near the kitchen; José heard the end of the meeting while he cleaned the cooking surfaces. *I must speak with Pastor Rich and Reverend Tony soon.*

CHAPTER 8

The refugees got off the bus and were greeted by Mayor Marcus Hamilton and his wife, Susan. She gently hugged each lady. Marcus shook the hand of each man and boy. He beamed a smile.

Reporters from the Carlisle Guardian, WWNS, and a couple of other news services were on hand. Susan knew Marcus would show for a great photo op as she recalled their discussion a few weeks ago.

"Can you believe the Governor wants us to take a bunch of Syrians from the Feds? The subsidy is good. The PR will be good for us, but we're a country town at heart. We like Christians, if they're not too fundamental. These guys are Muslim. I'm not even sure what all they believe. What if we end up with terrorists in town? I hope to run for greater office someday. I can't have terrorists in Carlisle."

When she heard it, she just knew they had to come here. "We could use an old abandoned apartment complex down the river from Villa Maya. We just need a dozen or so units. I'm sure they won't send hundreds. You can control that. These people are in such need. We can't turn our backs on them. It's not Christian. The Bible tells us about welcoming strangers, remember. You know I studied the Middle East in college. I can be the goodwill ambassador. I'll get some others from the church to help. Think of the PR. On top of that the Governor will owe us one. Our national party will appreciate it too.

"I see the news stories of these people getting shuffled from camp to camp and country to country. It's so sad. I see the photos of the children washed up dead on the beach. Marcus, we have to do something!" She reached out her hand to touch his chin and turn his head to look into her eyes. *I know he loves it when I touch him.* I knew I could draw the humanitarian in him to the surface.

"Besides, you know they vetted these folks closely. They're Kurds, for crying out loud. We fought alongside them in the civil war! There's no way there're terrorists in this bunch. I doubt they have many men at all."

Marcus caved in fast. *I suspect it was the humanitarian and the politician in him.*

Susan found out that the folks up the hill didn't like having *terrorists* in their midst. When she presented it to their church, Susan found a few like-minded people who would help.

A group of fifty to sixty people arrived, families broken up by the war. All were Muslim. Perhaps more would come later once these were settled. Their able-bodied men and older boys died in the conflict, forced to fight on one side or the other, gone without a trace.

The group formed a close-knit semicircle with the bus at their backs. Eyes were wide but hollow, hope drained away. The children looked down at the ground, not at her. The women went where directed but never far from their remaining children. *Small children don't even cry. They must be used to this constant shuffle from one place to another. How sad.*

What few old men and teenage boys there were stayed at the front of the group. *Bus protecting their backs, men in front. Dear God what have these people been through. I can't bear to see children with missing limbs, wheelchair bound.*

José watched them arrive from a distance. He saw gifts given to the refugees. The echoes of the comments of his Latino neighbors rang in his head.

"They came with legal immigration we didn't have access to."

"We can't get access to the city services these guys get for free."

"Didn't we travel and leave home, family and friends to be here too?"

"Where was the mayor and his wife when we got here?"

"They speak a strange language and worship Allah."

"We'll stay away from them."

He hoped that others ignoring the refugees would avoid conflict between the groups. However, José would not ignore them.

José knew the black community in Broken Wharf didn't care much for the Syrians either for some of the same reasons they didn't like the Latinos. But they were a larger voting block and had been around longer than the Latinos. *They wouldn't see the Syrians as major rivals but didn't feel the need to help them much either.*

José was glad to see a few progressive thinkers like Susan Hamilton reach out to the Syrians in the name of God and humanity. He wasn't sure which was first with Susan. *She and her group were a powerful but small minority of the affluent. At least they're willing to engage and help.*

José, Susan, and all those assembled could see the white conservative groups protesting nearby. Signs read, *Terrorists Go Home! Muslims Don't Integrate, They Dominate!; Mohammed Not Welcome Here.*

Jackie Hyatt, on the scene, interviewed one tall, lean protestor who asked, "Were they really extremely vetted?" He answered his own question, "If they were, they'd have been kept out altogether. We don't need radicals here who kill our families. What're the politicians thinking? This isn't our problem."

A rotund protestor pushed the first one aside and said, "We speak English, pray to Jesus, wear normal clothes. These guys worship Mohamed, speak Arabic, believe all Americans should be killed . . . " Jackie cut the mic. She walked a few steps away from the small band of protestors to say, "Well, it appears emotions are high. The protestors are a small, but vocal group. Let's go back to the mayor."

She moved back to Susan and the mayor for a final word.

Susan and Marcus were stately symbols of Carlisle. They were both dressed well, Susan in a purple dress with big sleeves and a patterned scarf flowing off her left shoulder. She was a former homecoming queen that kept her good looks even while she aged. Her long chestnut brown hair, dark brown eyes, dark eyebrows, olive skin and comely figure drew attention to her wherever she went. Marcus the statesman, lean, with thinning, salt and pepper hair. Always in a jacket, and trendy tie. Both had perfect teeth.

He looked at the Syrians and said with a federal translator repeating in Arabic, "We welcome you to Carlisle. This is your new home. We will do all we can to help you settle in this place, despite those who do not agree. Welcome!"

Susan thought it best that most of them couldn't speak English and thus didn't understand the protestors and their signs. *They can't read them but they know the sentiment behind them. This is so embarrassing.*

After the news crews packed up, the protestors dispersed.

✠ ✠ ✠

José approached the male leader of the Syrians. He assumed it was the older man the mayor greeted first.

In Arabic, he said in a slow deliberate cadence, "I am Yosef. Welcome to Carlisle. I am new here also. I will help you get settled. This can be a good place for you and all of your families. It is much safer than where you have been."

Sami Jaziri smiled like he'd seen a long-lost friend. Yosef knew they would love to hear someone speak their language who wasn't a government official. Sami greeted Yosef with gusto, shaking his hand and giving him a hug. Several others gathered around and began asking questions. Yosef raised his hands to calm them and with a smile on his face said, "There will be a time for these questions later. For now, I think you need to get settled in your new homes and rest from your long journey."

Susan Hamilton came over to see what all the noise was about. Approaching José, she cocked her head and asked, "Who are you? What did you say to them?"

He looked in her eyes and said, "I told him my name was Yosef and I welcomed them to this place. I cook for a restaurant in Villa Maya, but I speak most Semitic languages. Theirs is a very proper dialect of Arabic. I told him I would help him and the others if I can."

"Please be the translator for our group while we help them?" She didn't wait for his answer, and continued, "I thought communication would be the hard part but you're a godsend. You just can't turn me down!" Yosef perceived she was used to getting her way and today was no exception.

"I'll have to check with my boss to see how much time I can give to you. I'll help when I can. If you want to speak with Ramone Hernandez at Restaurant Tapas, that may help."

Her eyes lit up at the name. "I'm sure I can work something out with my old friend Ramone." She chuckled after she said it.

Jackie, now in the news van about to drive away, noticed Susan Hamilton with her arm on an attractive man. He wore blue jeans and a dark pea coat. *I'll call him Mr. Pea Coat for now. She made mental notes, dark wavy hair, average build.* She motioned to Bradley to stop the van. Susan had the reputation of being a flirt or perhaps more. *He didn't get off the bus with the others, so he must be local. Mr. Pea Coat didn't belong to the Hamilton entourage either.* Susan laughed and turned to walk away. *I can see why Susan chatted him up, very handsome man. But there doesn't appear to be a story here about them, at least not yet.* She motioned to Bradley to drive on.

José could see that the Syrians were transplanted into a difficult situation. They moved into an old apartment complex, too run down to be repaired without the federal subsidy. The apartments weren't close to grocery stores or bus lines. *I'm sure they don't speak English much less Spanish. Their children will attend the Latino schools nearby and be bullied and ostracized for their clothing, religion, diet and language.*

He also knew that despite all that was against them, the hope and strength of the human spirit does shine through. They made it out of the camps and across many miles. They had a new home. A small group is all the Master needs to make them feel welcome.

When I was a stranger you welcomed me . . .

CHAPTER 9

It had been a few weeks since the riot and the criminal justice system now needed to process all the evidence. Jackie had her questions ready. *I just hope the presentation will answer them. Who would be charged for the deaths of the officers? Would anyone be charged for the deaths of the rioters? Would there be any charges for the shooting of Lamont Wilson? Would more unrest ensue if the rioters didn't like the answers?*

Jackie and her new cameraman Bradley Cameron walked the streets where the riot occurred. She wanted footage of the repairs in progress. The broken plate glass removed. The charred street memorialized the location of each of the burned cars. She didn't see the blood stains from all the injuries. *I wonder whose job it is to clean all that up. That could make for an interesting interview.* Storefronts and doors still had their plywood covering. The shops that had insurance money reopened already. The ones that didn't remained closed.

"What happened to your other cameraman?" Bradley asked.

"Leonard didn't have an adventurous spirit," she said with a coy smile. "He didn't like getting stuck in a mob or in a men's bathroom with me waiting for the police to rescue us. I thought it was cool. We're part of the history of Carlisle. On top of that we had indoor plumbing while we waited. Not a bad hide out. He didn't see it that way and he quit the day after. They tell me you're a man of high energy. Is that so?"

"I'm a cameraman who enjoys some fun and adventure. Not sure I would've liked the mob thing either though. You're the talent, I'm the support. Here to make you look good on air. I go where you lead."

She pointed her finger at him. "You're young and a suck up. I like that. We're going to get along fine, Bradley." She quipped with the same coy smile. "Now get some images of the repairs in progress and the stores still closed," Jackie shifted into business mode.

After some photos and commentary, they made their way to District Attorney McCluskey's news conference. He was going to announce charges today.

The conference room had a sterile tone. A podium set up to the right of center. He put some blown up photos around the room. Mayor Hamilton was there to make opening remarks. Sheriff Ward was on hand too.

No full Hamilton smile today, this is serious business.

Mayor Hamilton, first to the mic, started the presentation. "We're here today to discuss the tragic events that took place in mid-September. I understand many people are skeptical about our investigation. To address those concerns, we used resources from the State Bureau of Investigation. I know that much of what we show today will be distorted to meet some people's agenda. I ask that we all listen with open minds to the facts we know. Some facts cannot be known since we don't have witnesses or legible camera footage or other reliable physical evidence of those events. I turn it over to DA Ike McCluskey now for his announcements."

The DA had thinning hair and a thickening belly. He wore a gray sport coat with black slacks, a black patterned tie. *He must've known that white doesn't show so well on TV so he went with a light blue dress shirt. No, just dumb fashion luck,* Jackie thought.

"Thank you, Mayor." He took a deep breath. "As you can see from the photos to my right, the events in September—while confusing— did allow us to collect enough evidence to file charges in many of the offenses culminating with the September riot. Just like the Mayor stated, we asked the SBI to help us so that there was no local bias in these matters.

"I'll start with the shooting of Lamont Wilson. For those who've seen the amateur cell phone video, and for those of us who've seen the body camera footage, it's apparent that Officer Byrum acted to prevent injury to a fellow officer and a potential victim. While no weapon was found on Mr. Wilson, it's apparent he was a threat to those around him. It was believed by the officers that he had a weapon. The resulting use of lethal force while regrettable was justifiable. In light of this, no charges will be filed and no further actions will be pursued against Officer Byrum.

"I'll take questions now on this matter before I move to the riot itself."

"What about prior allegations of Officer Byrum's racially motivated use of excessive force?" Jackie asked.

"While Officer Byrum has had prior inquiries into his service and has been disciplined for at least one of those, the reality is that there is no basis in this matter to indicate that he did anything wrong."

Sheriff Wade stepped to the podium. "Officer Byrum is still on administrative duty and won't go back in to the field until we believe it is safe for him to do so."

"When can the public see the body cam video? Don't you think that would allow us to draw our own conclusions?" Jackie continued.

"It's department policy backed by state law not to release this. That release tends to be more inflammatory than calming and we have decided to follow the state guidance on this matter." Sheriff Ward responded.

Mrs. Wilson's attorney, William Randolph Hill, was a large African American man who talked in the steady cadence of a Missionary Baptist preacher, stood up from the front row and stated with a booming voice, "Whether we agree with the DA's conclusion or not, we understand that no criminal charges will be filed against Officer Byrum. However, it is clear to me and my client that he has a history of racist behavior and that was a contributing factor in the untimely death of my client's husband. Our intention is to pursue a civil action against the Officer and the city for putting a man with such a history in a domestic disturbance in the Wharf. Regardless of Officer Byrum's actions, Black Lives Matter in Carlisle and in our nation. We will see all the video in court when the time comes!" There was some applause from the group around him.

Can I get an amen? Those comments won't do much to keep the Wharf quiet tonight. I hope there's better news to come, Jackie thought.

McCluskey stepped back to the podium and resumed his presentation. "As you can see from the photos behind me, Officer Desiree Houston died near the corner of Commonwealth and Eighth Street. Cause of death was head trauma with a blunt instrument. Based upon body camera footage, we can see that she was attacked by a group of young men wearing masks and carrying clubs. Mr. Jalen Stone of Carlisle has been arrested for her murder. He's seen here in this photo with a club and during the video responds to his gang alias when it's yelled by others nearby. Mr. Stone is a known leader of the Wharf Rats gang. His gang alias is Stonecutter and it is repeated often in the footage. He was taken into custody early this morning without incident."

He took a drink from a plastic water bottle. His hands trembled when he put the bottle back down.

"In the death of Officer Wayne McCaskill, who died at the scene near Commonwealth and Ninth Street. Cause of death was a gunshot wound to the neck that cut his carotid artery. You can see from the artist's rendering to my right, the angle of the shot came from behind." He pointed to the photo with a red laser pointer. "Based on the caliber of the weapon and ballistics analysis, Officer McCaskill was the victim of friendly fire. He was wounded while the Riot Team was being assaulted and returned fire. He was a rookie officer who shouldn't have been on the other side of the riot police. While we are unclear why he was there, we believe he was killed by Officer Harold Foster. We did recover the bullet at the scene. It contained Officer McCaskill's DNA and is a ballistics match for the weapon Officer Foster used that night.

Officer Foster was acting in self-defense against an aggressive crowd and was under orders to stand his ground and fire. While he won't be charged in the unfortunate accident, he has chosen to resign from the Carlisle Police Department."

Sheriff Ward stepped to the podium again. "We want to thank both officers for their service to Carlisle and are grieved at this tragic event. We encouraged Officer Foster to remain on the force, but he has chosen to leave us."

DA McCluskey returned to the podium, "Officer Craig Forsythe was burned over 60 percent of his body by an improvised incendiary device commonly called a Molotov cocktail. He appears to be out of position based on the photos on the wall to my far right. This was taken a few moments before the incident. He succumbed to his injuries later that night at University Hospital. Based on video footage available and some eyewitness accounts, the device was thrown by Clement Robert Garinger of Carlisle. He is still at large but a warrant has been issued for his arrest. His last known whereabouts were the Knollwood Apartments, the location of Mr. Wilson's incident also."

The DA paused for a moment and took another nervous draw from his water bottle before continuing. Jackie could see the sweat glisten on his brow as he continued his presentation.

"Mr. Rodney Clark was a life-long resident of Carlisle. He died in the middle of Commonwealth near Ninth Street from a gunshot wound to the head. The video evidence is inconclusive but the ballistics and forensic reports indicate this was also a Carlisle Police service weapon. Officer Anthony Scott fired at the direction of his captain to disperse the crowds. One of the rounds struck Mr. Clark killing him. Officer Scott is a black officer. He won't be charged with any criminal wrong-doing in this incident."

The DA turned his notes over and continued. "We also have Mr. William Putnam who died at University Hospital from burns and internal injuries from the mob stampede away from the gunshots. It is conjecture at this point since the evidence is hard to follow, he was apparently knocked into a burning vehicle and he then stumbled backward, and was knocked down by the retreating crowd. There are no credible witnesses to this incident and no physical evidence to tie anyone to the death of Mr. Putnam. Therefore, no charges will be filed in his case.

"I'll now take questions on these findings. And then continue to speak about the charges for the other injuries, property damage to buildings, Hart Park and several vehicles."

The reporters all clamored for attention.

⊰⊱ ⊰⊱ ⊰⊱

Da Wyz watched the news conference on the 86" TV in his office with Jalen Timmins and Tonya Harrison of the Carlisle chapter of Black Lives Matter. He smiled because he already knew the outcome. He knew his guests didn't want to be here. He enjoyed having people squirming around him.

Da Wyz was dressed in a white suit with a black shirt and black handkerchief in his breast pocket. Well-groomed as always. He sat behind his large wooden desk with gold trim. He preferred to stay seated, so his stature didn't diminish his commanding presence. He made his office over the top to accentuate his success to any who entered.

"There will not be any more riots tonight," he said in a quiet and firm tone.

"Did you see that? No officers charged in killing three black men. Two black men arrested or at large for our demonstration. This ain't right, Wyz. We got to do something." Jalen said.

"I agree; the people got to speak. Do it in the churches tonight or at the community center. No more demonstrations at the Park. Too hard to control. Whitey did this to us I know, but we're just playing into his hands if we take to the streets again. Nothin' gonna change. 'Cept more black folks going to get killed or arrested. We can send a message that this is wrong. We can sue in court where we'll get lots of Whitey's money. They hate that. We don't have a good plan for counterattack unless you're ready for loads of violence. All we gonna do is stir things up and confirm what they already believe. We have to live to fight another day. This day is not ours. Our day will come." He continued in the firm and quiet tone.

Tonya leaned forward in her seat. "So, we just lay here and let them walk on us. I don't like it one bit. We have people dead and in jail. The Wharf is frustrated and angry. You want us to tell them to just get over it?"

"I'm not here to tell you what to say. You two are the great mouth-pieces. I'm here to tell you this got out of hand before and needs to stay under control now. Unless you don't like those pretty mouths of yours. I can fix that."

"Jalen, he can't talk to us like that," she said. "We got a following in this town too."

Jalen capitulated, "We'll keep it to the community centers and the churches this time. We do this favor for you; a time is coming when we'll need one too."

Da Wyz smiled, "Now that is why they call it the Biz. I like to ne-gotiate with smart people. Tonya, you can learn something from this young man ... like how to get older. If this gets out of hand tonight, I'll hold you two responsible. I like to negotiate, and I collect my debts. I'm not a good man to owe. Best if I owe you. Let's leave it at that."

"I understand but don't hold us responsible if the cops do some-thing else stupid tonight. We got to find a way to get some justice here. You gonna help us with that?" Jalen said.

"I'm all about dispensing justice brother. Tell me who to shoot and I can make it happen, clean and tidy. As it is, we have to shoot everyone up the hill or all the cops. That ain't gonna work. That's bad for business. Let me dispense justice when the time is right. It won't be with riots and us burning our own neighborhoods. Do this and I'll owe you both. Let this get out of hand tonight and I'll collect from you both. Then I'll know who to shoot."

After some frustrated glances back and forth, Tonya and Jalen agreed to the terms. "We got to get this organized," they said as they got up to go.

"I'm sure Reverend Tony over at Commonwealth would love to help and would be more than glad to have a rally at his church." Da Wyz watched them leave and smiled.

"Get Mario in here," he told his assistant, Julia over his speakerphone.

Mario filled the doorway as he entered the room. He was six feet tall and wide like a wrestler. With a full head of close-cropped hair and full beard, broad chest and hands the size of a catcher's mitt, he exuded the image of a classic brawler. While not as smart or subtle as his other lieutenant, he was good with a gun, a knife, or his bare hands. Da Wyz was proud to have him as one of his top confederates. When he went on a job, it got done. In addition, his size and the brutality of his methods made it only necessary for Da Wyz to send him places once.

He came in and wedged himself into the chair vacated by Jalen Timmins.

"We got some justice to dispense." Da Wyz knew Mario liked dispensing justice. He dialed the Sheriff's Office on his burner phone.

"I did what I said I would. Now you need to deliver. Give me Byrum. There won't be a body. He's mine now. We agreed, no investigation."

Da Wyz jotted down some notes from the call and handed it to Mario. "Like he was, you get to be judge, jury," then he paused for effect, "and executioner."

Mario took the notes and said with dead eyes. "When?"

"Set it up, wait for next week. Do what you like but there won't be any trace found. Whitey got to suffer something for this. Officer Byrum got to pay his debt to the Biz. Close the door as you go."

Da Wyz, alone now, heard the voices again. It never used to bother him when he ordered a killing. He did many himself. Now the echoes of the cries of the mothers of the dead were gnawing at his soul when it got quiet around him. He had the fix—work harder and longer. But he was tired now. He shook it off and grabbed the phone to get Julia to send for Deion.

CHAPTER 10

"The Rats are restless since Stonecutter got nailed. They been looking for action now for a couple of weeks. Got to blow off some steam," said Deion.

Deion Washington was a tall slender black man. Clean shaved, including his head. He was seated with Da Wyz at their main office in the Wharf. Unlike Mario who was more of a hulking presence, Deion, had the finesse of the two lieutenants and posed an ominous presence in his own way. He also enjoyed the ladies, always having a new one around. Da Wyz thought they all could've been models. He didn't realize there were that many beautiful ladies in Carlisle. Deion didn't discriminate. These days, he seemed to prefer Asian women although Da Wyz had seen him with women of all colors. Loyal to a fault and altogether trusted.

Da Wyz responded with a wry smile, "Well it's Halloween, let 'em go trick or treatin'."

"You know that won't do. Besides, they got no action for a while since we been layin' low after the riot."

"We still need to leave the police alone for a while. Tell 'em go shoot some Mayans. Just gangbangers though. No women and children or the cops'll get involved. Cops won't care much if it's a fair fight. They'll think it's just gangs killing gangs. The brothers could use some practice anyway. Might thin the Mayan ranks and get our guys ready

59

for a fight when it's needed. Call it target practice. No wait, call it *a war game*."

After they got the all-clear sign from Deion, the Rats headed out to create mayhem. Shots rang out from the small gang of young men in the midst of the MX 60 barrio. It was late at night and José was on his way home from work, he missed the last bus home. In all the commotion, he didn't know whether to retreat or advance. After a brief prayer, he decided to advance.

As he got closer, he could see a group of five or six men firing in several directions. They were yelling at each other. *Calling out targets? Was it random?*

He noticed one of the shooters near a streetlight, just as another shot the light out. It was a black man. A rival gang, looking for trouble in the MX 60 territory. *This will go badly.*

José knew the MX 60s would be here before long and with plenty of firepower.

The after-lunch trainees told him the most aggressive black gang called themselves the Wharf Rats. This was a bold move to come into Villa Maya and start shooting. The shooters were aiming at storefronts. *Wow! It's loud when plate glass goes down. They're trying to draw the 60s out. They want a fight.*

The 60s obliged. They came from down the street opposite from where José was taking cover in an alleyway. A bright purple hoopti, was blitzing down the street with bright lights on, shots coming from the windows. Foot soldiers came from opposite alleyways in advance of the hoopti. They were well coordinated enough to stay out of each other's way and keep the Rats in the crossfire.

A Rat, Isaac, got off a good shot and took out one of the headlights on the fast approaching hoopti. The car swerved and hit a light pole. Sparks rained down on the battle below. The driver righted the car and continued to accelerate toward the Rats. Guns resumed firing from the car.

The superior firepower of the 60s began to overwhelm the half dozen Rats. José could see them go down, one by one.

The Rats weren't bad marksmen either and José could see the fire-fight was taking its toll on the 60s. Several of their foot soldiers on José's side of the street were down. With all the firepower José could now smell the scent of fireworks and bad cigarettes, as the odor of the shooting filled his nostrils.

The Rats closed ranks and grabbed their injured. They couldn't run toward the hoopti. They couldn't go toward the far side of the street since the 60s were at full power there. They retreated toward where they stashed their van, right where José hid. José slid to the inside of a doorframe and prayed they wouldn't see him while they dragged their compadres to safety. It worked. He got a good look at the faces of three Rats. The other three were either limping or being dragged by the first three. José now realized they concentrated their firepower to clear their path to their ride. As they got close, the vans automatic doors opened and everyone piled in.

It took the 60s a little time to figure out where they went. Cautiously they tried to ferret out their enemy. Once they heard the tire squeal, they realized the Rats were running.

Four of the 60s charged down the alley but could only see the van disappear. They fired a few vain shots in the direction of the dimming taillights. The 60s cussed and yelled threats at a vanished threat. The hoopti couldn't get down the alley due to parked cars and debris. The Rats got away.

Coming back through, one of the 60s spotted José in the doorway. He leveled his weapon. "You one of those Rats, señor?" José stepped into the little amount of light available and came face to face with Carlos Rodriguez. He was one of José's students that afternoon.

"You know I'm not."

He looked at the other gangbangers and said, "He's cool. Not one of them."

"Will he turn us into the Man?" one asked.

Carlos looked at José with his hands open and head cocked to one side. "You gotta answer, man."

"Why would I do that? They don't like me anymore than they like you. I saw who drove out the Rats. I'm still waiting for the police to show after dozens of shots fired," José said.

"He's alright. Illegal like my mom. He's not going to the cops. Did you see who they were?" Carlos said.

"I saw three faces pretty clear. I have no idea who they were. Never saw them before. They're all black teens, I guess. But I'm not going to tell you so you can even a score. Looks like you won anyway."

The sound of police sirens became louder. Carlos looked at José and then at his gang. "We got to get our homies and get 'em treated. No need to stick around for the Man. José, you know they aren't your friend. We take care of amigos who take care of us." At that, they all dispersed into the night. Multiple police cruisers arrived with lights flashing and sirens blaring.

All that was left were a lot of shell casings, broken windows, and blood on the street.

José decided to skirt the area down another side street to avoid detection as he started home again. *What are these boys doing? What is the point of all this?*

Ten minutes later, a police cruiser pulled up next to him. Officer Jim Lemoyne got out. He was over six feet tall, clean-shaven, and overweight. His white skin, stark in the dim light, was very different from all the colors José had seen tonight.

"You been out long tonight, señor—?" he asked.

"They call me José Sabio. Si, officer, just walking home from work."

"Where do you work?"

"I'm the cook at a restaurant on East Boulevard," José said.

"That's a long walk from here. Did you come through the war zone earlier tonight?"

"I did hear some gunshots, but I huddled behind a wall till it was over."

"Did you see anyone?"

"Si, officer. I did."

"Want to make a statement?"

"No, officer, I want to go home and sleep."

"I appreciate your honesty, if not your cooperation. Was anyone killed tonight?"

"No, officer. I saw some injuries but didn't see any deaths."

"Any idea what this was about?"

"No, officer, I don't know. I'm wondering that myself."

"Any idea who the 60s were?"

"Si, officer. I know them. I suspect you do too."

"Yeah, it would be helpful to have a witness though."

"I'm not going to do that, officer. I'm trying to help them in other ways."

"You've been working all day. I'm sure you're tired. Here's my card. Call me when you have a moment tomorrow. I need to get a statement. Nothing we do tonight is going to change what happened now. Call me tomorrow, José of Restaurant Tapas."

As he turned to leave, José realized he still wore his name badge. *He knows my name and my workplace. No wonder he didn't ask for my address.*

Officer Jim stopped and then looked back. "José, I hear you run a cook's training school for the gangbangers at Restaurant Tapas. I didn't make the connection till I saw your badge. You're doing something to make a difference. I work the Wharf mostly, but responded to this call for back up. Figured it was the Rats. I got pictures of them I can show you. No stationhouse. I want to help them just like you want to help the 60s. Give me some positive ID on the Rats and I'll know who to speak with. We won't save many, but we can save a few. We're on the same team. Call me tomorrow, please. Don't make me come find you. I'll stop by the restaurant if you like."

"No, officer. It would be best if I ride the bus to see you. At which stop will you meet me?"

"Take the mainline to Hart Park, we can chat on a bench or in the car. I'll bring the mug shots.

"You may have already figured this out, José, but in Villa Maya, our fight is with the gangs. They seem to be everywhere. They organized along national lines. But the large Mexican population splintered into several different ones. The strongest and one of the most brutal is MX 60. Seldom do the gangbangers live to thirty. They make their money running the area they possess through protection, prostitution, drugs, gambling. They keep the order, so they're tolerated. If things get too bad, we get a call and we try to take out the leadership. That happens every so often. The guys never go without a fight, which seemed to be fine with some on the force but not with me. I hate this part of the job. I know if I don't do it though, more young men die and often-innocent bystanders too. It's the tough part, but part of why I'm a cop."

José said, "I'll call after the breakfast rush tomorrow."

At last, an ally in the Wharf.

CHAPTER 11

José got to the picnic table near the parking lot in Hart Park before Officer Lemoyne the next afternoon. The park was almost empty. Trees were naked with mounds of leaves on the ground needing to be raked and composted. Officer Jim arrived with his mug shots of the known Rats. José swiftly identified the three he saw the night before.

"I know the Saunders kid. His name is D'Andre, but he goes by D. His gang handle is Fixer. The other two are Isaac 'I-Man' Dixon and Jamal 'Super J' Stewart. They're hard-core. D's still salvageable, I hope. We can go talk to him if you have time. I know where his grandmother lives. Sweet lady, Ms. Roberta everyone calls her. We can be there in a few minutes. She's bound to be home," Officer Jim said.

Before he could say *no, I need to get back to work;* the two were riding through Broken Wharf in a police cruiser to see D's grandmother.

"I like Reggie, her oldest grandson and Ms. Roberta a lot. You will too. They're both victims of their environment and the system to a degree. Sweetest person you'll meet in the Wharf. Although she's almost blind these days. She was a force for good in this area for a number of years."

José didn't like being in a police cruiser, but preferred the passenger seat to the one in the back. "What about the boys?" José asked.

"Reggie and his brother D are well known in these parts. Reggie for being smart enough to get up the hill. D'Andre known more for the trouble he gets into. Not sure if he goes looking for it or if it just finds him. Where're you from? What's your story?" He was making idle chat for a cop, but José was on his guard.

"I came from out west to find a better life in Carlisle. I was a farm hand for many years, but others told me I cooked well. I started doing that instead of harvesting. The work was easier on the body and I was older than most of the other hands. I found the money to take some classes but now I just cook what I like and found that it agreed with most people's tastes. I like Mediterranean food these days." *Who am I kidding I've liked it all my life.* "I like cooking for people. I enjoy talking to the customers and meeting so many of the people in the community. Sooner or later everyone has to eat. It's a good way to get to know a new town. If it's good, it didn't have to be expensive. Sooner or later all the important people in town come by and I get a chance to meet them and talk to them."

"Sounds like you've done this before."

Moving into preaching mode, José said, "I believe like Hippocrates and Augustine said that *food is medicine.* So, I try to be sure my dishes use fruits and vegetables and limited meat and grains. I know what the American diet is like and how the poor have a hard time finding healthy food to eat. It's ironic that the poor receive lots of canned foods loaded with salt and other additives because they keep long and don't have to be refrigerated. These are some of the least healthy things for any of us to eat. Especially, the ones with no health care. Then the rest of society wonders why these people are overweight and why they have so many health issues. We do such a poor job educating folks on these topics. If we can keep things from farm to table more, we would do well to extend our lives and eliminate so much misery in the working classes. Not to mention improve children's lives for good, help their young minds develop.

"OK, sorry I asked. You can get off your soapbox now, amigo." Jim said.

José wasn't sure he understood that but went quiet for a moment. He was pleased his food commentary threw Jim away from more probing questions about his past. He often talked about food when the situation was uncomfortable. Such a neutral topic distracted most casual questioners.

They arrived at Roberta's house and parked in front. When they got out of the car, Jim told José to wait. "I need a cigarette." He offered one to José. He shook his head.

He smoked while they continued the conversation. "Well, I'm not one to talk about nutrition." He took a long draw. "You know the stereotype of cops, donuts and coffee. I get my exercise, but something has to keep this six-foot three-inch frame filled out." He looked at his cigarette with contempt. "I've tried to give up these things for years. Coffin nails my mom used to tell me. Well, sounds like something I can resolve to do after New Year's."

He finished his smoke, crushed it out on the tire, and dropped the butt in an empty coffee cup inside his cruiser. On the way to the front door, José said, "Why wait until New Year's? Why not give it up now?"

"Yeah sure, I have a few other areas of frustration in my life right now to focus on." Officer Jim gave an annoyed smile.

José reached out and touched Officer Jim's shoulder as he turned to knock on the door and said, "I believe you can do it this time."

Jim turned his head slowly, "Thanks. Best not to touch a police officer on duty, amigo."

"I didn't mean to offend," José said, withdrawing his hand with care.

"Just don't do it again."

"Ms. Roberta, it's Officer Jim Lemoyne and a friend. We need to speak to you." Officer Jim knocked hard.

The porch had dust thick in the corners with cobwebs all over. This one hadn't been cleaned by anyone, other than the wind, in quite some time. The paint was peeling in large spots. A yard area had sparse grass and a couple of big scraggly bushes that grew out of control.

Roberta came to the door and greeted the officer like an old friend. This wasn't their first meeting. Officer Jim smiled at her. It was obvious from the dark glasses, she couldn't see well.

"Hello officer, how nice of you to stop by and visit an old woman. Who's your friend?"

"This is José Sabio. He works with the troubled youth over in Villa Maya. He's been working with some kids there and he had a run in with D'Andre and his friends last night. Is D home?"

Ms. Roberta smiled at José and welcomed him in, along with Jim. They stepped into a very structured living room. Old photos on the mantle were well arranged, if not well dusted. The furniture was covered with sheets that no doubt hid holes and exposed springs. The bare old wood flooring needed refinishing. No tripping hazards visible.

Ms. Roberta wore an old light pink housedress with brown slip-on shoes and white socks. She was well groomed for someone in her condition. Her smile welcomed them but also showed that she was missing several teeth.

With everyone seated, she asked, "May I get you something?"

"No thank you, ma'am," Jim said.

He must want to get straight to business.

"Is D'Andre here or nearby? I don't want him on the street another night without him knowing that he was a suspect in last night's disturbance in Villa Maya. Is D'Andre here?"

Ms. Roberta glanced down at the floor like she could see it.

"No. He hasn't been here in a few days. He likes to hang out with a new crowd. Someone called Isaac or Jamal or some such names. I heard him talking on his phone a few weeks ago. He hasn't been home much since then. Not sure where he is. Lord how I worry about that boy. He should be growing up. More like his brother Reggie than his dad. What did he do?"

"Roberta, you know there are gangs over in Villa Maya. You know they have real strict ways to deal with outsiders in their territory. It's amazing to me what people will get offended about and what little they will kill for these days. Anyway, D'Andre and his group crossed the line of the MX 60 gang. They started shooting up the place. Not sure if they came on purpose or by accident, but a legion of gangbangers went after them. They got away but not before some stores got shot up. We're convinced some people are hurt and don't know where they are. They haven't gone to University yet. We want to stop this before it escalates. The MX 60 bunch feel like they won the fight I'm sure, but they also got dissed in their own territory and sustained some injuries too. They may want more blood. Might be best to get some folks off the street, kind of like protective custody for a while, until temperatures cool."

"This Isaac kid hangs out around Seventh Street, I hear. Used to be a good kid but got mixed up with the Biz. Then they had him dealing or collecting or running girls. All bad and makes you worse. I tried to get D to stop it but you know how boys can get when they're frustrated and see no other way. They go where the money is. They go to the Biz," she said.

She sounded like she was repeating a sad recruiting slogan.

She looked at José and said, "You're not from around here, are you?"

"No, I came from out west a couple of months ago."

"That's not what I meant." She fixed her gaze on him through the dark glasses.

He'd seen it before, some folks just knew he was different. *Often the unsighted had a different sense of life. Like they were tuned into a different wavelength of awareness. We can all hear it, but none with sight spend enough time in solitude to listen.*

"I came from South America before I landed in the west. Traveled around there a lot. Working farms and being a cook," trying to give her a little more without making Jim suspicious.

Please let this go. I don't want to talk much with the police around.

"Oh yes, perhaps that's it. Your accent didn't seem to be from out west. I listen for such things you know."

They got up to leave and she asked again, "May I get you a cup of coffee or tea?"

They politely declined again. She showed them to the door. Officer Jim gave her a big hug and said, "We'll get D'Andre safe if at all possible."

José reached out to give her a side hug and shook her hand. She looked at him again like she could see his face and said, "Please call again when you can spend some time. I would love to hear about the mission he has you on. Officer Jim, please give this kind man my phone number." With that, she smiled and closed the door.

"She's a sweet lady but a little eccentric. Call me if you really want her number. Sounds like she's alone a lot these days. Reggie should take better care of her. Let's go to the Seventh street *zoo* and see if we can get these boys someplace safe. It should make everyone safer. We need to get D'Andre out of the Biz quick before he gets too far in."

They headed toward the car while the sun rose high over the buildings of downtown.

"I need to get to work Officer. Can you drop me at the nearest bus stop before you go talk to the Rats?" José said.

"Happy to but it's just a block or two down the road." He pointed with his right hand. "I'll take you to Villa Maya if you like."

"No need to drive all the way back there. You have some boys to find. I'll make my own way." José was glad to be away from any further probing questions. He walked to the stop, but knew he needed to come back to speak with Ms. Roberta.

CHAPTER 12

Tony awaited D'Andre in his church office. He had a large desk, bookshelves as well as a sitting area complete with coffee table. Not much natural light due to where it was situated in the building but he made up for that with well-placed lamps and overhead lighting. Tony leaned back in his creaking chair and prayed for the words to come. *You'd think I'd get tired of this after pastoring the same church for fifteen years. But I find energy here among our families, widows, orphans, and even members of the Biz including Da Wyz himself. I wish we had more diversity though.*

Tony liked to speak often in the pulpit and in community meetings about the plight of the poor in the Wharf. The lack of movement by the community jaded him. When he prayed on this topic it seemed to be more by rote now with little expectation, but he continued to do so.

He challenged Da Wyz from the pulpit a few times and learned better of it over the years. Still he felt it was better to have him hearing God's word than not, so he dropped the public confrontations. Da Wyz could do some good and he did provide some protection from the outside oppression so, he gave him a pass on a few other matters that bothered him. The guilt from that conflict felt like a heavy load on him at times. Lately, he focused more on social issues than preaching against the Biz.

Ms. Roberta and her family attended the church for years and he knew them well. When Reggie got into the Carlisle State University

MBA program, he celebrated with them. Now he helped to counsel her when D'Andre got into trouble. Officer Jim and Ms. Roberta both told him about D getting into the Biz, which grieved his heart. *I know I should be more vocal on the Biz.*

Despite his imposing presence, he had a gentle spirit that made him a good counselor to the downtrodden.

Today, he would meet with D to try and talk some sense into him man to man.

D'Andre was a cool nineteen-year-old man with a couple of tats visible on his neck. He was wearing a sweatshirt and blue jeans. Lean and good looking, he was fit, obviously worked out, but at five feet nine inches he was short for a gangbanger. He wore red tennis shoes with short white socks, trying to look tough but, not so much to a six-foot plus man of God. D, now slouched in his chair on the other side of the desk showed Tony his tough guy face.

"D, what're you into these days? How you making your way in this world?" Tony said.

D looked at him like he didn't care much for this whole conversation and said, "I got stuff around the Wharf keeps me busy. What's it to you?" D looked away. "Officer Jim said I had to come see you or he was gonna lock me up for the shootin' in VM last week."

"I've known you, your mama, your half-brother and your grand-mamma for years. This isn't what any of us want for you. We want you getting a good education and a good job like—" Tony said.

D's eyes narrowed as he looked back at Tony. "Like Reggie you mean? I don't like Reggie; he became a white man that lives up the hill now. He don't have time for us and talks so big like he's better than us. He's the same old Reggie, too good to get his hands dirty and too soft to live in the Wharf."

Tony took a deliberate breath, unclenched his jaw, and said, "I was going to say like others in the area who've made a better life for themselves. They're on the right side of the law and make a good living for their families. Yes, Reggie is one but not the only one. You don't have to move up the hill to make life better. You need to make your own way. I live here and have for years."

"Maybe I spoke too fast, but you know you can make it good here without getting the schoolin' you talkin' 'bout. Look at Da Wyz and his brothers. They do well. Have all they want. Lots o' respect and lots o' cash. Lots o' pretty women too."

"D, you know that isn't all there is to it. They die young. They live hard. They fight all the time. Leave widows and lots of kids with no father. That's not what you should be looking up to. They do time. They become addicts. Kids end up homeless. They beat up those pretty women. Is that really what you want?"

D looked at the floor and then back at Reverend Tony. "Well, you know this world is hard for a young black man. The Man don't like us; look at what happened to Lamont Wilson and the marchers. They just want us to go away. We ain't going away, we a problem they got to deal with. We men same as the ones up the hill. They can't just kill us. They can't just cut off the jobs," raising his voice, "They can't just take our pride and self-respect without paying. I want justice! I want a fair chance! I want a good life!"

"I hear you D, but you're becoming what they want you to be. A rowdy black man they can put away for crimes committed. You've not done much bad yet, but you're heading that way. I'm trying to stop you. I told Officer Jim and your grandmamma I'd talk to you and try and get you out of the Biz before it goes too far. I'm pleading with you, D, let's work together to find another way. This isn't all there is, son. Go home to your grandmamma. She wants to see you and she will give you a talking to I'm sure, but she loves you, D. She wants what is best for you and the Biz isn't it. We got jobs programs and night school. You have time. You don't need to take the easy money. I'm afraid for you, my brother. You not that tough or mean. This bunch will let you die just like the Man will if you let them. You need some friends that aren't part of the Biz. I can help there to. What do you like to do? What do you want to be?"

D thought about that for a moment and said in a humbler tone, "They call me Fixer 'cause I like working on cars and trucks. I can hot wire 'em, fix 'em when they break . . . what's the use, I can make a lot more doing the other stuff. Easy money is good money if you don't plan to live long. The life of a black man isn't long in this world. You know that. How many funerals you done this year alone?"

"D this ain't going to be easy. You can live long, many do, but not the ones in the Biz. Stop this, look at the facts. I've done a lot of funerals for those young men. Just like ones killed by the Man. What I'm telling you isn't the easy way, but it is the better way. One that will make you happier in the long run, but you got to put the Biz behind you. I can get you out. You're not even very far in right now. Please let us help you."

"I'm goin' home. I'll think 'bout this but don't get your hopes up. I'm gonna make my own way in this world. If it's short so be it." With that he slapped his legs and hopped out of the chair.

"May I pray for you, son?"

"Yeah," D said, as he turned to go.

"I mean right now, D."

Tony got up and walked around the desk and put his hand on D's shoulder and prayed for Jesus to move in his life. He could feel D lean into his touch. It must've been a while since a *father* type had shown interest.

"Thank you," D whispered under his breath and walked out.

Tony continued his prayer for the young man like he'd done for so many others in this office. Some listened, most didn't. He hoped it wouldn't be a short life for this young man. At least he had someone who cared for him at home. "Lord, what will be next for this troubled young man?"

CHAPTER 13

José, Susan, and her small band of humanitarians arrived at the Syrian refugee apartment complex. José translated. Meeting in the home of Amena Khani, they used chairs and sofas that seated everyone except one. Yosef went to sit on the floor between the refugees and their benefactors, but Sami Jaziri, another of the leaders, objected.

"No, you're our guest. You sit in a place of honor." He moved his own chair and took a seat on the floor.

Yosef remembered the Middle Eastern customs of hospitality and knew that resisting Sami at this point would be an insult. He took his seat.

The living room, though sparse, at least had new carpet. Mismatched chairs from the kitchen had been brought in to accommodate the guests. The whole place smelled of new paint mixed with old mustiness. The aroma of fresh baked manoushi bread came from the kitchen. *I'd love to taste some of that again.*

There was coffee and tea for those who wanted it. While they were being served, they exchanged pleasantries as best they could among strangers with little language in common.

The meeting finally got started and began with brief introductions. Yosef discovered that the refugees created an informal leadership group, headed by a three-person committee. Amena, an attractive forty-year-old with medical skills helped many in the community. He later found out that she had lost her husband and two teenage sons in the war. Two to the bombings and the other to the fighting. *She must be their doctor.*

Rima, a mother of three, had lost her husband and two children to the regime and the fighting.

Sami, a wise older man with only a few teeth, also had lost most of his family in the fighting. All he had left was a wheelchair-bound daughter named Dijlin. Yosef didn't see her at the meeting. All were dressed in traditional Muslim garb. The ladies wore long dresses with hajibs covering their heads. Amena's was black while Rima's was off white. Sami wore a long black robe that buttoned up the front with black pants and a black and white head covering.

While Yosef assumed Sami to be the leader, it was now clear that Amena was the one held in highest esteem. A rarity in Muslim culture but this was no ordinary situation anymore. Yosef translated as she became the spokesperson and started the meeting.

"We created a school to teach the young ones the ways of Islam and the culture of our old home. We try to enlist the older children to help. Some enjoy it, but most want to be part of the American culture. They say the old ways are what got us here. We should embrace the new country we're in."

"Amena, that sounds like you're settling in. What're your most pressing needs? Is the reconstruction of the apartments to your liking?" Susan asked.

"They still have much work to do on five of the units. One, Unit C of Building Two leaks bad in the rain. Another, Unit E of Building One doesn't have running water. The others we can help to fix if we have some tools. We want to help them. It'll teach us how to do things and maybe we can make some money at it. Either way, we don't want to be helped all the time. We want to do it ourselves."

"There is a time for charity; now is that time while you get settled. I'll speak with the contractor and get the pressing matters fixed. What're your other needs?" Susan said.

Yosef paused a moment and moved over to speak to Susan with discretion. "I think we should see what they have. What talents and abilities? Let's see who they are before we start fixing things for them. They're a proud people, like you or I, that have endured a disastrous crisis. They don't want to be a charity case very long."

"Thank you, Yosef. Thanks to me, you're able to join us after I spoke to Ramon. We're trying to help these refugees. We want to be sure they have enough food to eat and proper shelter. We can't make them all college graduates in the next few weeks. You're here to translate, not lead. I require your cooperation, not your input at this time." Susan said through tight lips in a whisper.

Yosef stared at Susan. He could feel the arrogance in her comments.

"I don't want to demean you, Yosef. I thank you for being here, but I've done relief work before and know how to go about this. Please don't question me again."

Yosef recognized that Susan had her own agenda and planned to work it. So, he went back to the center of the room, sat down, and resumed the group conversation.

"We need jobs. We need hope and a purpose," Amena said.

Yosef only translated the first part, then spoke to Amena in Arabic directly and said, "I will help you with the second part. This group only wants to meet your physical needs today."

After receiving a list of things to bring later in the week and a list of construction deficiencies, Susan and her team got up to leave. They left clothing, shoes, and several boxes of canned goods.

"I wish to stay with them for a time. I'll get back to Villa Maya on the bus," Yosef said.

Susan touched his shoulder and gazed into his eyes, "Thank you for being here today. I hope you weren't hurt by my comments."

Yosef got lost in her dark, chocolate brown eyes and enticing facial features. *Despite her arrogance she has a heart for the needy. Could she be the dark-haired lady of my vision?* He realized he had left her comment hanging as his mind drifted. "No, señora, I know what you're doing. I'll stay awhile. I want to speak to Sami's daughter and Rima's son."

Rima's son, Hamsa, stood near the stairs observing the conversation. Yosef had noticed this sullen, quiet boy when they arrived, guessing him to be sixteen. He couldn't be sure if it was his just being a teenager or if deeper thoughts troubled him.

Now that Susan and the humanitarians were gone with their to-do list, Yosef could spend more time and get to know the Syrians better. Susan had gotten him a day off. *What did she promise Ramone to make that happen?*

"Tell me about your son," he asked Rima.

"His name is Hamsa. He's sad and moody much of the time. He doesn't understand why Allah spared him when his siblings were killed. He says he doesn't understand this new land or why everyone seems to hate us. He doesn't matter in the world and won't find happiness. He says he's scrawny and girls didn't like him much. He must've been spared for a purpose, but he doesn't know what it is."

"I thank you. You must be close to your son for him to open up like that. May I address him directly?" She nodded yes. "Hamsa, what's on your mind?"

"I don't know you. Why should we trust you? I don't trust anyone anymore." Hamsa said in English as he got into Yosef's face

Rima put up her hand. "This man is our guest today. He's the only one around who speaks our language, and doesn't treat us like we are a problem to be solved. Respect him!" she said in Arabic.

"He's quite right. I'm sure you've been through many things to test your trust. Let me tell you some of my story so we can all know each other better. First you must know, I'm not a soldier, nor am I with any government agency. I'm sure the Syrian secret police would tell you this too, but I'm not a police officer. I try to stay away from most of them. I have my own reasons for that. I've spent time abroad and traveled all over the Middle East early in life. I was raised there. You must know that I'm not Muslim. I follow a different Master. We can live in harmony together, just like they did down through the ages in places like Spain and Palestine back in the day. I'm not wealthy but will help however I can. I see you are learning English. You should learn Spanish, also. I can teach small groups who can teach others. I live in Villa Maya and cook at a restaurant there."

"Thank you for telling us that. We've many stories to tell, but let us focus on what we have. Mrs. Hamilton's group wanted to focus on what we don't have. Hamsa and I are from the rural Kurdish area near the Turkish border. My husband and extended family were farmers before the war. I still enjoy working the earth with hands and tools. Something very blessed in raising food for your family and others," Rima said.

"I come from the city of Rojava. My husband was a doctor. We met in the hospital. I worked the women's section. The regime bombed the hospital and he was killed saving patients. After that, my oldest son, Karim, became part of the rescue group whenever there were bombings. He died when a building collapsed on him trying to save those trapped by debris. My youngest, Salim, was captured by the regime's troops. I never saw him again. He was just a boy. No older than Hamsa." Amena recited this without much emotion. Yosef could tell her heart was seared.

"We need jobs, something to do. We can't bear idleness. We're hard workers. We just need a place to help the community. The English and Spanish lessons would be wonderful. We have four who speak a little English. Some who speak French. That's similar to Spanish. When can we start classes? We will pay somehow."

"I would love some of the manoushi bread I smell baking. I haven't tasted that for many years."

Amena pulled out a bag and began to load bread into it.

"No please, not too much. I couldn't bear to see it wasted, and I can't eat that much," Yosef said. "Let us have some now together."

As they shared the bread infused with thyme and a light dusting of cheese, Sami asked, "Why don't they like us here. We've done nothing to them. Our children are shunned in school. We're isolated in this community downriver, away from needed things. We have little transportation and stores are almost too far to walk. We need to be sure our children are educated so they can adjust to this society. This is our new home. We want to be a part, we want to contribute."

"I'll work on this, but it'll take time. People don't like newcomers here. Remember what happened in your old land when new people came to stay. They're welcomed at first but then the locals are slow to adopt them. You must be patient with these people also. Many, like Susan, mean well and will do much to help. There are also those who wish you harm. We'll try to keep them away," Yosef said.

Sami shared his story. "My wife and son were killed in a chlorine gas attack by the regime. Dijlin and I were away at a computer symposium. She loves computers and I took her to Rojava for a seminar. The attack came while we were gone. After that she sustained a spinal injury in one of the many bombings. I'm just glad she survived. She went quiet for weeks but came around after a few months. We fled to the camps to avoid the bombings. I'm a university-educated electrical engineer. Now, I'm a refugee with nothing except what others give."

Yosef showed empathy for each person telling his or her story. They spent another hour or so chatting about Syria, their journey, Carlisle, and more.

"I'd like to return soon and bring some clothing, books, and food. I work with a church in Villa Maya, and they help the impoverished. It's part of their mission. They're not wealthy but they do good. I'll try to get some tools also. I know how much you enjoy growing things. The soil is fertile here and you can plant in early spring. That will be here before you we know it. Before I go, Sami, may I meet your daughter?"

"She is resting at this time and not ready for visitors. I plan to bring her to the next meeting. It's hard to get around in these rooms with a wheelchair, but we manage."

They all thanked him for his concern and wished him a safe journey home. He left with a small bag of manoushi they insisted on giving him.

"I don't expect you'll need charity for long, but there is a time for it. Like Susan said, now is that time. Let us help and then you can help the rest of our city one day."

Yosef smiled and made his long way to the bus stop. Because of the refugees, the city put one closer but still, a hike was required to get to it. He admired the strength of the human spirit. He could only imagine what they had gone through to get here and now what they were enduring. They were ready to get on with life. He was sure they still grieved their losses. Healing would take time.

As he walked to the stop, he walked past two young white men in a pick-up truck idling on the road a couple of blocks from the refugee area.

Stu Powell and Jimmy West cased the Syrian apartment complex. They saw the people milling around. A squad of kids playing soccer. A red, white and green flag with a golden symbol in the middle. "Can't you just see a mosque near the main clubhouse?" Jimmy said.

"Something has to be done. These people can't stay here," Stu said.

CHAPTER 14

The Thanksgiving Parade idea caught fire with the whole city. The civic leaders said they were thinking about something like this already and were thrilled to have the churches come alongside. The committee blossomed into a much larger group with the local TV station chiming in for publicity.

Jackie Hyatt did the promos. She never announced a parade before and got the job because Suzanne Fleming, the lead female anchor, had Thanksgiving plans and persuaded Mitch to let her go. Jackie was announcing along with Bob Cullen, whom she respected. However, he had that news reporter arrogance she didn't like very much. She viewed the assignment like a backhanded honor, so she agreed.

While Jackie drove in this morning, she recalled the planning meetings she attended. Mayor Hamilton insisted the parade start at 9:30 AM so everyone would be home in time for a big Thanksgiving lunch and so no one would miss the football. They had a couple of floats, four marching bands, a few clowns, the local Shriner's little cars, a local horseback riding club, and the Whitaker classic car collection. The mayor, city council and others had fun debating who would ride in each of the four classics. The sheriff's office decided to show off their cars and motorcycles, and the fire department had a couple of trucks on display—a modern one from Station One and a classic no station wanted but would be useful in the parade. Hart's store sponsored a Santa float at the end, just like other parades this time of year, adding a touch of tradition to the first annual *Carlisle Thanksgiving Day Parade.*

Carlisle turned out in force to see it. The crisp, fall morning invited the crowd out. A few street vendors came to town to peddle their candy apples, popcorn, and soft drinks, and blow up reindeer and Santas.

This is so different than the strife displayed on these streets just a few weeks ago. I guess I won't have to hide in a bathroom today. She smiled to herself and watched all the kids gathered around adults of every color and class together. People were chasing the street vendors and families were setting out folding chairs along the parade route. It made her heart warm. *Maybe it's just the ugly sweater and knit hat the production crew made me wear.*

"Jacqueline Hyatt, WWNS News at the Carlisle parade. You can see, thousands have lined the streets this morning." A small dog barked nearby. Never daunted, she added with a smile, "Even the dogs are happy to be here."

Before the start, Bob Cullen interviewed Pastor Rich Taylor of the Church of Carlisle who was credited with getting this going.

"This is a great day for our parade and I'm so thankful to God to see how the community came out to support this. It's a real blessing to see how Carlisle came together with only a few weeks to get it going," Rich said.

A band was tuning up in the background; there was the thumping of the drums out of rhythm with the others while they got them ready to start.

"Yes, we have a lot of variety for our little parade. No balloons this year, but we're just getting started," he continued.

"Rich, take us through the whole idea of the parade," Bob said.

"Well the glory goes to God first but he used a lot of different congregations around the city to pull this all together. . . . "

Rich ran long so Bob wound the interview up fast with, "Thanks for your time and enjoy the show."

"I will, I hope you do to. Happy Thanksgiving!" Rich said.

"Happy Thanksgiving." They parted and cut over to Jackie.

✤ ✤ ✤

Sheriff Roman Ward was waiting his turn on camera to talk about security.

"Jackie, we've got plenty of officers here today. We don't expect any trouble, but we're ready for it, just in case. We're on the job and have a great group of officers participating in the parade today, too." He waved to someone off camera.

"I understand you're going to show off some of the department's new equipment today?"

"Yes Jackie, we have some new bikes, motorcycles and police cars riding in the parade. We even found an old CPD car from the 1960s someone was restoring. It's not 100 percent, but it looks good. You're going to hear a few blaring sirens just for fun."

"Thanks for the update, Sheriff, and hope you have a wonderful Thanksgiving." She knew Happy Thanksgiving would get worn out on the broadcast this morning, so she was trying to mix it up.

✤ ✤ ✤

Yosef brought a group of the Syrians to the parade. The leadership group of Amena, Rima, and Sami all came. Some of the youth attended as well, including Hamsa and Dijlin, Sami's wheelchair-bound daughter. While the adults all wore traditional garb, the youth had already gone to the dress of the West. Sami knew the wheelchair would create challenges for transport, so they started early. Now all of them settled in near an area by the grandstands.

✤ ✤ ✤

Jackie noticed Susan Hamilton's attractive friend whom she dubbed, Mr. Pea Coat, from the refugee welcome ceremony. Heading straight toward this group that looked so out of place, she asked if she could interview them on camera. Yosef deferred the question to Amena who waved the idea off holding up both hands.

"Her English isn't good enough to be interviewed," Yosef said.

Mr. Pea Coat looked at Jackie and smiled with his hands turned up hoping to deflect without offending.

"It's just a couple of questions, I don't bite," Jackie said.

"Alright, but not sure we have much to say."

Jackie had Bradley take a quick pan around the group. "Pause on the girl in the wheelchair," she whispered. In broadcast voice, "I'm here with some of the newest members of our community, a Kurdish group that just relocated from Northern Syria. How are you enjoying your new home?"

"This is very new for them. We were speaking on the trip over that such parades back home often had a military purpose. This is very refreshing to see just a community gathered to celebrate a time to be thankful to God for all he has done for us."

Well said, Mr. Pea Coat.

She held her hand to her earpiece and said, "What's that?" She looked back at Mr. Pea Coat said, "Thank you." and backed away to an open shot of the parade ground.

"We're just about to get started." She waved to the Syrian group now a few steps away and said, "I've got to go." Then she scurried up to the temporary broadcast booth overlooking the route, she realized she forgot to get the name of the interviewee. *Can't call him Mr. Pea Coat.* Bill was already in his chair with a headset on over his knit hat.

✢ ✢ ✢

Yosef watched this delightful lady flash her smile and dash away. He didn't watch TV much but did catch her stories on the TV news at the restaurant sometimes. In person, she captivated his attention. While she walked away, Amena tugged his arm, and he refocused on her. She leaned close to him to thank him for rescuing her from the camera and wanted to know what he told the reporter.

✢ ✢ ✢

Back in the booth Bill said, "Here comes the opening band. Let's have a listen."

The leadoff band from Hillcrest High, up the hill, dressed in their well-pressed blue and white uniforms, blasted "God Bless America" all the way down the street. Flag girls with flags twirling fast and furious set the proper mood for an opening act. The crowd cheered the majority white group while it marched by. As they marched away, the band switched to a spirited rendition of "Jingle Bells."

Jackie and Bob did the usual play-by-play, along with getting in the well-rehearsed, off-the-cuff quips each had written down. Jackie could be sardonic at times, but she kept it under control based on the jovial atmosphere. *Am I getting into the festive spirit, for real?*

From her elevated vantage point, she watched people taking photos and videos with their phones, selfies with a clown, and dogs barking from time to time when the bands took a break.

The next band, Benson High Marching Lions from Broken Wharf, showed a lot more spirit than Hillcrest. Uniforms of burgundy and gold were well used and faded. Instruments of varied colors had dings and dents. The color guard of flag girls twirled their banners in complete unison, but their uniforms didn't all match. The cheerleaders led by doing gymnastics. The band played an up-tempo version of "Santa Claus is Coming to Town" while the flag girls gyrated with flair and danced in sync. When the band paused, they danced along, also full of energy and zeal. Everyone seemed to be high stepping along the way. The band, almost all black, was composed of more girls than boys. From her vantage point, Jackie could see the Broken Wharf crowd cheering with whistles and shouts. The more subdued groups nearby looked annoyed.

Reverend Tony and his family were there enjoying the Marching Lions. Sporting a black fedora, a long black overcoat, and leather gloves, he noticed a lot of his congregation in the crowd and waved and smiled to all. Ms. Roberta, Reggie and Deirdre were there across the route, but he couldn't get over to speak to them. D stood nearby and tried to look cool. As Officer Jim passed by on parade duty today, Tony wished him a Happy Thanksgiving.

A convertible classic car drove by with Mayor Hamilton and his wife, Susan, waving to the crowds. Jackie never could get straight the year and make so she focused more on the occupants. Later, a classic Corvette came by with Karl Shuford, the city manager. *He's a good contact and fun to be with, but I know why he's single.* She would meet Karl later for Thanksgiving Dinner with a few friends. They spent a lot of holidays together, both of them were divorced with no children or family in town. *Keeps the loneliness of the holidays at bay.*

Next, came the high school band from Villa Maya. All Latino, they played a salsa version of "Jingle Bells" while the cheerleaders and flag girls *sambaed* to the beat. Then went into a spirited version of "Feliz Navidad." The crowd seemed to enjoy it just like Bill and Jackie did. Again, the uniforms of green and white lacked the shine of Hillcrest, the numbers lacked those of Benson High but none of that seemed to bother the members. They had a good time, based on their energy.

Father Menendez smiled and swelled with pride when they came marching by. He made his way to José, who introduced him to the Kurds over the roar of the crowd and parade. The Father reminded José that the parish Thanksgiving dinner was at three and he could come and bring all his friends.

Da Wyz sat in his office with his wife and two young daughters. He didn't go out in public with this crowd. Too many variables to control. However, he wanted to share this with his girls. Since his office overlooked the Wharf, they had a bird's eye view right on the parade route.

The Carlisle State University Marching Red Eagles played just before the last couple of dignitaries and Santa. They blasted out the best sound of the day, playing "I Saw Mommy Kissing Santa Claus" and a more traditional version of "Santa Claus is Coming to Town." The cheerleaders, both young men and women, walked on their hands and did front and back flips. They gave an impressive display for the crowd who roared in approval.

At the planning meeting, the committee didn't allow a *battle of the bands* since the churches thought that may breed unneeded competition. Local businesses liked the competition idea and offered to sponsor it, but the leaders didn't think it had a place this year. Everyone was cheering loudest for their own group except for Hillcrest, which had more reserved fans.

Toward the end of the route, where the participants finished and began the journey back to their vehicles, Isaac Dixon stood with his pit bull Spike, on a leash. With all the activity, he struggled to hold onto him. Isaac decided the parade was a good place to show off Spike and let folks know the Wharf was Wharf Rat territory. He was proud of his dog and liked the fact that many people were nervous around him.

But he tired of controlling him. Isaac yelled at Spike, over the noise, "Calm Down!" and he jerked his chain. Hard. Kids got scared. Spike, spooked by the crowd, the loud music and everything else happening nearby, didn't want to be there.

Jake Baucom, in town on a rare holiday break from his truck route, looked at Isaac and said, "Get that menace outta here."

Isaac snapped back with a few expletives, the gist of which said, "You get outta here or he'll come after you."

At the veiled threat, Jake's eyes widened. He flagged an officer and said, "Someone needs to get that dog out of here before something bad happens."

Isaac stood with his homies, Jamal, and then D came to join them. Each guy had his well-tattooed girlfriend nearby, staring down any who dared linger on them. Isaac noticed the group of Mayans that were dancing to their school band earlier. *Those Mayans shouldn't be in our hood. They headin' this way.*

Carlos and Juan of MX 60 saw Isaac and the other Rats across the street and decided it was time for some fun. Pushing and shoving each other closer to the Rats where the parade route finished. *Our girls won't like this but I got to have my fun.* As Carlos got closer, he shoved Juan, into Isaac's group. Juan fell backward, into Isaac causing him to let go of the leash. Spike lunged at Juan and took Isaac off his feet. Spike caught Juan on the upper thigh and took a twisting bite out of him. Juan yelled with the fire from his leg and Carlos kicked at Spike to let go. Spike backed away toward Isaac to protect his master while he regained his footing. One of Rats laughed at the bite and closed ranks to keep the Mayans from hurting the dog.

The Red Eagles were still blaring, and the crowd was now starting to spread into the street to avoid the fight and the dog. More dogs started barking in the time it took Officer Chelsea Kepley to respond.

She saw blood, a vicious dog, teens punching and shoving, Rats and Mayans facing off, and the crowd making space for it all while the university band arrived on the street, not knowing any of this. The band kept their lines and their discipline just like at a rowdy football game.

Carlos and the Latinas dragged Juan away from Spike and crossed the street.

Isaac and the Rats tried to contain Spike. The leash trailed along the ground like a snake just out of reach. There were too many people running in multiple directions to even see where the dog went now. Isaac decided it best to go after the bleeding Mayan. Then he saw that Spike stopped in the middle of the road for a moment very close to a lady cop. Spike barked at everyone and readied for another attack once he could focus on who to go after. Isaac called for Spike in vain over all the noise. The crowd moved, and he could see the officer draw her baton lifting it above her left shoulder and lowering it with all her might, right at the dog's head. The dog didn't see it coming and went down immediately with a loud yelp. She stood above the animal, now convulsing from the head injury.

It seemed to Isaac that everything moved in slow motion. He couldn't get to Spike fast enough. Couldn't hear anything but Spike's cry, the loud crack of the baton on his skull, and himself yelling "No!!" The Rats froze where they were while the dog whimpered and floundered in the street. The Mayans got lost in the crowd. The band, no longer advancing, marched in place with the drumbeats all you could hear now.

Isaac fell on his knees near Spike.

In the crowd, some covered their faces, some had their mouths wide open, and others covered their children's faces and moved away from the scene.

Isaac cupped his hands around his dog's head. "Hold on boy. It's going to be okay." The words rang hollow, he could see the blood all over and the dog twitching. He looked at Officer Kepley after cussing at her, "Why'd you hit him?" She had her baton out, ready, if Isaac charged her. She didn't approach them.

"This is on you, buddy. You shouldn't bring a violent animal to a parade. You should've kept it under control," she said.

Three other officers arrived from three different directions and cordoned off a small area. One told the university drum major to disperse the band down the nearest street toward Commonwealth. Officer Jim now joined them and helped move some barricades back one block to stop the parade before it got to the battle zone.

The Mayans were long gone. Isaac was holding Spike's fractured skull while the dog died.

Isaac vowed under his breath, "They gonna to pay for this. No one kills my dog for free. They got to pay."

※ ※ ※

Jackie and Bob heard some reports about the commotion at the end of the parade through their headphones. They kept on the game face and smiled until Santa came by. After they were off the air, Mitch came into the booth and told them what happened.

"Some gangbanger's dog got killed by the cops at the end of the route, but not before it took a bite out of one of the VM kids. Sad, we can't even celebrate without these hoodlums getting out of hand."

"Let's get the full story before we conclude. I guess we'll have a story for tonight's news other than the feel-good fluff. It keeps us in business, eh?" Jackie signaled for Bradley to come over so they could get to the scene. She checked her watch. *I can still make dinner.*

Bob just shook his head in disbelief.

CHAPTER 15

Ms. Roberta answered the door for José. He called yesterday request-
ing a visit to continue the discussion they had begun with Officer Jim.
Having guests delighted her, especially someone as interesting as this.
She smiled as he came inside off the cobwebbed porch.

"Please take a seat on the sofa. Reggie tells me, it's lumpy but also
feels like a warm, welcoming lap of a loving parent."

"I made you some coffee. I hope it's how you like it. I have to ask in
advance these days or I spend more time fixin' food than visitin' with
my guests. My mama told me 'it ain't right to have company over and
nothin' to offer'. Downright inhospitable. Got you some cookies too.
Store bought. You don't want nothin' I'd bake these days. Used to be a
good cook now I can't see enough to tell what I'm puttin' in stuff." She
chuckled to herself and shuffled over to her favorite chair.

"You're a special guest I know. Thank you for coming to gossip with
an old woman."

"It's I who should thank you for your hospitality today and for
agreeing to see a man you barely know in your home. I'm grateful for
your time. Tell me your story. How did you get here? What's happened
in your life journey so far?" José said.

"Oh, where to start? Well, I grew up in Carlisle. This was my parent's house. When they passed years ago, I took it over. I raised my
children here. My daughter, Casandra, such a beautiful girl . . . " Even

though she couldn't see, she pointed to pictures on the mantle. She figured they were dusty and faded. "She got pregnant in High School and had Reggie when she was seventeen. Then went on to get married to a different man a couple years later. Marvin was his name, such a cruel man. She had D'Andre by him almost twenty years ago.

"Marvin left after a few years, so Casandra came to live here. D's last name is really Prince but no one calls him that. He goes by Saunders, like his brother and me. Cassandra became a single mom with two boys. Got hooked on heroin and died of an overdose when D was 10. I didn't even realize she had an addiction to the stuff until it was too late. My sight wasn't failing at the time, but I couldn't see what my baby was doing. I was too focused on helping with Reggie and D. Raising them like my own. I never believed that stuff could happen in my house."

She paused a moment and took a deep breath.

"My son Lucas was a different story. Always a good boy who didn't much like school. He joined the army after his senior year at Benson High. I insisted he graduate since his sister didn't. He fought for our country in Afghanistan. Got killed by a roadside bomb on his first tour. He never married, didn't have no children. You can see the flag and picture on the mantel." She dabbed a tear when she said it, almost without knowing.

She cleared her throat and changed the subject, "Me, I worked as a CNA for many years while the kids and grands grew up. Praise the Lord, the house was paid for so we could make it on what little I made most of the time. Got some help from the government. Still do. I had to quit working when my vision faded.

"After Casandra and Lucas died, I still had Reggie and D'Andre to care for and to care for me.

"I've always been active in the Commonwealth AME Zion Church down the street. I can still walk there although they usually send someone for me. The Lord gave me great comfort after Casandra passed. My vision started to fail too. Then with Lucas making the ultimate sacrifice just a little while later, I was in a bad way. If it hadn't been for the Lord and his church I don't know if I would've made it."

She paused and took a sip of coffee.

"He gave me Reggie. What a beautiful and smart boy. Good in so many ways and at so many things. Always busy. He didn't let school issues get in his way. He spent time at the library and studied hard. He got a scholarship to the University. He studied business and got his MBA through their program. He was the first in our family to graduate college much less with a master's degree. He joined the bank and now stays busy all the time. He's making a good life for himself. I don't see him much no more. He got out of here, which is good, but I do miss him. He and his wife Deirdre came to see me on Thanksgiving. We went to the parade. I couldn't see much but just enjoyed being there with everyone. He has his own family now. No kids yet but one on the way. A great grandbaby. I'm so looking forward to that."

She smiled like a proud grandparent should when she said that.

"D's a different story. Amazing how brothers can grow up so different. I guess it's how God made them. I wish D was more like Reggie, but D is D. We need to get him out of the Biz and on the right path before something bad happens to him. Now, you know about me. What about you?"

"You didn't mention your husband. What happened to him?"

She crossed her legs at the ankles and pursed her lips. "He was a good man to start but developed a drinking habit. Not good. He was hard on the children. He got full of rage and began to take it out on us. He beat me. That's how I lost some of my teeth. He just had to go. We couldn't take it anymore. I heard he died in prison in another state a few years back. I don't like to talk about that."

"No need. I've heard all I need to."

"Me, I made my choices in life and have to deal with it. We need more chances to get ahead. The schools aren't great here and the boys see easy money in the Biz. The girls want to be with the boys, so they don't do what they're capable of either. People lose hope. Me, I just keep praying for things to get better. With the shooting and riot, not to mention the parade mess, not sure anything's going to." She paused a moment and then went back to José. "You're not getting away with distracting me. Tell me about you please."

José took a deep breath. "Roberta, the Master has heard the prayers of this place. There are many righteous people who want to do his will but aren't enabled to. The leaders aren't speaking the full teachings of the Master. Nor are we following in all his ways. He sent me here to help. I answered the Lord's call long ago to protect the downtrodden in the world. That's why I'm here. I'll stir things up some to make that happen. Change always requires some death and rebirth. Many died before I got here. I'm here to help with the rebirth. You know, there are labor pains in such efforts but the joy that comes after is worth it.

"I prefer if you call me Joseph. That is my given name. I go by José because I spend so much time in the Latino community. It fits that culture better. I prefer Joseph with you."

"You're here to help us be reborn? How will you do that? If you are from the Lord like you say, what're you planning to do?"

"I can't speak of all that is coming because it isn't all clear to me yet. That will come over the next few weeks and months. I know you've been through a lot. You've come to terms with the death of your children, something no parent should endure. You had a difficult relationship with your husband who is gone now. You're faithful to the God of your youth who always enjoys the fellowship of those who love him. Tell me, Roberta, do you want your sight back?"

Her face went expressionless as she cocked her head to the right and turned toward Joseph and asked, "What did you say?"

"I asked if you wanted your sight restored."

"The doctor told me early on, it's macular degeneration. It's irreversible. Yes, I'd love to see again . . . another sunset . . . the faces of my grandchildren. But I've reconciled that it won't happen this side of glory. Please don't tease on old woman, Joseph."

"May I approach you and touch your face and pray for you?"

Not sure I like that idea. A stranger touching me. He's a man sent here by God. I sensed that when we first met. I feel truth in his words like I've not known in a long time. Could he have the gift of healing?

"Yes, I'll let you touch my face."

Joseph stood and walked the couple of steps to Roberta. The floor creaked while he approached. He held out his hands and asked her to take them and place them on her face. She took off her dark glasses and angled her face up toward where he was standing. She put his fingers to her temples and closed her eyes to pray.

Joseph prayed in a low voice and a language that was foreign to her. He prayed, and a calm came over her. When he said *Amen* he moved his hands away from her face. She opened her eyes and saw his face looking at her. What an amazing sight! She could see again!

Blinking over and over, "Am I dreaming?" She looked around the room. Joseph was smiling at her. Her heart was thumping a mile a minute. "How could this be? They said it would never happen. They said it was impossible."

"Your faith has made you whole. Please don't mention me to others. I still have many things to do and need anonymity. Give God the glory."

She could barely hear what he was saying, so many new sensations flooded her mind. "I can see the mantle, the pictures, the flag for Lucas. I can see the room. The sunshine through the window. I see the door, the hallway to the kitchen." She was afraid to move for fear it would go away as fast as it came.

"You are healed, Roberta. Use this for his glory. He will be glorified in your life, if you'll let him. Please don't mention me in your story, though."

Roberta nodded in agreement with great vigor. With the impact now hitting her, she jumped up and gave Joseph a giant hug. She almost knocked him down. "Praise God, Praise you Jesus. Thank you! Thank you! O my goodness, praise you Lord."

She walked around the room looking at the walls. Looking at the floor "What a mess! What an amazing beautiful mess!"

Fumbling in her pocket for the phone, she had to call Reggie and D. Before hitting the speed dial, she looked at Joseph. He smiled at her again and said, "I must go now. There is more to my mission than this. Use this for his glory. He can do remarkable things through you. I must go." After another big hug, he went out the front door. "I've never seen more lovely cobwebs. Look at the trees, look at the yard. It needs work and I can't wait to get at it."

"Call your family. Go see your minister and let him know God is working in this place. He has heard his prayers, too."

She looked for the phone in her pocket again but realized it was in her other hand. She dialed the speed dial and saw the number on the phone for the first time ever. "Praise the Lord! Thank you, Jesus!"

A PSALM OF THANKSGIVING FOR GOD'S WORK IN THIS PLACE

Praise you Adonai Rapha for bringing sight to the blind
Thank you, El Roi, for watching over us
For using me in your work

Praise Hashem for his loving kindness to His children
What an amazing Father who loves us so
El Elyon makes a way where none can be found
His Comforting Spirit abides with us in desperate hours

Praise Yeshua, the Messiah who saves us by His sacrifice
Praise Elohim for who He is
Praise Father, Son and Holy Spirit

CHAPTER 16

Reverend Tony met with Roberta, Reggie, his wife, Deirdre, and D'Andre, in his office. He had received Roberta's call about being able to see again this morning with great joy. His amazement at her healing made him want to get the facts so he could better understand.

He offered to come to her home, but Roberta wanted to get out of the house after being stuck there for so many years. They were coming to his office where he had counseled D just a couple of weeks ago.

Smiling from ear to ear, he greeted them when they entered. "Does anyone need coffee or tea?"

Roberta asked for green tea with milk. The others didn't take anything.

Tony asked his assistant, Shakiah, to get the tea and a black coffee.

Roberta, always well dressed at church, looked very stylish today. *I don't know all the tricks to dressing for the visually impaired, but she won't need that anymore.* Her clothes, though not expensive or new, had been well cared for. Her makeup applied just right. She seemed a well-organized woman with understated elegance now even more than before. *I guess living blind requires one to be neat and organized so you know where things are.*

Reggie wore his usual banker's attire, an expensive suit and tie. Deirdre, a beautiful lady with a smooth complexion, wore a purple and white knee length dress with a small baby bump showing. Her coat lay over her arm.

He smelled a wisp of sweet floral perfume when she moved past him to her seat. D'Andre even cleaned up for the meeting, wearing a nice jacket and khakis, doing without his usual sweatshirt and jeans. *Not sure all Roberta had to do to get him in that outfit, but it worked. He looks good.*

"What a beautiful family you have, Ms. Roberta. You look great, too," Tony said.

"Thank you Reverend, I always knew they were beautiful, but hadn't been able to see that for so long now." She smiled with beaming pride at the three of them.

Shakiah brought the coffee and tea in nice, but unmatched, cups with milk on the side. Roberta leaned forward and poured some milk in her tea, stirring it gently. Reverend Tony reached for his coffee, but Shakiah, always the hostess, got to it first and handed it to him with a smile. He took it and sat back in the chair. Shakiah lingered in the room, knowing something miraculous had happened. "You can go now," said Tony. "And thank you for the coffee."

Tony settled in for the conversation right next to Roberta. They gathered in an oval shape around the coffee table.

"How is this possible, Ms. Roberta? What did it feel like? How did it happen?" Tony asked.

"I've been praying for D and Reggie for a long time. Hoping they would come to know the Lord better, get more involved in church, and be a force for good in our neighborhood. I believed the doctors when they told me about my failing vision and didn't hold out much hope of ever seeing again this side of glory. However, my faith was strengthened, and my prayers still went up to heaven each day."

She leaned toward Tony now.

"You must promise to keep this confidential. I've sworn the kids to secrecy already. It was the request made by God to me." She paused and took a sip of tea, "Do you promise?"

"How can I promise when I don't know what you'll say?" He thought for a moment and said, "Yes, I'll keep your secret." He leaned toward her in anticipation.

"Last month I met a man with Officer Jim. He was concerned for D being in the Biz." She glanced in D's direction, and then turned back to Tony, "I could tell there was something special about him. He wouldn't talk much with Jim there, so I asked him to come back when he had a chance. Not sure he'd ever come again, but he phoned a couple days ago and we met yesterday. He told me God sent him here on a mission. After we spoke for a time, he touched my face and I could see."

Tony opened his mouth to speak but out of respect stopped there. She hadn't finished her story.

"I went to Dr. Shapiro, my eye doctor, this morning. I called and said I had to get into see him. The nurse told me he had a full schedule and couldn't see Medicaid patients on short notice, would two weeks from today work for me? I told her to just let him know my blindness was cured. I could see everything now. She put me on hold and then, what do you know, I got an appointment for 12:45." She laughed.

"He looked me over and thought I was a different patient. He thought he had the wrong records. He said my eyes showed no sign of the degeneration. 'They're beautiful, like new.' He wanted to know how. I told him God did it. I didn't tell him all of the story. I only told him, that I opened them yesterday and I could see. He told me about how the body had ways to heal itself, which remain a mystery to us at this time. 'Perhaps you had a recent revelation about something that removed some long-suppressed pain.' I mentioned that I remembered that I was blind to Casandra's drug issues and perhaps felt guilty about not seeing it. I'd been forgiven for this, but perhaps still harbored some deep repressed issues. Dr. Shapiro said 'Perhaps.'

"He did ask if he could study me more. 'It could help others.' I told him, 'No'. I don't want to be a lab animal. My healing was unique, and I knew God did it. Science may be able to explain how, but not why. He persisted but I remained resolute. I want God to get the glory. Not Dr. Shapiro or anyone else."

Reverend Tony listened to the Shapiro commentary with eager anticipation to get to his questions. He laughed along with the others while she described her appointment. He appreciated what she said but wanted to hear more about the healing. He asked with great anticipation, "Who was this man who healed you?"

"Remember you promised not to tell. I fear that if I don't do what he says, I'll go back to being blind. So please don't reveal his name to anyone."

"I promised. I'll keep it to myself. The God I know won't take away this healing. I don't believe he did this to test your resolve. From what you describe, he did it to reward your faith. You've been through too much and proved faithful over the years. You don't need to fear him like that."

"The man's name is Joseph. He works in Villa Maya. He said they call him José but he prefers Joseph. He said he had much work to do and did this for God's glory. He said he had a message for you too. He wanted you to know God heard your prayers and is moving in this place."

Tony hoped his mouth wasn't wide open for long while he listened to the story. He almost dropped his coffee at the last comment. "This sounds like a Bible story of old."

She paused a moment, then asked, "So how do we use this for God's glory?"

"Well . . . " Tony rubbed the back of his neck and exhaled. "First, I wanted the story, which I have now. Let me pray over this and think about it. I'm not sure how at this point. Is it okay if I speak with this Joseph?"

"I don't think so. He told me not to tell so I think God will show us how to use it and give Joseph his anonymity to continue the work. Please don't contact him. I suspect he'll seek you out soon."

"I'll do what you ask. God has done an amazing thing here; he'll show us what his will is for it soon, I suspect. He already is being glorified. Just look at you guys together and happy. May you go with God."

They devised an official story that left the messenger out. Then they shared some other stories and reflected on life; the Reverend prayed for them and sent them away. They left, still rejoicing in Roberta's sight and in the work of God yet to come.

Around 6:00 PM that night, Reverend Tony found himself in the office of Da Wyz. The office was on the top of one of the old Wharf warehouses overlooking the river. *High enough to avoid any shots fired at street level.* The office had over-the-top décor. An overabundance of what seemed like velvet and leather. Deep colors and dark woods everywhere with gold highlights in places. *No doubt designed to reek of success and over reward a poor childhood, now so far away it was almost forgotten.* The ceiling was high around twenty feet. *It makes the man look smaller than he is. Doubt anyone tells him that.* The smells were of smoke and musk covered with some type of incense. Tony had no idea why he'd been summoned. Jeremiah came to see him when he wanted something from the church. *Never been in the lair before.* Tony was flattered that he was trusted enough even to know its location.

Da Wyz kept him waiting, to show who was in charge. He entered the room from a side door, dressed in a black suit with a pink shirt open at the neck. He had a pink pocket square in his breast pocket, smoothly ignoring Tony while taking a seat behind his desk. He was now holding court with Tony.

"I suspect you're wondering why I called."

"We've spoken before but never here. Yes, I am wondering what was so urgent that you had to see me today."

"I know you met with Roberta Saunders today and that her blindness is gone. I want to know how it happened."

Tony told the story he and Roberta rehearsed, "She had been praying yesterday and when she opened her eyes she could see. She went to the eye doctor today and he verified all is well. He thinks it's because the body heals itself and she let go of some repressed issue in her life. I think God moved and wants to let us know he loves us even with all the mess in our lives."

"That's the story for the church. What aren't you telling me?" Da Wyz smiled unconvinced.

Tony feigned surprise. *I don't speak half-truths well.* "God sent a man to her. He healed her with God's power."

"Now we're getting somewhere. And the name of this man of God?"

"I promised I wouldn't tell. I promised Roberta before God in my office just a few hours ago. Please don't ask this."

"I respect a man who keeps his word, but I need to know what's happening in my Wharf. I can't have people chasing after folk heroes. I need to know what his intentions are. I want to meet and speak with him. How can I do that if I don't know who he is?"

"I don't know how to resolve this. I can't tell you and keep my word. Yet you're not gonna let me out of here without a name, are you?"

"You're an insightful man, Reverend. I've no desire to harm a man of God. Especially my own minister. So, let's play a game. What does Roberta want from this?"

"She wants God's glory. That's what the man told her."

"You both want D out of the Biz, too, I've heard."

How does he know this stuff? "Yes, that's true."

"How about I trade that for a name. You get what you want. Roberta gets what she wants, and I get what I want. It's a win all around. No one gets hurt." Da Wyz grinned.

Tony looked down and began to wring his large hands. He loved the idea of getting D out. *That must be God's will. What could Da Wyz do to someone who could perform miracles?* He muttered almost under his breath, "I promised not to." He looked back up at Da Wyz.

Tony felt his resolve weakening. He knew Da Wyz wasn't known for his patience either. *This is hostile territory. Da Wyz had home field advantage. That's why I'm here.*

Da Wyz came across the room and stood in front of him. "Tony, I have to know. If you don't tell me, I can lean on someone else. Reggie or D know, I'm sure. Do you want me to do that? In addition, you get what you want, too. I could even make a nice contribution to the church on top. You're bound to need some extra money these days with all the trouble going on."

Tony looked up. "No money! You make me feel like Judas. I'll do this to save a young man. I won't be bought with silver and gold."

"It's simple. Freedom for D for a name from you. No pain, just a small concession. Just a few syllables."

"No one gets hurt right. I couldn't live with myself."

"That's right. I just want to talk to the man. Give me a name. I'll find him."

Tony breathed out an audible exhale. "He goes by Joseph. He works in Villa Maya. He'll have to tell you about the healing. Roberta didn't say much after the encounter."

Da Wyz's face changed at the mention of VM. He lost his smile and raised an eyebrow. "See, that wasn't so hard, and you spared a young man from the Biz. Which happens to be my Biz. But I'm not insulted. He's a promising recruit. We both gave up something we value. Let's keep this talk to ourselves. Your secret is safe with me. May I get you anything before you leave? We have lots of pleasures around here."

Tony wanted to go take a shower now. *Lord, please get me out of here.* "No. I want no part of the Biz. I'll pray for you. You know this is wrong. All the killing, all the prostitution, all the drugs. How can you do this in the neighborhood you grew up in? Think of the good you could do if you turned to the Lord."

Da Wyz let out a big laugh. "You want me to turn away from all this, brother, you're crazy. I have everything a man wants and then some. Please save your words for Sunday. If God didn't want me doing this, he wouldn't reward me so well."

"But do you have peace?"

Da Wyz's smile left his face again. "Tony, you need to go. I'll keep my word. D is out of the Biz. That's our deal. You have other souls to save I'm sure."

Tony got up and was escorted to a limo that took him back to the church.

✠ ✠ ✠

Da Wyz sat back down at his desk and rang for his assistant, Julia, "I need to know who this Joseph character is, from Villa Maya. He must be new, or we'd heard of him before. Get Deion in here now."

CHAPTER 17

Pastor Rich shook José's hand and welcomed him into his office. "What may I do for you my friend? Please be seated. Father Menendez says wonderful things about you. He told me how you work with the troubled youth of Villa Maya. He said you run a training kitchen at a restaurant there. Why do you want to speak with me today?"

The pastor's office was quite modern. A bright, white, U-shaped desk with sit-to-stand features, a black leather desk chair and comfortable black fabric guest chairs. The back of the U had a bookshelf with volumes of all shapes and colors. The room was awash in light from the windows on two sides of the corner office overlooking the playground outside one floor below.

José looked at him and said, "My name is Justus Sabbas. Just like you say, I work at Restaurant Tapas. I'm the head cook. I go by José Sabio in Villa Maya because it allows me to fit their culture better. You must understand 'being all things to all men.' I overheard your pastor's lunch meeting back in October and told Father Menendez I wanted to meet you. Thank you for finally agreeing to see me."

"Sorry it took so long; the parade took up a lot of my time, but now that's over, I'm able to get to a few other important matters I had to delay."

"I work with the Latino gangs and the Syrian refugees. I come today to see if your church is willing to support either of those missions in the Master's name. You must be able to see God is bringing the world mission field to us. We have a chance to do international missions without leaving town. We must meet him on that field he brought to us and watch what he does."

"We already support many causes in the impoverished communities of Carlisle. But before we go there, tell me about yourself. Who are you? How did you come to be involved in these ministries? I need some background . . . context."

"I'm a lay minister of sorts for these communities. Like I mentioned, I cook to support my ministry focus. I haven't any family other than my mission field and I'm very passionate about it."

Rich smiled in understanding, sat back in his chair, and began to twist from side to side. "I admire your commitment, few would make those sacrifices for their mission."

Sitting back in his stationary chair, Justus said, "I try to reflect the Master's love to people who live in despair. I've found the poor are much more receptive to the Word and work of the Master than the comfortable. I've traveled many places and have always had a passion for those in need. I work for the defenseless. Children and women are the usual focus of my work, but I see here that men who are illegals are also at risk. They're often taken advantage of since they can't cry out to the police for fear of deportation. They, not to mention the women and children, seem to be a forgotten group by our affluent communities. Treated more like cheap labor than like the Imago Dei."

Rich responded with apprehension in his voice, his chair now stationary, "I see, go on please."

"The affluent wall themselves in with private schools and community activities that have them interacting with their own. I suspect that many in your congregation were amazed at the riot I'm told happened this September. I suspect they condemned the rioters—ungrateful people who don't know how good they have it. They condemn the gang activity too and do all they can to further insulate themselves. Who could blame them unless there is a missional focus? They hide away up the hill rather than engage. They no doubt decry the Thanksgiving parade incident as more gang activity they're happy to avoid. Few will be sensitive enough in the Spirit to be able to ask why this is happening in their city. You must raise these questions to your church."

"Okay, then, you're here to make me uncomfortable I see," Rich leaned forward now with his hands on the desk.

Justus also leaned forward, "Mostly because the affluent busy themselves with providing for their families, paying private school tuition, and so forth. They have no margin in their lives. What they give is to their schools and other community organizations to further selfish interests and then wonder why the impoverished don't work harder and can't get ahead.

"You know just like I do that in this system very few will get ahead. We've forced *slavery* on the impoverished. We put them in aging neighborhood schools with like-minorities and not enough funding or parental involvement. We keep them in these neighborhoods by pricing housing outside those areas too high. And we keep the public transit system to known routes without expanding it to service other places, which, in effect, keeps a cycle of poverty going from generation to generation. I've read the reports of affordable housing trying to be placed in other areas of Carlisle and all the objections by those in the areas nearby. Many, who I suspect call themselves Christ-followers, but in reality, they are more self-followers. That is why they lead and support those protests. Some of these I suspect are even members of your church, Pastor."

Rich now engaged with mind and body, his passion stirring. "Keep going, my friend."

"We build big churches and church schools and keep the children from the real world. We don't allow the impoverished in and then borrow so much that we can't afford to help them. The result is that we've created clubs that look like churches and don't reach out to the poor and downtrodden. What would the Master say?"

"Is that all?" Rich said, as he leaned back in his chair again folding his hands together in front of him and stroking the inside of his palm with his thumb.

Justus nodded.

"Well, you're passionate about your mission, there's no doubt. I think you're being hard on the affluent though. They aren't mean and evil. They live in blissful ignorance at times."

"With respect, sir, ignorance is no excuse. They choose it. Just like I chose to be a part of these communities and choose to be educated about their lives. It's our jobs, as ministers of the Master, to not allow their ignorance. We must declare the truth and they must deal with it. I'm here to comfort those in distress and to make the comfortable uncomfortable. I fear that includes you.

"I'm being very forthright with you sir, in the hopes that this will move us all to action. This community can't survive on the backs of the poor and disenfranchised. It will eat away at the foundation of our city until all the castles come tumbling down. We can't rely on the police to keep order for groups that don't respect the law. We can't ask people to respect the law that was made by those who oppress and disregard them. It's our task to stand with the powerless. You must see that in the Master's message."

Rich unfolded his hands and leaned back further in his chair. He turned to one side toward the window without speaking. What Justus said rang true in the back of his mind, but he felt it wasn't fair. He didn't think this community was about to create more trouble. He paused and looked down at the floor and turned back to respond in a thoughtful way.

"You're over the top with this high and mighty talk. Our church protects the unborn. It's one of our key initiatives. Who is more op-pressed than that?"

"You should do that, but we can't forget them once they are born. Remember our Master says, 'You should do the one without neglect-ing the other'."

Rich was caught flat-footed by this stranger who spouted truth with such ease and conviction. He felt the Spirit prompting him to lis-ten, but really wanted this to be over now. If the goal was discomfort, he already succeeded. Now Rich was rubbing his right temple with one hand. He took in a deep breath and exhaled slowly.

Justus continued, "God still judges unrepentant sin. You know that. But it's not God's judgment that will come here. It is the logical outcome of humanity's sin nature. If we continue in sin against our fellow man we should not be surprised when they rebel also in sin. Is that not an outcome of the free will we exercised in Eden? God doesn't bring judgment at this time, he brings mercy. That's why I'm here, to show his mercy."

Rich held his tongue, not sure what would come out if he tried to respond. He made a circular motion with his right hand now encouraging Justus to continue.

"You, no doubt, want to dispute what I say. I suspect you'll come up with arguments that help you deal with this. Perhaps you already have. I'm asking for help from those who can, on behalf of those who cannot. It will show God's mercy to them and allow others to participate in this wonderful blessing. It's the holiday season and thus budget time. Please consider not just a gift of money, but of time. We must build community here with those who love the Master, no matter where in town they live. Ask the Master what you should do. I'm doing so and he led me here to you today. He gave me the words this day. My task was to declare it. I must speak what he places on my heart. Listen or don't."

Rich could feel his clenched jaw as well as the muscles on his back tighten. Defensive thoughts began racing through his mind. *Who does this guy think he is? Why am I on his call list? How does he know so much? He has passion for sure and is unapologetic when he confronts complacency. But our church does a lot of good things for Carlisle and has for years. What does he want? Not sure if I can preach on this. Who would listen? What would the elders say? What does the Word say? How can one church impact the needs of the Wharf, VM, the Syrians, not to mention our own congregational needs. The task is too big. There are so many.*

This man has come in here and knocked me off of a comfortable perch, and I don't like it at all. I need to end this conversation now and get him out of here.

"This task is too big. Our Carlisle Church alone can't solve all the issues for the Wharf, VM, and the refugees. It's too much."

"You're right, it's too much for your church, but not the Church. I thought from your lunch meeting you had a vision of uniting the churches of the city to help heal its scars. Was it just words?"

This guy has an answer for everything. I've got to stop this conversation now!

"Justus, your words are harsh and quite disturbing. I see that you're trying to get a reaction from me. I won't give you one today. I've too many other things happening here now. I need time to go over this with my elders and staff. We'll take your thoughts under advisement. I do like a challenge and I do like to challenge our church, but I won't do it like you've said. There's too much good that we've already done and are continuing to do in our city to accept all that you say. I need time to see what the Church of Carlisle will do to support your missions, if anything. I do wish you well with them and will pray for you."

Justus lowered his gaze. He took a deep breath and exhaled with deliberation. "Pastor, I respect you and what you do for the Master, but I'm trying to let his people know that trouble is coming to this city. What you've seen so far is a foretaste. I don't know what it will be, and I'll do all I can to keep the human suffering to a minimum, but we must respond to this or it will wash over us like a flood. These are not my words. Listen—or don't."

With that, he got up to leave. Pastor Rich stood and shook his hand. "Justus, I'll take this to our elders. I make no promises. I'll be in touch after the holidays."

Justus left the Pastor alone in his office. Rich shoved his chair back until it hit the back of the U leaving an indentation. He plopped into the chair and rolled it forward again slamming his hands on the desktop. After several deep breaths he rubbed his temples with both hands growling under his breath.

He had a powerful presence and a convicting message. It seemed grounded in truth. What am I missing? Was trouble like that coming? Is he just an alarmist? What can I do to stop it? The task is too big.

Listen or Don't rolled over in his mind. *This guy is no politician. He comes across arrogant. Not sure I like him.*

Rich spoke out loud to himself. "We need our Christian school. All the assaults on our values in the secular schools have driven us away. We use it to maximize the use of our buildings, so we don't waste resource. We need more space. We need to raise money and build more school and church space when each grows. If we don't do it some other group will. We're good stewards of what God gives us."

Now he was trying to solve the challenge Justus made. "Where do people get their values if not from school? Should we be surprised the poor are not like us if we don't teach the same materials and values? Maybe we could add scholarships for the working-class poor? Would they fit in? For that matter, how would they even get here? They could be their own clique, I guess. Does that even help?" He shrugged and shook his head. Too many questions without answers.

"We do so much for them now. Or do we?"

"Who does this guy think he is? Coming in here. He's a cook not a minister. He doesn't know what I have to deal with in this church. Easy for him to be challenging. It makes him a bigger deal in his mission if he gets more money."

He ruminated on the Justus' comments. "He sure had a strange way of going about it."

He picked up his cell phone. "I'm going to text Menendez and thank him for this."

"I'm getting a headache. I have other meetings today. No more time to think about this one."

… Listen

  or

Don't …

CHAPTER 18

Jesus Esteban proposed to Maricela Rodriguez just before Thanksgiving. The families decided to celebrate with an engagement dinner that also doubled as a Christmas party. They booked Restaurant Tapas for the second Saturday night in December. Jesus and Maricela came from two of the wealthiest families in Villa Maya. Not the kind of wealth of the families up the hill, but very prosperous by Villa Maya standards. Both families stayed in VM despite having enough money to move out. They liked living among their people and wanted to make it a better place.

Maricela's father, Francisco Rodriguez, a city councilman from the district, considered himself the unofficial mayor of the area. Most of the locals agreed with him. Known for his fiery stances defending his district, but also reasonable when it came to the greater good on issues. Endowed with rugged good looks, thick wavy salt and pepper hair complemented by a lean build and great taste in clothes set him apart from many around him. He knew many of the powerful up the hill too. The Rodriguez family owned a thriving cleaning business that employed many locals. Ever the extrovert, he made good friends without forgetting where he came from.

His enchanting daughter graduated valedictorian at the local high school and received a full scholarship to Carlisle State University. Maricela studied medicine there and became the first Latina doctor to come from Villa Maya. Jesus' father, Dr. Juan Esteban hired her straight out of residency to practice with him.

Dr. Juan had a following all his own in Villa Maya. While lacking all the connections of Francisco, he determined to keep his pediatric practice local in Villa Maya. He had an excellent reputation of being able to look at a sick child and diagnose him fast often even before the test confirmed his thoughts. Despite taking a lot of local charity cases, the Estebans flourished. Due to their philanthropy, he and his wife, Lucina, attended most of the high-end charity events in town.

Both families wanted to have the event in the Villa Maya. After the reputation acquired by Restaurant Tapas over the past weeks, they just had to rent it for their gala.

Ramone remembered how he quoted a price for the night and they told him to double it. They wanted it to be very special. With almost no limit on price, he rented special uniforms for the staff and had José and the other junior cooks talk about menu options. After all was set, José said a prayer to calm the nervous staff and owner. It seemed to give peace to the whole group.

Ramone provided valet parking using his brother Hector's lot nearby.

José and the team prepared appetizers with both a Latin and a Spanish flair. Ramone knew that José was very good at creating things they hadn't seen before but were succulent and satisfying. *I wonder where my cook learned so much about Spanish cuisine.*

People began showing up at seven for cocktails and appetizers. Ramone dressed in his finest black suit, white shirt and pink and black striped tie, oozed charm and pride. He gave out glasses of Cava at the door when the guests arrived. One of his favorite parts was watching all the pretty ladies in their finery.

With Francisco's connections, he had people representing a Who's Who from all over the city, including almost all the city council. A number of the wealthy from up the hill couldn't attend due to a conflict with the Stanley Builders Christmas Party.

"Welcome Mayor and Mrs. Hamilton. It's good to see you again. Your table is just there, near the head table." Susan Hamilton gave Ramone a big hug and complimented him on the look of the restaurant tonight. Once she gave her coat to the coat check girl, Ramone observed that she sported a sleeveless, V-necked, holiday green dress with a thin gold belt, handbag and shoes to match. Her dark chestnut hair was feathered out past her shoulders. Marcus was in a black pinstriped suit with a matching green solid tie and pocket square that were identical to the green of Susan's dress. *She must be cold in that.*

The Hamilton's were greeted next by both sets of parents in addition to the happy couple. The bride and groom-to-be looked like they came from an awards show. Jesus in a black tux with purple bow tie and cummerbund; Maricela in a white, strapless, form fitting, sequined dress with dangling pearl earrings and spike heels with ankle straps. She was slender but not small and this showed off her curvaceous figure well, Ramone thought.

The well-dressed waiters sported short, white jackets along with dark pants and thin black ties. They brought around plates of simple, toasted paprika almonds to start. They also had cheese stations at various points throughout to promote the mingling of the guests.

"You must try the manchego. The salty taste with the Cava is wonderful," Susan told Marcus while she took another bite.

"What is the soft white cheese on this table? Is it mahon or tetilla?" Marcus asked a waiter.

"The tetilla is on the table over there, señor. That is mahon."

Jackie told Karl Shuford, her date, "I love this—each cheese table has dried figs and honey. Look over here, they have an olive station with all kinds of ripe and green olives."

"Yes, we have olives in orange peel, bay leaf, and hot red pepper sauce," Ramone said.

He was walking around with a bottle of Cava to top off the drinks. "Be careful my friends, the olives are not pitted." *This portion of the meal has gone wonderfully.*

He couldn't help but notice Ms. Hyatt in her red dress stretched over her curves all the way to her knees. It had a nice gathering of fabric at the waist just off center. She wore low-heeled silver shoes that twinkled with rhinestones, designed to show off her French pedicure. Long lacy sleeves rounded out the ensemble.

People began to sit down, when the first wave of plated dishes arrived. The staff brought out artichoke hearts in garlic sauce.

Sheriff Ward and his wife Melinda were seated at the same table with the Hamiltons, along with Karl and Jackie. Melinda cast a more mature look than the other women at the table. Ramone thought she would not fit Jackie's or Susan's dresses but she was tastefully adorned in a long gold dress that shimmered when she moved.

"I've never had ham quite like this," Ward noted.

"According to the notecard here, these are serrano ham wrapped plums and melons. Wow, the saltiness with the sweetness, very nice," as Jackie took her last bite covering her mouth with her hand.

Ramone watched this table with great interest and couldn't resist. "That is Jamon. Imported from Spain for this occasion. It is hard to find but very savory."

The small hot dishes followed, with mushrooms and ham croquettes. Jesus and Maricela were enjoying each course that arrived first at the head table. Ramone delighted in overhearing them say, "This is like a fine symphony. Each course adds to the next. We're building to a crescendo. Look at this, here comes the seafood from heaven."

"According to the menu card, these are salted cod fritters, salty yes but offset with just the right amount of light breading ..." Mayor Hamilton said.

Each started taking turns announcing a dish from the menu card.

"Next, we get tuna carpaccio on lemon aioli, followed by garlic and parsley squid on crusty bread," Susan added.

Ramone thought they sounded like kids awaiting a fireworks display.

Ramone knew each dish was small enough to savor and left everyone looking for more. If someone didn't like one, there was another dish coming up right after. The wafting aromas from the kitchen each time the servers came in, the beauty of the colors on the plates along with the exquisite wine pairings all made for a dining experience his restaurant had never known.

He knew what was next. The climax of the meal—fresh paella with chicken, shrimp, scallops, clams, and mussels. Ramone learned from José that paella was a rice dish accompanied by the various meats and vegetables. The rice must be right or the rest wouldn't matter. José made it to perfection tonight. It was like a Spanish-themed Thanksgiving dinner. Ramone looked around the room. He saw people closing their eyes in delight while they reveled in each bite. The conversations paused to say how wonderful each dish tasted. When the paella arrived, the room went silent. People quit talking to just enjoy the food.

After only sampling some of the dishes, Ramone could no longer resist all the compliments and scents in the room. From a plate at the bar, he ate paella too. His taste buds were in over drive with each new sensation and flavor. Isabella, a waitress, came by with some red wine pouring a glass for the boss.

"We are running out of the Rioja. All the others are holding out well," she said.

"Move it to the back and promote some of the other reds, please."

The wines were from all over the Spanish-speaking world. There was an excellent malbec from Mendoza; cabernet and carmenere from Chile; and albariño, tempranillo, and rioja from Spain. Ramone didn't stock these wines, but he began to think he should.

This was a true celebration of the senses, and since the dishes were small, there was room to enjoy many of the wonderful desserts and after dinner drinks.

Before dessert arrived, each family head made a speech of welcome to their friends and well wishes for the bride and groom. The temporary lull allowed dinner to settle and made the guests lustful for the desserts.

Dr. Esteban clinked a spoon on his glass and struggled to stand, one hand on his protruding stomach, groaning with pleasure. Ramone laughed with the rest of the crowd. He thanked the Rodriguez family again for a beautiful evening and an even more beautiful daughter. The crowd applauded.

"This was the best meal I can remember eating in a long, long time. You should be proud of your whole staff for the way this came together."

Ramone beamed with pride.

The doctor started to sit down but changed his mind, "Ramone, bring everyone out here. I want to meet the people who prepared the orgy of food we've enjoyed."

Ramone, ever happy to please the customers, went back in the kitchen and told everyone to come out for a bow. José was still making sure the desserts looked right and were arranged on the trays perfectly. He suggested to Ramone they take the deserts out for the bow. Like the end of a cruise ship dinner, each server exited the kitchen with trays filled with sweet delectable treats, and the whole room erupted in applause and laughter again. Each server smiled and tipped their head modestly at the crowd.

The desserts consisted of light as air tiramisu, coconut flan, and gelato for guests who needed to cool the spiciness. For patrons desiring a liquid desert, they served five-year-old Madeira and thirty-year-old Port along with fine coffee.

Ramone flushed José out of the kitchen. When he exited at last through the doors, Ramone grabbed him by the hand and lifted it high like a champion boxer. Everyone was smiling and laughing, and even the servers seemed glad to be a part of this special and grand affair.

The bride and groom-to-be and then the whole crowd, gave them all a standing ovation. José pointed toward heaven to thank the Lord for his blessing then folded his hands near his chin and bowed from the neck.

⁜ ⁜ ⁜

These families indeed had the community out tonight. I can see Mayor Hamilton with his wife, Susan, Sheriff Roman Ward, the striking news lady Jacqueline Hyatt and a score of others I don't know. Did Susan Hamilton wink at me? They're all dressed very well. Those dresses and outfits might be a little tighter now. José smiled to himself. *I wonder if they realized much of the staff were gang members now gaining a trade. This night was a wonderful blessing on these families and on this place. May it continue.*

After dessert, the crowd began to break up. The staff came out once more to thank the customers for coming while they exited. People collected their coats and waited for the valet to retrieve their cars.

Susan Hamilton complimented José on this triumph and gave him a big hug like a long-lost friend just back in town. After a kiss on the check, she thanked him again for the work he was doing with the Syrian refugees. This embarrassed José more than the grand entrance from the kitchen. *I must be blushing,* he thought.

Jackie noticed Susan speaking with Mr. Pea Coat. *Or is it Chef Pea Coat. My, my they do seem friendly. I must get closer, perhaps there was something going on.* Mayor Marcus was clear across the room speaking with the hosts. She told Karl to get the car from the valet and went back to speak with José as Susan headed over to join Marcus. "So, you and the Mayor's wife are quite a pair?"

José just smiled.

"What I really want is your recipe for that paella."

José smiled at her again. "Ramone wouldn't allow that, señora."

"What are you doing here? In a place like this? You could be making a lot more money up the hill. And it's señorita or ex-señora, whichever fits," and she smiled at him.

José returned the smile, but he didn't enjoy the spotlight, especially when it came from beautiful women. He hoped his blushing from the Hamilton kiss was gone but wasn't sure if it was lingering or happening again. *She is stunning in that red dress. Those alluring eyes must be a door into a beautiful soul. Am I staring at her?* The memory of a dark-haired woman in the visions that brought him here flashed to mind. Previously, he'd wondered if it was Susan or Amena. *Now, I believe, I've found her.*

Jackie turned her head to the side, like she wanted to hear him better and said with a smile, "I think this is the second time you tried to avoid my questions."

He gathered his thoughts, "I'm sorry, so much happening in here and I'm tired from all the cooking. I'm here because this is where my mission brings me. Thank you for your kind words. I wish you a blessed evening. Peace."

"We haven't been introduced, I'm Jacqueline Hyatt." She extended a lovely hand with a French manicure.

José didn't know whether to shake it or kiss it. "I know who you are, I see you on TV. They call me José Sabio." He wiped his hand on his towel and shook her soft, warm hand.

"My evening has already been wonderful, thanks to your culinary creations. I'm glad I had a chance to meet you." Karl signaled from the door that the car was coming around. *Is she staring at me?*

"You always seem to hurry away just when I start speaking," José said.

She lingered for one more moment, "Perhaps a time will come for us to change that . . . I should be going."

As they left, he overheard Karl say, "Did you have to flirt with him like that. I think he was blushing."

"You know I don't flirt. I was interviewing. It's what I do. I haven't seen you jealous before, Karl."

"I hadn't seen you in that dress before, Jackie."

She smiled while they made their way to his city-issued Ford Focus.

José couldn't take his eyes off her as she walked away. *What a remarkable señorita or ex-señora whichever fits.*

CHAPTER 19

And so it began. I-Man, Fixer, and Super J, also known as Isaac, D and Jamal gathered together with other members of the Wharf Rats in a small empty warehouse on the waterfront. The cold bit at their backs while they stared at each other over the flames coming from the metal trash barrel. The fire heated their faces in equal proportion to the cold on their backs. Time for a strategy meeting.

I-Man, his language laced with expletives, spoke, "Spike got killed by that lady cop. Thanks to those Mayans. I'm gonna go kill me some dogs. Spike was worth ten of theirs. Got to get us a police dog too. They got to pay."

"Bro' we'll cause a bunch of stuff if we do this. The Man'll be all over us if we kill a police dog. We better check with somebody at the Biz. They got to know what's 'bout happen," D said.

"They ain't gonna care. We got a score to settle; we don't need no-body's permission. We do have some other business to settle though." I-Man said.

"What's up?" Fixer said.

"You're out, Fixer," I-Man said.

"What!"

"You heard me, you're out Fixer."

"Says who? What'd I do?"

"Don't know. Mario came by today to tell me you're out. You know when Mario says it, I do it. You're out, D. The Biz has fired you."

"No man! Who can I talk to? This ain't right!"

"You can't fix this Fixer. I think you should just walk away. Don't know what's happenin'. Never seen nobody get this treatment before. Be glad you can walk away. Most folks get fired don't breathe no more. Bye!"

D walked into the cold night. Spurned by the Biz.

"That was cold bro," Super J said.

"We in the Biz, that's business. Now, let's get back to the dog business. You in with me on this, my brothers?" I-Man said.

"Dogs, gangbangers, what is the diff? We need a couple of others. With Fixer gone let's get Acer and Dreads to help," Super J said.

"We got to go to VM and find us some dogs. We need to pop two or three tonight to send a message. They'll be out after dinner doing their biz 'bout now," I-Man said.

The Rats arrived in VM in a gold van Fixer stole from there before he got fired. The van looked local so it wouldn't draw attention before the act. A ride meant they could hit and run. On foot, the local gangs would put them down quick. Armed with handguns and knives, it was time to hunt for dogs in the barrios.

Acer drove as I-Man spotted a teenage girl walking her big, black, shorthaired mutt down the sidewalk. They passed by and waited down the road with the sliding side door open. I-Man thought, *Man, it's cold.*

"She sees us. She's ain't stoppin'. This is gonna be easier than I thought." She gave the van a wide berth.

Thinks the dog'll protect her. That's why she's walking with it. This is gonna work out real good. She ended up giving them a cleaner target on the dog without getting too close to her. This was not a night for killing girls. As she approached the van, the dog started barking at the gang. I-Man had his hand on his gun, out of sight. He raised it and squeezed the trigger twice. She ducked for cover. The dog yelped loud and then fell silent. The girl screamed so loud it almost scared them.

I-Man slammed the door, and Acer hit the gas as they sped away from the scene. The smell of the smoke from the shot still lingered in the air. I-Man liked it.

"Cool bro, that was easy. She thought we was after her," Super J laughed as he spoke.

"Take off down another street and see if anyone else is out walking," I-Man said.

"I get to do the next one," Super J shouted, hopping around in his seat trying to get into position.

Acer drove about three streets and saw another dog walker. She was walking away from them, with what looked like a German Shepard mix. They passed her and stopped at a stop sign. Super J rolled down the front passenger window and waited for her to catch up. She got to the corner, and two more shots and another scream was heard. Acer gunned the engine and took off like a bullet.

"She was a slut with a big butt and a dead mutt," Acer said as the whole gang roared with laughter.

"One more for tonight," I-Man said. I'm sure the VM gangs are scramblin' by now. Cops may be, too."

The van approached an area near the edge of VM. "We got to get back to the Wharf but I want one more shot, one more thrill," Super J said. They parked and got out.

"Somebody got to have a dog 'round here," I-Man said. "Ace, stay in the van, keep it ready in case we get some 60s."

I-Man and Super J walked down the street, hoping someone's dog would start barking. They didn't have to wait long. The sidewalks were close to the front stoops and within a few minutes they heard barking from both sides of the street.

"We're running out of time. You two go that way. I got this side. Shoot if you get a shot. Don't want to kill nobody. This is about payback for Spike. Want to send that message," I-Man said.

I-Man's adrenaline was high after two successful kills and now the hunt on foot—he was filled with bloodlust. His senses seemed sharper.

Was it the cold or the task at hand? Guerilla warfare in enemy territory. *Do the job, don't get caught.*

I-Man spotted his prey through the rusted chain link fence. Eyes reflected streetlights. A big boy, based on the bark and the shadow. He got close enough to see it was a pit bull mix. A lot like Spike.

"For Spike." he squeezed off two shots. A loud yelp and then nothing. The lights came on in the front of the house. He ran like the devil was chasing him back to the van. He looked back and could see some of the MX 60s chasing him. Super J and Dreads were hauling back to the van, too, from across the street.

"I got one over there," Super J yelled.

Everyone jumped into the van laughing and pumping fists.

"This is great! We got to do this again!" Jesse said just as shots rang out behind them. The back window shattered and glass sprayed through the van when they squealed away rocking from one side to the other. They made plenty of turns and left the van in an old alleyway back in the Wharf. When they got out, Acer set it on fire.

All the way back to the warehouse they bragged about their bravery, showed each other how they held the guns and fired. Talked about the screaming girls.

"Wow, what a night!" I-Man said.

"We shoulda stayed and shot some 60s too," Acer said.

Dreads relit the trash can fire and each took some hits of cheap coke and scotch before they called it a night.

"I'm gonna go get my girl and have some fun now," Super J joked as he left.

✠ ✠ ✠

The killing spree made the news that night. Not a major story—dogs dead in Villa Maya. They sent a junior reporter, BJ Quinn to cover the ugly crime.

"Four dogs killed in Villa Maya in less than 30 minutes. Bullets flying all over the neighborhood endangered several people, some witnesses said. I interviewed one of the teenage girls whose dog was shot. She was terrorized and inconsolable, and didn't want to be on camera."

He cut to an image of her hands, still gripping the now empty leash. "How could this happen? This time of year? Who would do such a thing? Oh, dear God! Why my sweet little Chico. Why? Why? He was my friend since I was a little girl. Who would do this?"

The camera cut back to BJ Quinn on street with the police lights flashing in the background. He showed the picture of the gold van with a broken taillight someone took and posted on Facebook.

"The assailants are alleged to be three young black men . . . "

As I-Man watched the eleven o'clock news, he smiled at the notoriety, did another long line of coke and said, "For you, Spike." *Dead dogs in Villa Maya wouldn't be a story for long.*

⚜ ⚜ ⚜

The meeting of the MX 60s was called by Carlos, the new leader, since several others were either arrested or deported. Three of the dogs died in their territory and it was time to decide what to do.

José arrived, uninvited just before the meeting began.

Carlos knew José from the restaurant. He also knew he worked with the church in some fashion, so he didn't address him like he would have most intruders. He cleaned up his language and spoke to José.

"What do you want, señor? We've business to do here and don't allow outsiders. You leave now, we'll all agree you just got lost and stumbled in here. No debts owed."

José stopped but didn't turn to leave.

"Gracias, Carlos, but we both know I'm here for a purpose. Before your business gets underway, may I speak as a guest? I don't want to know your business, but I do want to say something that must be said. I can say it to you alone or to all here. Which do you like?"

Carlos admired José for this. He showed respect for the boss, but also didn't back down. He was visibly nervous shuffling from one foot to the other. The gang quieted down. Carlos motioned to Juan and they both walked toward José in the back of the room.

"What you got to say, señor?"

"This dog killing is bad news. Wharf Rats shooting up Villa Maya and killing our animals. We need to look at it right though. I think they're getting revenge on the parade killing. Some of you were there. The dog killed at the end was a shame. It shouldn't have been there, but Juan, you still have the bite healing from that day, si? You shouldn't have been messing around with them that day either."

Juan nodded. He grabbed his leg near the bite.

"Seems to me the Wharf bunch got some of their own back. If we go after them now, it's going to get uglier. Right here at Christmas time. No one wants that. I think we know who did it. Let's wait and see what they do next. I doubt they're coming back here. Not sure the next move, but it'll be for the cops to deal with. After all, it was a policewoman who killed the dog. We can be smart, have a wonderful Christmas, and if nothing happens before January, you can go after them later.

"While they wait, they'll wonder what's going to happen. Let those Rats sweat this over Christmas, while you know nothing else is going to happen here. I bet the cops'll solve this one soon."

"J, you ain't right. Comin' in here and given your ideas on what's gonna happen with the cops and the Rats. You telling us to stand down when we got Rats shooting up the Villa. I don't like it, man. Not sure you givin' good advice. But, this is a gutsy thing you doing here. You know I can pop you and no one knows or cares, but you're down here trying to do us good. I gotta respect a man for that. I like the idea of giv'n my team some time off for the holidays. Makes me feel like the good boss. I also like letting the cops do the job on the Rats if they will. We do enough for them 'round here. For now, we got bigger things to do than hunt dog killers."

Carlos reasoned this out. He wanted action, but it could wait. "Besides if the cops take out some of the Rats, that makes it easier for us later.

"Tell you what J, we'll hold off for a while on this. If the cops do their job and make this right, I'll be happy to agree with what you say.

If nothing happens by New Year's we're going after this boy and his homies. No dogs, we'll kill Rats," Carlos said with a menace they all knew was real.

"Gracias Carlos, for hearing me out." José said and backed away a few steps before he turned to leave. Carlos and Juan headed back to the meeting.

"Hey man, be careful out there. You know this is a bad barrio," Carlos yelled. They laughed as José left the building.

Officer Jim found a burned-out gold van while on routine patrol in the Wharf warehouse district. He could see some shell casings but any other evidence was all burned up on what was left of the interior. Tires melted to the street. The van matched the description of the one he had from the detectives in charge of the dog killings. He ran the VIN and found it was stolen from VM a week ago. Nothing much left, but it had to be the van from the dog killings two nights earlier.

I-Man, Super J, Acer, and Dreads gathered a few nights later to talk about next steps.

"It got on the news for a while, but no one seems to care that dogs die in Villa Maya. What we gonna do now? Have you had enough?" Super J said.

"We got more to do. Still need to take us out a police dog." I-Man made the *po* syllable last long. "I kinda liked making the news and not having any heat. Can't believe those Mayans aren't coming after us. They all cowards, anyway. We got away with it. You homies want to go get some more of those VM dogs?"

"Nah, that's too easy. Not much splash either. How we gonna get a police dog? I say we go get some of those dogs up the hill. That'll put some heat on the police to deal with over Christmas. That should bring the police dogs out. We can hit a few of them and watch the news. No gangs up there to come get us either. Only the Man. They got too much else to deal with instead of dogs this time of year," Acer said.

"I like it. We can't go up there, guns blazing though. We got to be smart about it. Let's get another van and some antifreeze. We can do it careful-like; make our point, the news, and still not get caught. It woulda been nice to have Fixer here to get us another van. Dreads, can you handle it?" I-Man said.

Tuesday was the big night. Dreads learned enough from Fixer to steal another late model van, and they headed up the hill.

"These houses are too far from the street," Super J said. "We'll get made halfway up the driveway."

"You see all these dog watering stations in the park and on some of these wide streets. Let's go fill a few with antifreeze and then we can go hunting in some of the apartments. They have fenced walking areas," Acer said.

They filled five dog-watering stations with antifreeze and then headed to a large apartment complex that had a fenced dog walk area near the road.

"This'll do. The gate's on the far side. We just have to wait. You guys stay in the van and park it down the street. A crowd's gonna draw attention," I-Man said.

They waited. I-Man wanted to go after a big dog since they were easier targets but also didn't want to go after big guys. *The dogs can't stay too close to the owners or I might shoot somebody. I'm just after dogs. This is a great set up. With a high fence facing the street and the gate on the opposite side of the area, anybody inside would have to come all the way out and run around the entire area before they could get to me. By the time they get here, I-Man be gone.* He moved over toward one corner just outside of the fencing near a wall opposite the entry gate. From his position, it wouldn't be a straight shot at the owners standing near the gate on the far end. With the wall behind, no one could come up and surprise him from that direction either.

There was a constant stream of folks coming and going. Dogs barking and sniffing each other. Owners chatting. It was a cold night, so people didn't linger too long. At last, there were three large dogs loose in the doggie park with the owners inside the gate at the far end. *They don't want to walk in too far for fear of stepping in something.* I-Man came up to the fence and the dogs all headed his way. One had a growling bark, but the other two seemed playful and curious. The owners must not have noticed him; they chatted about the cold and the season, he guessed.

Once they got into range. I-Man pulled the handgun from the small of his back and emptied the clip spraying bullets across the field where the dogs stood. He killed the loud dog instantly. He dropped the second one with two shots as it turned to run. The third dog bolted away from the noisy flashes, back toward its owner. He only got one hit on that dog, who kept running back to his owner. The owners ducked for cover at the noise.

The owners regrouped quickly. One was on his cell phone; another was grabbing the injured dog. The third owner was screaming in distress. *She musta been the owner of the big loud one.* With the magazine now empty, he turned and ran to the van, and they squealed away into the dark.

⚜ ⚜ ⚜

Billy Cosmo always took Max out for his final walk of the night around the neighborhood. He liked a crisp walk at night and so did Max, who was a mixed-breed beagle with a doggie sweater on. When they came to the watering station, Max gave it a smell and started drinking. Billy tried to stop him, but it was too late.

"I guess we'll be going out again later if you drink too much, buddy."

Max was dead by noon the next day from antifreeze poisoning. This was repeated three more times with three more dogs. One owner always dumped the bowl before he would let his dog drink. This saved the dog from death, but he still got sick from the residue.

The eleven o'clock news was all about the dog killings at the Essex Square Apartments. The deaths of several dogs from antifreeze poisoning came out the next afternoon. It took the police until late the next day to make the connection. It was the lead story on the six o'clock news.

⚜ ⚜ ⚜

"Jacqueline Hyatt, WWNS News, reporting from the Essex Square Apartments. In the dog walk area just behind me three dogs were shot by an unknown assailant last night. Reports also came in today about several dogs being sickened or killed after drinking antifreeze out of the doggie watering stations in Dearborn Park and the Wellesley neighborhood less than a mile apart. Both neighborhoods are only a mile from the site of the shootings. This is a heinous crime, especially at this time of the year when families are gathering for the holidays. Animal control has issued a warning about not using the outside bowls without rinsing and inspecting them."

They cut away to show an earlier interview with poor Billy Cosmo who was so upset over his dear Max that he could barely speak. He just said, "He was my best buddy. He would never hurt anybody. This ain't right. Someone must do something. Sorry." He sniffed and wiped his eyes while the camera cut back to Jackie.

"No question Max was well loved," she said. "There are no suspects in custody at this time, but witnesses say they saw a black male near the Essex Square dog lot. No video evidence exists of the incident. There is a doorbell camera video of a man pouring something in the watering station in Wellesley, but it is too dark to be of much help. This has a similar MO to the shootings of dogs in Villa Maya last week. The police are asking anyone with knowledge of these crimes to please call Crime stoppers at . . . "

I-Man clicked off the news and smiled.

⚜ ⚜ ⚜

Jackie asked BJ Quinn earlier about the VM dog shooting the week before to make sure she was well informed.

"Something ugly is going on in the city and the dogs were the targets not the people. Since VM and the Hill had been hit one had to think it was coming from the Wharf or maybe the Syrians," BJ told her.

✠ ✠ ✠

Sheriff Ward didn't often get involved in animal control cases, but based on the public outcry, he had to this time.

The next morning at the briefing with his officers, he said, "This looks like it's coming from the Wharf. I need answers fast. The Syrians aren't a viable suspect. We haven't had any issue with guns from that group since they arrived."

"It could be the kid from the Thanksgiving Day incident?" Officer Kepley said.

"Follow it up. Find out if Da Wyz knows what's happening here. We need answers before this gets any worse," Ward said.

✠ ✠ ✠

Da Wyz got his team together. Speaking in colorful language, he asked. "What the devil is happening out there? Who did this junk? We got other things to do than kill dogs right now. I want 'em found and took care of. I didn't care about this in VM, but now the Man is crawling all over us after what went down up the hill."

"Looks like the Wharf Rats did this. Hearing I-Man be braggin' bout it," Mario said.

"Go find out and tell him it's over. I-Man and his boys have done good work for us before, but he needs more discipline. If he won't stop, stop him. Break something anyway to let him know what happens if he gets out of line again."

"Got it."

✠ ✠ ✠

Officer Jim found the van used in the Essex Square shooting the next day. Burned out like the one used in the VM shootings. He hoped it was over with the first van, but now he was going to probe deeper to keep it from happening again.

✠ ✠ ✠

I-Man heard the knock on the door, more like a pounding—or was that his head after last night's party? It was hard to tell?

"Yo, I-Man, we know you're in there." I-Man looked out the window and shook the fog out of his brain. He knew these guys, but he didn't know what they wanted. *Should I run? Maybe they're here to congratulate me on this dog stuff.* He decided to answer the door.

He cracked it open. A gigantic muscular thug with a bald head and thin mustache shoved his way in, knocking I-Man backward as the door slammed against the wall. I-Man hit the wall behind him and bounced forward to steady himself. The second thug, smaller and nimbler than the first, came in with a bat and took I-Man out at the knees just as he braced himself to keep from falling forward. Based on the crack and the nausea, I-Man wouldn't walk the same for many weeks, if ever. He fell forward with the impact and balled up awaiting the next hit that never came. The man-mountain thug leaned down and said, "This dog stuff's over. I-Man, this dog stuff's over. Got it? Let me hear you say it."

I-Man couldn't breathe much less speak. His head was spinning from all the junk he had done last night and now the pain made him want to vomit. He knew better though, and best he could muster was to breathe in deep and out slow then in a whisper, spit out, "Over, yeah it's over."

They left him in the door way unable to walk and scratching his way down the hall for his cell phone. He had to warn Super J and ask him to get over and help him. After leaving a message, he puked until the dry heaves came.

CHAPTER 20

Yosef got a nice bonus from Ramone for the triumph at the engagement party. He decided to use most of the money to create a Christmas celebration for the refugees.

The construction crew finished making the apartments habitable in late November. They left some small, well-used hand tools for the group to tinker with and do some of their own repairs. It cut down on the punch list, and the contractors could turn the tools in for reimbursement claimed on the federal subsidy.

Sami used his engineering skills to get the clubhouse kitchen up and running. With the help of the tools, spare parts from the electrical boxes in units that weren't restored, and labor supplied by the legion of Syrian ladies, they got the clubhouse power on. They pulled old stoves from the unrepaired units and were able to cobble together a working community kitchen. They needed running water to power the toilet and the sink, and found a way to pipe it in from one of the neighboring units. There wasn't much pressure, but it was better than a bucket brigade.

Yosef was impressed at what they'd done and could tell these were educated, driven people who just needed fertile soil to grow again.

They'd created a prayer niche, a *qibla*, in one clubhouse antechamber as far from the kitchen as they could make it. Yosef saw an arrow on the wall that pointed out the direction of Mecca. There were no minarets to shout the call to prayer from, but he was sure all the devout also had a directional arrow in their homes pointing to Mecca for daily prayers. *Islam instills discipline, that's for sure.*

Today, the clubhouse became the celebration center.

"This is a time of celebration. You've made your way in a new world. It's not been easy. I bring you food to share. I would like to work with some of you who enjoy cooking to create a meal using what I brought and what you have," Yosef said.

There were six cooks for two stoves. In the end, Yosef just did traffic control. He brought plenty of fruits and vegetables he'd purchased from the wholesalers at Restaurant Tapas. The group joked and laughed together. There was a lot of joyous hand clapping and some happy music to celebrate the gathering. The ladies were all dressed in their finest, some in traditional Muslim attire and the younger girls in western dress as they danced with each other to the music.

They made all types of dishes from baba ganoush, hummus, salads and pita bread. They served plates full of muhammara made with Aleppo pepper some saved during all their journeys.

Amena sat next to Yosef and attended to all his needs. He was flattered by the attention and decided to let her demonstrate her gratitude this way. Unlike the ladies at the engagement party of a few days earlier, she adorned herself in modest dress, always a dark hajib. Yosef wasn't sure he knew what color her hair was but he guessed it was dark since she was Kurdish.

The group was stuffed like a feast at the end of Ramadan's fasts. Sami pushed back from the table as if to say "no more for me." Yosef took some time to explain the Christmas story to the people, speaking Arabic. Most knew it, but never heard it explained in such detail before.

"In the Christian view, we believe Yeshua came to earth in such humble surroundings to make himself accessible to all, no matter how poor. It was Hashem reaching as far down as necessary to touch the hardest to reach in our world. You must have heard already that the story doesn't end at Christmas. Yeshua grew into a man and taught the ways of the Holy Father. After a few years of ministry, he was mistreated and put to death by the authorities. On the third day, he rose from the dead to prove his status with the Father. Fully God and Fully Man. I thank you for giving me a chance to share this with you. I know it's not something Islam embraces. I feel compelled by my Master to share it. I thank you for listening."

"Yosef, Isa is in our Quran too. We don't believe that Allah would allow him to be treated the way your Bible says, but we revere him as a great prophet. We like to hear what those around us believe. You're our friend, one of the few we have in this land. We know you respect us, and we give you the same respect. While we may not all believe the same, we know that Isa, your Jesus, and Islam teach that acts of kindness are to be cherished. Thank you for what you've done for us," Sami said.

"I do what I can out of love for you and for my Master. I give him the glory," Yosef said.

"Tell me Yosef, where are Susan Hamilton and her helpers today?" Rima asked. "They've been good as angels to us as well."

"They couldn't come. This time of year is very busy on the Christian calendar; many travel, and have lots of family over. She sends her warm wishes to all of you," Yosef said.

As they began to clear the dishes, Yosef noticed they had several labeled jars of seeds on the counter. "What's this?"

"These are the seeds from many of the fruits and vegetable we've eaten over the past few months. We saved them to plant in the spring. You, no doubt, know Syrians are excellent farmers. We have many from the rural lands with us. There is land here we can use. We aren't sure what will grow, so we'll try many different crops. We learned not to waste anything after we were displaced," Amena said.

"I've worked in farms all along the way here. When the time is right, I can advise on what might grow in this area," Yosef said.

Amena took an armful of dirty dishes into the kitchen for cleaning and Sami took the chance to mention to Yosef, "She seems to be quite fond of you. You should give her a chance to be with you outside the group."

Yosef smiled. "I've much work to do these days with the restaurant and the ministries I do. No time for such things. I'm sure she is quite a strong woman to have come through all the trials so far."

Yosef looked over in one corner and noticed Hamsa on a computer. "Where did that come from?"

"Susan's group gave us a couple of used computers. Dijlin managed to make one good one with parts from another. She was able to get Wi-Fi working in here with a score of different pieces. Susan's group is paying for us to be able to get online. It allows us to keep up with family on a screen bigger than our phones. It's also easier to apply for jobs here. While it's slow, we make it work. In addition, we have sign-up sheets for computer time, to keep people from fighting. Now is Hamsa's time. He loves the screen time. We can't get him away from it.

✠ ✠ ✠

Hamsa learned areas he could access on the dark web while in several camps on his way to Carlisle.

He had connected to some of the more radical Islamist sites and was impacted by their propaganda more than he realized. These were sites used to recruit and radicalize young Muslims.

Hamsa listened with great interest to the Christmas story earlier. He was a young man looking for answers about his worth, his purpose and his future. What he'd seen in his young life would've traumatized anyone. Now more than ever, he needed to calm his troubled mind. Would peace be found in the community, the dark web, or in scripture?

CHAPTER 21

Officer Jim finished his lunch of a burger and fries in a diner off Commonwealth Avenue and began to think about the next phase of the dog killing investigation. *I often want a cigarette after lunch, but I haven't had one for a few weeks now. I guess I can kick the habit after all. Now I guess I should give up burgers, too.* Across the room he noticed Mario when he entered.

Because of his immense size, it took some effort, but Mario slid into the booth opposite Jim and grabbed the grease-stained, white and green ticket from the table.

"I got this. Crime pays better than police work."

Jim could fight him for it, but he knew this wasn't a social call. "But the career longevity is a problem. Those long vacations in a room for two with no room service and iron bars can drive a man crazy. What do you want, Mario?"

"I came to deliver a message from Da Wyz."

"And?"

"The dog killin's over."

"I don't follow you."

"Da Wyz took care of the people involved in the dog business."

"So, we should stop looking?"

"No need to look; they've been tried and sentenced. Justice is served. We don't need Carlisle's finest down here in our Biz. You know we got this now."

"Not sure it'll work that way. The folks up the hill are looking for an arrest and conviction. They want assurance this isn't going to happen again. I can't just go to the sheriff and tell him Da Wyz said, 'We are good.' I need a name and address."

"It was a stupid kid. He's been dealt with by the brothers."

"I bet he wishes we got there first. Am I going to hear about assault charges against some of your bros? Or am I going to find a body?"

"Nah!"

"I must be getting close if you're here to wave me off. I'm going to keep looking. I need a face to hang this on or the news won't let it go. We got a face from the Thanksgiving Parade incident; I've been socializing in the area. No name yet, but I'll keep trying."

"Shame we can't work this one out. You ain't gonna find a name. People ain't gonna talk. You know that."

"I guess we're still gonna have to do some detecting to be sure. I still need to turn over some more rocks."

"Crime pays better, and the job isn't anywhere near as aggravatin'. Jim, you in the wrong line of work. You turn over some rocks, but don't dig too deep or too long. This is over." Mario slid out of the booth and left the ticket.

With the new information that Mario and his bros took care of this, Officer Jim obtained a search warrant and pulled a favor with a supervisor at the emergency room of University Hospital. He checked the logs starting the day before Mario came to see him. He figured if the kids weren't in the morgue, they needed medical help. The injuries would be *accidents*. The explanations would be thin but plausible. The injuries would be violent. He found a young man with broken kneecaps two days before and another with broken hands. *That looks like Mario's buddies.*

He asked the emergency room supervisor about them. They came in two different times of day. Brought by different people. The one with the hands said he got his hands slammed in the car trunk by mistake.

Officer Jim looked at her over his reading glasses and said, "You believed that?"

"I don't debate an injured male in his late teens or early twenties. He is too old for child abuse, and there were no gunshots or knife gashes. Nothing to report to the cops." She shrugged.

He showed her the photo he had. She shook her head.

"What about Isaac Dixon and the knees. What was the cause there?"

"Said he fell down the stairs at home."

"Let me guess, no gun shots or knife marks . . . "

She nodded. "We get all kinds of crazy accidents in here. If it's not a kid or an obvious crime, we don't have time to worry about causes. We may roll our eyes, but what difference does it make what the cause was? We still have to get them patched up."

He showed the photo again. "Could be this one, I just see too many people and we don't take photos of them all to compare."

"May I have the addresses?" Officer Jim said.

"I need to leave my office for a few minutes. This is an emergency room, no telling how long it'll take." She bumped her computer screen on her desk when she left, and it turned toward Jim. He took the opportunity to jot down the addresses.

Isaac's turned out to be a vacant lot.

Jamal's mom, who brought him to the ER, didn't know to lie about the address, so Jim got lucky with that one.

Jamal stayed at his mother, Whitney's house. The emergency room said his hands would be immobile for four weeks and then they would recheck. The tips of his fingers stuck out of the casts, but the hands were too sore to move very much. *Bet he can't even text right now. Must be driving him crazy.*

After some legwork, Jim learned that Jamal's mom worked a cashier's job at the local market. She could be home regularly to check on Jamal since she had a set schedule. *She, no doubt, gets out-of-date food to bring home. Hard to make it on a cashier's pay.*

Jim went to the door and knocked. "Police. Please answer." He thought he saw movement around one of the window curtains, so he persisted. No answer. *I'll try back again at other times of day. If that doesn't work, I'll go see Whitney when she's working. Hate to do that without trying at home first.*

Carlos got word from an informant, about who did the dogs in Villa Maya. He needed to do something to let the barrio know they were protected. The promise to José was to wait until the New Year. With the information and the lack of progress by the cops, Carlos decided it was time to act.

Carlos phoned Juan, who brought his car up. Armed with addresses and times Jamal and Isaac would be alone, they set out to settle the score.

Carlos made his way up the two flights of stairs of the dingy apartment complex. *Lucky for me the lights are almost all burned out. No need for a mask here.* He could hear the TV through the door. He shot through the locks and barged in.

I-Man grabbed a crutch and tried to get up to take cover somewhere. It was in vain. The crutch slid out to the side and he just plopped on the floor hitting the table that had his gun, beer, and pills on it. The gun skittered across the floor and hit the wall under the TV stand. He tried to claw his way to cover, but without the power of his legs to move, he made little progress.

Carlos knowing that gunshots would bring others soon, had to act fast. *With gunfire people always move away to start then the curious come closer.* He saw I-Man's feet on the other side of the sofa. *Why doesn't he try for better cover?* Carlos came around the sofa and saw why. Leg braces on both legs. Carlos felt a momentary twinge of pity for I-Man but he had a job to do. "I-Man, you been killing dogs in my barrio." It wasn't adrenaline infused; it was a statement of the charge. "How do you plead?" would be the next sentence if this was a court? But it was not a court.

I-Man began to plead. "Look at me man, I ain't been doing nothin' and not likely to be anytime soon. What do you want from me? Take what you want; I can't stop you. Wallet's on the couch."

Carlos knew I-Man was hoping he could convince him that he had the wrong guy. *Guess I would do that too under the circumstances.*

"You been killing dogs in my barrio man," Carlos said.

"No man, I can't get out of bed without help." He whimpered like he knew what was next.

"That's new. Someone messed you up. That's why it stopped. We can't have Rats in the barrio shooting things up. It is a sign of disrespect. You can't be dissing us in our home. Now I got to dis you in your home."

I-Man held up his hands trying to wave Carlos away, "No man, you got it wrong, it's not me, it's not . . . "

He didn't finish the sentence before Carlos shot him twice, just like I-Man shot the dogs. Carlos turned and headed back down to the car, where Juan was waiting and they drove away like they belonged there.

"These boys been beat up. Da Wyz got to 'em. He had his legs broke. I felt bad shooting him, but justice had to be done."

Jim got the call for the homicide at the Briarcliff Apartments. He lumbered up the two flights of stairs and entered the scene. He could see locks shot out and a black male with knee braces lying on the floor face up, shot in the chest and in the face. The wounds were fresh with blood still puddled nearby. A gun laid about five feet from the body near the wall under the TV next to a table that had been turned over. Beer and pills were all over the floor too. The TV still tuned to an NBA game. A quick check of ID Jim found on the sofa, confirmed his suspicion, this was Isaac Dixon. *Not a robbery—money still in the wallet.* He checked the rest of the apartment and found it belonged to Ramonea White. *Must be the girlfriend.* After a call to dispatch, he tried to piece the crime together while he waited on the investigators and the meat wagon.

"Isaac must have come up the stairs from the hospital. Bet that was lots of fun. Probably climbed them on his behind. Must've been camped out on the sofa watching TV, popping pain meds, and drinking beer. Alcohol and pills don't mix. Guess he thought beer didn't count. Not a good choice for a man who would struggle to get to the little gangbanger's room. Kept his gun nearby. Must've been worried about something. Da Wyz busted him up, not like Mario's bunch to revisit. Looks like they got the point across already. Feels like revenge to me. Could be a mad ex. Or it could be . . . a VM hit. The light went on in his head. Jamal will be next if I'm right.

⚜ ⚜ ⚜

They got to Jamal's mother's house. "This one's mine," Juan said while he donned his ski mask. Juan went around back, while Carlos donned his mask and went to the front door.

"Give me thirty seconds to get into position then we kick in the doors together. That way they don't know where to run," Carlos said.

The curtains and blinds were drawn so no one could see in. Juan could hear someone talking in the kitchen. He guessed it was Jamal on his phone. They both kicked the doors at the same time. Carlos came in from the front and Juan through the kitchen. Jamal's mom was fixing dinner at the kitchen table and she screamed at the intrusion. Jamal jumped up in front of his mother and put his hands up to shield himself.

"You Super J, man?" Juan said.

Jamal didn't answer.

Both Carlos and Juan had guns drawn.

Whitney was scared and crying but still had her wits about her.

"Yeah, he did the dog killin'. He told me. You here to kill him and now me since I seen you. When does it stop, boys? They was just dogs. This is my son."

"He knows the rules. He came to our territory, shot up our place. We got to have blood for that."

Super J dove at Juan while he was talking. Juan backed away. Super J hit the floor just short and yelled in pain when he tried to brace himself with his hands. Juan turned the gun down and shot him once in the head.

Whitney screamed a guttural cry that stopped both young men in their tracks.

Juan, now full of blood lust, pointed the gun at Whitney. "She just saw me cap her son. She got to go too, man."

"No more killing tonight," Carlos said as he stepped in front of Whitney. He went straight at Juan and pushed him out the door. "We got to go. This is over."

They got back to the car and drove away. No lights. They passed a police cruiser with lights flashing heading toward Jamal's house.

⁜⁜⁜

After leaving Isaac with CSI, Officer Jim was already heading for Jamal's house when the call came in. He called dispatch to get an officer there earlier, but they didn't arrive in time to stop the killing. As he entered he found Whitney wailing and rocking back and forth on a kitchen chair overlooking the lifeless body of her son, his blood on her hands. *Should've gone to see momma earlier.*

Sirens and flashing lights in the night again. The neighbors came to see what happened. As he looked over the scene, Jim thought, *I guess Da Wyz didn't like me poking around over the last few days. I bet someone leaked Jamal's and Isaac's whereabouts to the Mayans, hoping they would deal with the rest. Carlisle Police gets the bodies they want; the heat passes. The 60s get their respect back. Everyone is happy. That's how cold and calculating Da Wyz gets when the Biz is in the spotlight.*

He walked slowly back to the cruiser and kicked the tires in frustration. He slammed his note pad on to the console as he got in and then took a very deep breath and called the crime in. *Maybe I am in the wrong line of work. The bad guys are winning these days. They just need us to clean up after them.* He sat in the cruiser for a few minutes then went back to the crime scene. *I still got a job a do. There's a mother that needs comforting . . .*

⁜⁜⁜

Mario told Da Wyz that the Mayans did the job. "Did the one kid in front of his mother." Jeremiah paused a moment then took a long draw off his scotch. "They're all too predictable."

"Surprised they didn't kill her," Mario wondered. "I would've. We gonna do anything 'bout it?"

"Nah, they did what we expected. Things are back in equilibrium. The cops got their dog killers now, and the Mayans got some honor back. We got rid of two loose marbles. Now the cops are looking in VM, not the Wharf. A win all around."

Da Wyz closed his eyes and swallowed another drink of scotch. He didn't hear Whitney's cries but he had heard others like it. Cries that haunt you forever. *I know why they didn't kill mama.*

CHAPTER 22

Jackie went to the office of Dr. Larry Shapiro with questions about the healing of Roberta Saunders. She always had a professional skepticism with miracle claims. This one caught her eye, since this miracle claimant became an activist against the gang activity in the Wharf.

As she waited, she recalled her conversations with Ms. Roberta and her friends.

Ms. Roberta, as she liked to be called, began sitting outside her house on the corner with a few others in the neighborhood several weeks ago. They sat and talked and greeted folks when they passed. Weather made no difference. It was gutsy to be out there with all the gang activity in that area. Jackie's research with the sheriff's office showed that the crime stats dropped off when Ms. Roberta started sitting on the corner.

Jackie marveled at this spunky old lady who just sat in a lawn chair. In a short time, she became the neighborhood's grandma. She mothered the young moms at the corner. They exchanged homemaking, child rearing, and even political ideas. They talked about ways to save money. They kept up with each other's kids. It felt like a community coming together. Jackie sat there for an hour or so several times during the last week. Observing and then interviewing.

After gaining the group's confidence, Jackie asked, "Why did you start doing this?"

Danielle, one of the young women, said, "I saw Ms. Roberta sitting out on this corner one day. Her house is two down from mine. She looked out of place. People asked her what she was doing there. 'Are you lost?' She used to be blind you know."

"I've been cooped up for so many years and just wanted to get to know folks again. The ladies came and spoke to me. Different folks come out to meet here at the corner everyday now ever since. Usually a group of two or three out of a consistent group of eight. It depends on their work schedule and the kids' school," Ms. Roberta said.

She paused and took a drink of water from a bottle. "We noticed that the gangs didn't hang around this corner anymore. Not sure why, but I think they don't want to be reminded of mama looking at them. They moved elsewhere."

"If lots more folks got out and did the same, the gangs are going to have a hard time making trouble anywhere they want to, at least during the daytime," Danielle added.

She used to be blind you know, echoed in Jackie's mind.

Jackie waited for the right chance to talk to Ms. Roberta without some of *her girls* around.

"Were you blind?" Jackie asked.

"Yes sweetheart, I was blind for many years. Macular degeneration or something like that is what they told me. Vision started getting bad after my daughter died years ago and kept getting worse. I couldn't afford no doctor or surgery, not that it woulda helped. They just looked at me and shook their head. Said it was a shame," Ms. Roberta said.

"So how can you see now?"

"The Good Lord healed me. I was praying one day, and he opened my eyes."

"Who did?"

"God did."

"Why would he do that?"

"I asked myself that for many days. I talked to my preacher. Reverend Tony over at the AME church. Do you know him, sweetheart?"

"No ma'am, but I've heard the name."

"Anyway, he said God must've done this miracle for a reason. I started praying again asking what he wanted me to do now. I just got the idea of sitting out here and folks came up, started talking. Before you know it, we had our corner party going on. I see the gang boys stay away now. We thought that was good, so we keep on doing it. On top of that we enjoy each other."

"So, you just prayed, and you could see?"

"Well there was more to it than that, but I swore I wouldn't tell, so that's all you get, Ms. Jackie."

"Now Ms. Roberta, don't tease a newswoman like that. You know I need more than that. Did your doctor look at you afterward?"

"Yes ma'am, he saw me the day after. They weren't too keen to see a Medicaid patient quick until I told them I could see and just wanted a checkup. They got me in to see Dr. Shapiro within an hour or so.

"Dr. Shapiro looked me over and said, 'You have the eyes of a young woman. Why are you here?'

"I said, 'I wanted to be sure I was healed.' He asked if he could study me. You know, get tissue samples, and the like. 'No sir,' I said. 'Not interested. God didn't do this so I can be a lab rat.'"

"What's your doctor's first name?"

Jackie was jolted back to the present when the doorknob twisted; the door opened, and in walked Dr. Shapiro, an older man with male pattern baldness. *Somewhat round, not enough time in the gym. Doctors should know better.* He wore a white jacket to let everyone know he was a doctor. He had a few pens in his pocket and other handheld instruments on his sleeve. She stood and shook his hand, "Jacqueline Hyatt, WWNS News. I'm investigating a story and wondered if you could help me. Are you Roberta Saunders' doctor?"

"You know HIPAA doesn't allow me to tell you that. If you have a signed release we can talk."

OK, it is going to be one of those interviews. She took a deep breath and bit her lip.

"Please be seated," he said, as he sat behind his desk.

Jackie pulled out her phone and stylus. "Do you know Roberta Saunders?"

He looked at the computer in his office and after hitting a few keys said, "Yes, I do."

"Do you know that she claims to be miraculously healed from blindness?" She said.

"I heard that from somewhere."

"Did she have macular degeneration?"

"HIPAA again," he said holding up his hands.

Jackie re-crossed her legs and decided on a different approach.

"Have you heard of someone being healed of macular degeneration?"

"Not according to any medical journal I've read in the past fifty years. It's degeneration just like the name implies. It degenerates at different rates for different patients, but it doesn't regenerate."

Now he's condescending. This guy is a real charmer.

"So how would someone be healed?"

He sat back in his chair. "There's no known cure. I have no idea how it would be healed. The macula is on the back of the eye. It would require surgery, in theory. However, no surgical technique to date has proven effective. In some, we can slow the progress, but we can't repair or cure it. I don't believe in miracles Ms. Hyatt. If she can see now, it must be because she was misdiagnosed. Mac D doesn't get better. Perhaps her blindness was brought on by a psychological issue that has been resolved. It's quite possible that she was cleansed of this issue and her sight restored itself. The body has amazing ways of healing itself, if we let it."

"Mac D, as you call it, could be healed by forgiving ourselves?"

"No Ms. Hyatt, if a patient had Mac D she would not get over it. However, if she had psychosomatic blindness she could get over it."

"OK doctor, I think I understand. Let's talk off the record now." Jackie put the stylus on top of her phone indicating that she wouldn't record anymore of this conversation. "So, off the record Doc. Are you her doctor? She told me you were."

"Off the record Ms. Hyatt, yes I am."

"Did she have Mac D? Do you have her charts before and after? What do they show?"

"Why would I share that with you Ms. Hyatt?"

"There is something strange happening in our city. Lots of bad things and a few good ones. I just want to know what to believe about this kind lady. Is she a kook or is this real?"

He motioned her to his side of the desk. He showed her the eye shots from a year ago and a few weeks ago. Pointing to the macula area in the shots he said, "MD clearly on the old one and nothing on the new one."

"Is it a miracle, doc?"

"Ms. Hyatt, you're too levelheaded a journalist to buy that. Is it a miracle or just bad record keeping? Ms. Saunders is a Medicaid patient who comes to see me on occasion. I have so many patients that images can get misfiled. I can't even tell you if this is the same person. Based on the images, I would say no. If there is some miracle worker out there, why doesn't he heal others? There are lots of cases of Mac D in the US alone. Thousands in our state. Why did this one lady get healed by a miracle and not all the others? If someone has developed a cure, why don't they publish the findings? Why did it just happen now? Is there a new traveling miracle worker in town? No, this is more of a paperwork issue than a miracle."

"But don't the retina scans look identical?"

"Yes, they do at a quick glance but again, that doesn't mean we got all the right films in the right file. I would need to see her again and make a more detailed study of this to see where it went. What I recall is that I asked her to let me study this more, and she declined. I don't have the time to do these things for free.

"I don't believe in miracles Ms. Hyatt and suggest you avoid that road to disappointment, too. I suspect, she is a kind but, what was the word you used, *kooky* old lady who had a life-changing event and now wants to make the world better. We need more like her. However, we don't need to load people's heads with stories of God healing her. We either have files misplaced or she had a psychological event that removed issues from her life or maybe both.

"Now, this was all off the record and I'll deny the misfile claims if it gets mentioned. You know how hard it is to subpoena medical records, so this is all you'll get from me. No such thing as miracles, Ms. Hyatt. Have a good afternoon, I have patients to see."

She left the office with lingering questions. *Either a miracle Ms. Roberta refused to talk much about, or a psychosomatic illness now resolved. She spoke about her daughter's death. However, she behaves like the miracle occurred. Why won't she talk about it? Why did it just happen now? Was there a traveling miracle worker in town? I guess I could try to find all the new people in town since November.* She chuckled to herself.

Not the first puzzle I've failed to solve. But since no one is willing to talk on the record, not much I can do to follow up right now. I got deadlines and this looks like a dead-end. I can do the story on the ladies on the corner but no need to mention the healing.

CHAPTER 23

Pastor Rich looked out over the crowd in the fellowship hall. There were round tables for the dinner served just before the meeting and chairs along the perimeter for those coming after dinner. The packed hall still smelled of fried chicken, green beans, mashed potatoes, and bread. The tables cleared of most of the scraps but still spotted with drink cups and spills.

The hall was full of members and visitors who came to see the experts on affordable housing. Some were real estate developers, some were government officials, along with a couple of concerned leading citizens from up the hill.

He climbed up the stairs beside the stage and called the meeting to order. The panel all present and ready to speak was seated just behind him. There was a screen in case one of the panelists had slides to show. Everyone took his or her seat, and he opened with a word of prayer.

"Dear Lord, make us wise this night. Help us to be understanding of others' views that may not be our own. Show us a better way than what has come before now. Bring us peace in the midst of debate. Please help us hear you and respect each other now. In Jesus' name. Amen."

Pastor Rich started by introducing each panelist.

"First, we have Paul Stanley, president of Stanley Builders, a large home builder in our city. He has built homes here for two decades. He has developed neighborhoods and luxury homes. He does mixed-use developments too.

"We also have Louise Cantrell, our city planner. She has been with the city for twelve years and previous to that, served on various planning capacities in several cities up north. She has a Master's in Public Policy from Cornell University.

"Our third panelist is from Carlisle State University. Dr. Tobias Landry. He's the chair of the Department of Public Policy. He has been with the school for nine years and has been chairman for the past six.

"Finally, we have Teresa McGinty-Cline, the founder and president of the Center for Affordable Housing in Carlisle. She works with those in the underserved communities we refer to as Broken Wharf and Villa Maya. She grew up here in Carlisle before going away to school to bring us a fresh perspective on the issues of generational poverty and potential solutions.

"Please join me in welcoming our esteemed panel for tonight's presentation."

After polite applause, each panelist took his or her turn to speak. The crowd was eager for the solutions that would be espoused.

❦ ❦ ❦

José took the night off from the restaurant. January was slow for dinner traffic and he had some of his students covering for him. He would be up before dawn to cover the breakfast rush. He sat in the back, in a folding chair to listen and observe. The mayor and some of the city council sat center stage. Father Menendez and Reverend Tony also sat near the mayor. When he looked around, he thought he caught a glimpse of that TV reporter, Jacqueline Hyatt. *The turnout is excellent, and I'm glad Pastor Rich hosted this session. I guess he did listen. The Spirit can be very persuasive.*

❦ ❦ ❦

Jackie sat at a table near the front of the room with friends from the *Guardian*. She settled into her chair, with nowhere near enough cushion to be comfortable, and pulled out her phone and stylus to take notes.

Paul Stanley spoke first. "I've been in real estate development for a long time. One thing most people don't understand is that we have investors in residential projects that demand at least a twenty percent return on their money. These investors represent pension funds and others who require long-term, low risk returns. The only way I could add more affordable housing into projects would be for the government to reduce regulations that cause costs to be higher." He addressed the government contingent directly. "Mr. Mayor, we need zoning waivers and regs streamlined. We can incorporate housing like you want in our projects but I must have savings from these regulations or I just cannot afford it. The numbers just don't add up."

News flash! Business wants lower regulations. Jackie chuckled to herself.

The next speaker, Louise, the planner, began spouting numbers. Jackie jotted them down fast. "We need 8,500 new affordable homes in Carlisle within the next 10 years. We cannot concentrate them in one or two areas. They must be scattered around town, even *up the hill* to keep from creating concentrated poverty zones. Remember we define affordable housing as people who spend less than thirty percent of their income on housing. The smaller your paycheck, the higher the percentage for the rent becomes. You must remember, these won't be *the projects* of old. We must create these with cash-funded maintenance reserves up front, so that they don't fall into disrepair. We have learned that folks with little income are willing to care for their places, but just don't have the money to spare. Thus, after a time, they begin to look worn. If we fund the reserves to replace roofs, windows, and so forth up front, we avoid many ills from the old system we've learned to call *the projects.*

"We have enough neighborhoods in our city to keep this from being a burden on any one area. We can't have people opting out or protesting when these come to their area, because we are a community that must work together to solve this crisis."

She looked sideways at Paul and continued, "Before we go killing all the regulations, remember those are there to protect the little guy. That's who we're all trying to help with this meeting. We're happy to review them but which ones are you referring to that need to be removed? Perhaps we just need to update them. No question we must speed up the approval process, Paul."

I wonder where these stats come from and if she even understands them. Good jab on the regs comment.

As Louise took her seat, Teresa from the crisis-housing center stood to speak. "We must have public and private partnerships that will allow the affordable units to look no different than the market priced ones. They have to be near public transportation and near shopping . . . "

Jackie's mind wandered while the speakers droned on for the better part of an hour with so many platitudes and truisms, but no one willing to step up and commit to anything.

The question/answer session got livelier.

"Now the fun part comes. Watch all the crazies come to the mic," Jackie said to her colleague.

Those from Broken Wharf wanted to get out and get their share of the area up the hill. Those already up the hill were determined to keep their property values from being impacted by low-income housing. Everyone was asking the mayor what he and the city would do.

"I've seen low income housing," one tall white man said. "It brings crime and drugs to the suburbs. It drags down the property values. Seems to me we're just moving the poverty around. Let's leave it where it is. I moved where I live now to get away from all that. I don't want it near me. I'll just move out of the county. Is that what we want, all the rich people to leave the county?"

A lady from the Wharf got up and said, "I'm glad we're having this conversation. I've learned a few things. I want a better life for my children and me. Mr. Rich Man, I may not do everything the way you do, but I don't like having crime and drugs in my neighborhood either. Why can't I come and live near you? Why can't my children go to the wealthy schools? It's a matter of money. I need help. All I want is a better life. I can't believe my better life will cause you to move."

Another from the hill spoke, "Why don't those in the state capital help us with some state money. They could cut regs and give some of the millions we pay each year in taxes back to us to help with the crisis."

"All the same songs just different singers. Why are we wasting our time?" Jackie said in a whisper, and made some notes for the news report that night and began to gather her things to get out before the crowd. *Not a good use of time.*

At last, José asked to speak. Most didn't know him. When he stood, he almost tripped over the chairs near him. He caught himself and was handed a microphone.

Jackie turned around at the commotion and saw Chef Pea Coat. *No Jackie, it's José.*

He spoke with a slight Latino accent. "Neighbors, I've been listening to you for almost ninety minutes. You're determined to understand this problem. That's admirable. You should understand it better now than you did when you arrived. It appears many came with minds already made up and not open ears to listen. However, you're not asking the right question. We always ask the government to fix this, but they cannot. We ask the businesses to fix it since they have plenty of money and organizational skill, but they do not. We have not asked ourselves what we can do. Tell me, are all the houses and apartments in Carlisle occupied?"

Most people shook their heads no. "Some areas are more available than others I'm sure, but all have vacancies. Therefore, why don't we subsidize rents for those open houses and apartments to keep the costs below the targets mentioned? Where will the money come from, you may ask? Since people don't want to give the government more money for fear of waste or businesses for fear of greed, then I suggest the Church. We could prepare a campaign that targets the number of rents we need to subsidize and seek those amounts from church donations. It can be administered by a group of trusted representatives from the various congregations around Carlisle. We could use the Center for Affordable Housing and some of the people on the stage tonight to be sure the money is well spent. In addition, whenever a church has a capital building campaign, they should raise the money they can from the congregation and cut it in half. Build the church building with half and affordable housing with the other half. This is something we don't need government or business to do but, we, the people, can achieve this solution through the power of God in His Church. There're no doubt details that need to be worked out, but it is something we can do now! Listen or don't."

With that he handed the microphone back and went to sit back down. Almost tripping again. The crowd stayed silent for a moment then the murmurs started.

"We could only build half of our gym," one member said.

"We would have the *projects* around the church."

"It could work for an immediate solution."

"We would get people moved out to the burbs pretty quick."

"Is that what we want? They would be in our schools and in our stores. Do we want the poor right next door?"

"Isn't that what's needed?"

"It would make a concentration go away but who knows, the entire neighborhood might turn bad."

"I don't know about this."

✢ ✢ ✢

Da Wyz sat unseen in the back of the stage, behind where the panel sat looking out through the curtains. He didn't want to show his face in this place. He was so far out of his territory, but curiosity got the better of him. It went about the way he'd expected until that clumsy guy in the back got up and gave a very reasonable solution. *It could work. What would that do for my Biz? Might get me some new customers and territory. All those rich folks like my smack just like the poor ones do. I could have new distribution lines. Might be good for Biz. Times change, and we must change too. I like things as they are right now though. All the cops leave me alone, and I do well. But that guy had a point. Maybe it could work. Love to see the rich folk only build half of their plans. Nah, this ain't gonna happen.* Da Wyz grinned.

❈❈❈

Jackie had her own thoughts *Wow, there is more to this guy than good looks and great seafood. That is a remarkable but simple plan. It demands commitment, leadership, and good organization. It could work in a significant way. Probably doesn't solve all the issue but . . . I need to catch up with this guy. Maybe have an on-air interview.*

As the murmur began to slow, Pastor Rich got up, "I'm afraid we're out of time tonight. We've run long already. We'll schedule another follow up session to consider more ways forward. Let's thank our panel again for coming to speak. I also want to thank you for being here. It shows your concern for your neighbors and our community."

After polite applause, chairs started screeching across the floor and people gathered their coats to face the biting January air outside.

José began his long walk to the bus stop when Father Menendez pulled alongside and offered a ride back to VM. He accepted and they chatted on the way back about the proposal.

Jackie couldn't get her things and get to José before he disappeared.

Pastor Rich wanted to speak with him also but missed him. He listened while the crowd exited. Many expressed frustration and dissatisfaction. Others said, "Well I'm glad we got that over with."

Rich wasn't surprised to see Justus in the crowd. Nor did it surprise him that he spoke such sense. *There are strong forces to maintain the status quo. I now see more than ever that change must come. I didn't like Justus' comments last month. They challenged almost too much. I'm the leader of this flock; I can't wait for someone else to lead. Nothing changes if you are satisfied with things just like they are.* He said out loud to no one in particular, "That's exactly what others want. Status quo. I must shake us up now."

He had a sad feeling that things were about to change, and that change often came with great pain. *Father, have we missed our chance?*

CHAPTER 24

Hamsa spent his allotted time online looking at radical Islamic sites. He read the narratives. He saw the videos. He watched people make improvised explosive devices. Some of it was pretty cool. Some of it he found quite scary. *I must flush the memory before the next person comes along, so no one could trace what I'm doing.*

The Latinos in school didn't like him and showed it by mistreating him regularly. All the other teen refugees were girls. The Latinos liked the Syrian girls. They didn't like them as friends but more like objects to ogle, Hamsa thought. *The Latinas don't notice a scrawny little Syrian. He longed for someone his age to reach out to him. It had been almost four months since they arrived.*

Why am I here Allah? I pray my prayers, I read the Quran. I do acts of service. I try to be good. Why does this not get better? Help me to know what to do.

Stu and Jimmy had been friends since grade school. They grew up in blue-collar families on the outskirts of the Wharf. While the Wharf was majority black, there were poor white families, too. Stu listened to the conservative radio station and visited websites that spoke about the evils of radical Islam. Stu's dad got killed in the Iraq war. He didn't like having the Syrians here. *They kill and maim. They don't speak our language; don't worship the right God; dress funny.*

They're going to take jobs from us if they don't kill us first. They want America to be Muslim. He didn't dispute any of this he heard from these news sources. When challenged, he became combative. He refused to listen to anything or anyone that disagreed with his views.

Jimmy, the big kid of the twosome, wasn't a good student. They did everything together. Stu told him all about the bad things the Syrians would do now that they were here. Jimmy believed it, because Stu was the smart one.

Stu and Jimmy tried to make them unwelcome without people finding out. They left graffiti on the signs near the Syrian apartments. They mailed threatening letters. They talked bad about them to folks in school. *Most people don't understand how bad these terrorists are,* Stu thought.

Nothing they did got much traction. It'd been months and the Syrians were still here. They heard another wave would arrive in the spring. Stu was certain *Before long, we'll have thousands of them.*

One day Stu said to Jimmy. "Man, I guess they'll have to blow sump'um up before people see how dangerous these people are." Stu clapped his hands together, "Hey, wait a sec. I got an idea. Let's blow up sump'um and blame it on them. We need to figure a target and then get the stuff to make a bomb."

"That sounds like a lot a trouble. If it works, for sure the Syrians would be gone. Why don't we blow them up 'nstead?" Jimmy said.

"Nah, that gets traced back to somebody else. We got to make it look like they did it. Not looking to hurt too many people. Just enough to cause an uproar. Let me think 'bout where and how."

They got an opportunity delivered on a platter when Hamsa transferred to Benson High and landed in their homeroom.

At first Jimmy was going to take him out and beat him up. Stu stopped that. He had a more devious plan. He went over and began to spend time with Hamsa.

Hamsa, learned to distrust everyone along his journey, but quickly got past that with Stu and Jimmy. When one of the black kids picked on him, Jimmy stood up for him and scared him away. Stu took him around campus and showed him the ins and outs of Benson. Where to smoke and not get caught. How to stand just right near the girls' locker room in the gym and get an eyeful. Hamsa felt these guys were like him in that they were minorities in a majority black school.

Stu told him often, "We got to stick together. We can help each other."

Hamsa liked the attention from boys his own age. They were into guns and ammo as well as naked girly sites. Hamsa felt bad when he looked at those but he still did it. Finally, he had some friends in America. Besides, no one else his age extended any welcome at all.

During computer time, he still spent a lot of time on the radical sites, but he slept better.

⚜ ⚜ ⚜

Late in January on a cold gray afternoon, when Hamsa got off the city bus on his way home from school, he saw Yosef standing outside his apartment with his mom. Hamsa wanted nothing more than a warm snack and to get to his computer time, but he knew he had to finish loads of homework first.

"Hamsa! How are you? I want to invite you to my cooking school at the restaurant. It takes about two hours. It would be on your way home from school. Would you like to join my class?" Said Yosef.

Hamsa tried to look distracted by his phone and muttered, "Who else is in it?"

"Mostly Latino teens from the gangs."

"Not interested."

"Don't let that bother you. They're from rival gangs and don't like each other much. I have some strict rules about treating people with respect for anyone who wants to stay. The Golden Rule. It would also give you a chance to practice some Spanish and some English. I would like you to join it."

Looking up from his phone Hamsa said, "Tell me of this Golden Rule?"

"My Master taught it in his Sermon on the Mount that you should treat others the way you want to be treated yourself. It is in my holy book. Do you know any of his teachings?"

"I've heard that one, just didn't know the name of it. I like that teaching. What else does he teach?"

"Many wonderful things. It may be good for you to read some of his teachings. During your computer time. You can find it online. Pull up Matthew chapters five through seven sometime and give it a read. It's the Sermon on the Mount I spoke of. You'll find it fascinating. But, please join the class."

"I'll think about it," Hamsa said, and he walked away.

"It starts each afternoon at 2:30 and finishes before the dinner rush at 4:30. You would be home in plenty of time for homework and dinner. You wouldn't miss your computer time either."

"Maybe, but probably not." Hamsa said as he shuffled away with his head down.

CHAPTER 25

Jackie called Ramone on a cold day in early February.

"I want to stop by and speak to your star chef José about some comments he made at the affordable housing meeting a few nights ago."

"Señorita Jackie, feel free to come by anytime but please, it would be best between the lunch and dinner rush."

"Thanks Ramone, please let him know I'm dropping by."

"I'm sure he'll be delighted to see you."

As she hung up, she marked the appointment on her phone and crossed an item off her virtual to do list. *See you at three, Señor Chef.*

When she arrived, she asked for Ramone at the bar. He came out smelling of sweet cologne, just like he always did. He was smiling and always ready for good publicity.

"May I speak with José?"

"I'm sorry, but he's in the middle of cooking class. I must confess, it's been a crazy day since your call, and I forgot to mention you wanted to see him. He puts on a class for the local teens to teach them a trade and keep them out of the gangs. Gives them something to do after school. If they stay with it, I may hire them to help José. If you don't mind asking him questions in between sessions, I'll get him to talk to you. He doesn't like a lot of attention, even though it seems to follow him around. But I bet he'll talk to you, Ms. Hyatt." He walked away with a wry smile on his face.

Jackie followed Ramone into the kitchen, "I can work around the class. Who knows, maybe he can even teach me to cook."

The aroma was mouthwatering as they entered the kitchen. There were five young men ranging in age from thirteen to twenty, Jackie guessed. All wore stained white aprons and hair coverings. Some were putting vegetables into large stainless-steel pots full of boiling water. Others were making tortillas. José was instructing the group.

When he noticed Jackie, José came over and shook her hand. He looked in her eyes while she spoke, and she liked that. Many men looked at other parts when they greeted her. He had beautiful, intense brown eyes she got distracted by. But his welcoming smile put her at ease. *He must've learned that smile from Ramone. Maybe it's just genetic with Latino men.*

Due to the brevity of their earlier meetings, she hadn't focused too much on this man. He was a shade under six feet tall, with short dark wavy hair under his hair net and olive toned skin. She guessed him to be late thirties. A good-looking man with no BMI issues. He wore a short-sleeved uniform shirt with no visible tattoos—unusual for a Latino man his age. At their previous meeting, he seemed unsure of himself, but not here; he commanded this kitchen.

She returned his smile. "I'm Jacqueline Hyatt of WWNS News. I would like to ask about the things you said at the affordable housing meeting."

"I remember you, Señorita Hyatt, from the Christmas party."

"I'm glad I was memorable. Please call me Jackie."

She pulled out her phone and stylus. "Your name is José Sabio, correct?"

"That's what they call me, yes."

"José what you said the other night made a lot of sense. Where'd you get the idea? How can we make it happen? The big churches won't like the idea of cutting their capital budgets in half, but I liked the suggestion."

"In this country, we spend too much time focusing on the prize. We forget the reason we're here," he said.

"And that reason is . . . "

"To glorify the Creator and to care for each other. We often get the priorities wrong and get so busy that we lose sight of that. I often think the busy part is to help us forget and give us a good excuse to disregard the trouble around us. Of course, when the rich find a spot surrounded by those like themselves, they get caught up in outdoing each other and forget all about the poor. The poor become those people over there who don't work hard like me or aren't as smart as my friends."

"Are you saying the churches up the hill are too focused on themselves?" She was fishing for a quote.

"Yes and no. The church is the people in it, not the building. Some of the people are more focused on what they're doing and seeking the reward because they want to please their bosses and themselves. Then, when the time comes to help those in need, they just can't find the time or the money. There's no time to build a relationship with the poor. They may give money to salve the mind, but they're just trying to buy favor. God wants us to be in relationship with those around us. Not just those like us, but those in need. It's a shame because that's the reason he gave us time and money. It's not to spend it only on ourselves and those like us, but on those who are in need also. Don't misunderstand me. All church members aren't like that. Just the ones who don't know better or won't listen to the Kol Yahweh," he said.

"Excuse me, the cool what?"

"The K-o-l, Kol Yahweh. It's Hebrew for the voice of God. We don't listen for God to tell us what he wants to. We're too busy to listen to him. That's true of the rich and the poor at times. We approach God with our list of to-dos and don't bother to ask if he has anything he wants to accomplish through us."

"You hear God's voice?" Raising her eyebrow and hoping he didn't notice the apprehension on her face.

"Señorita Jackie, we can all hear his voice if we stop long enough to listen."

This guy is out there. She changed track.

"They should be working like crazy and give all their money away to those in need?"

"Oh Jackie, you're quick to turn my words into things I didn't wish to say . . . "

Before he could finish, one of the boys asked what to do next, now that the cactus paddles were done.

"I better come and show you. Will you excuse me a moment? Best for you to wait here."

"Cactus paddles? For real?"

"Yes, they're cheap and can be very tasty if prepared right. If not, they can be a touch slimy?"

"Not to mention prickly."

"Yes, the key is always to watch for the needles," he smiled.

As he approached the stove, one of the boys making tortillas flipped some oil at one of his compadres who jumped out of the way. The oil hit the open flame and made a big flash. José frowned at the boy, who looked away sheepishly.

He called back to Jackie, "This may take a few minutes. May we schedule this for a time when I'm not in a kitchen full of students?"

She yelled her agreement over the kids laughing and pushing each other.

"Come by one night after the restaurant is closed, and I'll talk to you more then. No classes."

"Which night works best?"

"All weeknights are about the same, but Monday is often a slow night for dinner, and we close pretty early. I can speak to you then. Say around 9:30, if that makes sense."

She agreed.

"I'll show you how to cook some genuine Latino cuisine. I prefer to cook and talk; it helps me concentrate. I don't eat until the restaurant is closed. I want to make sure you get my message correct. It's not new, but it can be misunderstood. Especially coming from a guy with a Spanish accent."

Is he asking me to dinner? This clumsy, shy guy who works with the gangbangers in the barrio?

"Is it safe—that time of night?" She asked Ramone.

Without losing his smile, he said, "Yes, Señorita Jackie, the monsters don't show up until after midnight."

Jackie thought about a comeback, but then decided she must've insulted him with her question, so she just grinned and said, "Thank you. I'll see myself out."

José was directing traffic with the teenagers now and was out of sight.

CHAPTER 26

Dressed in a t-shirt and checkered chef's pants, José cleaned himself up from the breakfast rush and sipped a cup of coffee while reading a copy of the Carlisle Guardian a patron left behind.

He liked to read the paper to keep up with local concerns. He never bought one so he never knew if it was all there. *Newspapers are so small these days; it's not hard to believe some part could be missing.*

A limo stopped in front of Restaurant Tapas around 10 AM on this beautiful February morning. José saw it through the window and knew he must go along. *A divine appointment?*

After the driver opened the rear door, a tall, bald, black man unfolded himself from the back seat and entered the restaurant. He moved with grace unbefitting his size. Ramone, always smiling, but very annoyed that the limo blocked his driveway, greeted the man to determine his needs.

"I'm here to see Joseph," the well-dressed passenger said with a hint of entitlement in his voice.

"No one is here by that name, señor. You must have the wrong place. Please move your vehicle. You're blocking the entrance," Ramone said.

"I'm not wrong. He's here." Deion looked past Ramone.

José stepped forward and said, "I'm Joseph."

"Come with me."

"Careful señor, this is my place. No one orders my staff around here but me," Ramone said.

Deion focused on Ramone with a hint of disgust and opened his mouth to retort . . .

"I'll go with you. Where are we going?" José said.

"We're going to see Da Wyz." Deion canted his head to the right, as if that was an obvious answer.

He seemed to like saying that line.

"Should I change? I didn't prepare to meet anyone today."

Looking past Ramone again, Deion said, "No, he wants to see you now."

"May I ask how long this will take? I have to be back for the noon rush."

"I bring you back, when Da Wyz is done."

"I need my chief cook back before noon," Ramone said.

"You get him back, when Da Wyz is done. You know the way things are here. Don't make Da Wyz mad. What he wants, I get for him. He wants Joseph. I'll bring him back later."

The man, an obvious threat to most of those around him, didn't like the challenge from Ramone. He was a pick-up and deliveryman with a schedule to keep and now was tired of the questions.

Joseph got his pea coat from the kitchen. He just got his first cell phone a couple of weeks ago so Ramone could better communicate with him, and it almost fell from the coat pocket as he pulled it from the hook. On the way out, he said, "It'll be OK, Ramone. I'll be back soon. I suspect he wants to talk. Otherwise, he would've picked me up with more discretion. If I'm not back by 11:30 have Carlos stand in for me. His number is on the board in the back. He's become my star pupil."

Joseph got into the back of the limo with Deion seated opposite him. He began to pray about what would happen next.

They left Villa Maya and headed to Broken Wharf. They went through a number of side streets with many turns to be sure they weren't being followed. Seemed like an overabundance of caution, but he'd never been an organized crime boss. In the Wharf, Da Wyz was king.

He touched the cell phone in his pocket for some added assurance. Then he laughed at himself at the thought of whipping it out to call the cops. A cook in the back of Da Wyz's limo calling the cops for help. He decided to make a different call. A peace came over him, when he asked for words to say.

They pulled into a warehouse, and a big garage door clattered down behind them.

"Come with me," Deion said.

They headed toward a long metal staircase. Joseph went up the stairs to what looked like an office.

As he entered he saw fine wood paneling, smelled the scent of leather and cigar smoke with some incense. There was a high ceiling with plenty of overhead lights, which weren't on. The window in the back of the office opened out toward the river. *What a view of the waterfront!*

The mahogany desk had a computer monitor and keyboard on it. He saw a small stack of papers in folders in a box on one side. A high back dark red leather chair turned with its back to the door must contain Da Wyz. He couldn't see anyone.

They closed the door behind them, and the click of the latch seemed to trigger the next few minutes.

"Welcome Joseph, I've been expecting you," came a voice from the chair. *Da Wyz must like to intimidate his guests. Must've made him feel like he had the upper hand. I've been in a more impressive presence than this before.* He decided to play along.

"Deion, thank you for escorting our new friend."

"Always glad to be of service, sir." Deion turned and left.

The latch clicked again.

Da Wyz slowly turned his chair around and smiled at Joseph. He had a lit cigar in his mouth, eyes shrouded by dark glasses, and sporting a white silk shirt open at the neck.

Taking the cigar from his lips with thumb and forefinger, he began. "I've been looking forward to meeting you, Mr. Joseph. Or is it José? Cute using different names. Made you harder to find. I apologize for the way you were brought here, but I've found people from VM don't always appreciate my invitations. Seems I have a reputation there. I guess I've got a reputation lots o' places. I'm pleased to see you. I hope you found the journey pleasant."

"The journey was smooth. Deion's not much of a talker, but that's OK. I use different names to blend with different cultures, not to hide myself. Why have you summoned me here?"

Da Wyz motioned Joseph to sit down in front of his desk. Joseph complied. He offered him a cigar or a drink. Joseph declined both. When he got closer he saw a man who wanted to be perceived much larger than his physical stature. *Now I understand all the surroundings. He's suffering from small man syndrome.*

Da Wyz looked at his desk, then looked at Joseph. "I didn't realize you were the man from the housing meeting who spoke so much sense the other night. I called you here because I heard something else about you. I hear you healed a blind lady in the Wharf, Roberta Saunders. Is this true?"

Joseph knew he'd bullied this information out of someone.

"Yes, I was there when it happened. It was the power of my Master that healed her."

"Who is this Master?"

"Jesus of Nazareth is how you may know him."

"I see." Da Wyz folded his hands in front of him on the desk. The cigar now in an ashtray nearby. "Tell me, Joseph, what else can you do other than heal blind old ladies and give wise advice? I may have a use for a man of your talents. You wouldn't have to work those crazy cook's hours. The pay is bound to be a whole lot better. Lots o' pleasures of home. No more boarding houses."

He's done his research. I wonder what else he knows about me. No way he can know it all. No one would believe it.

"Your offer is generous, but I'm a follower of the Master and can only do whatever he instructs me to. The power is his, not mine. I'm only the vessel."

"Well ain't you the humble one?" Da Wyz put on his folksy black man routine.

"Is it humility to know one's limitations? Or is it just reality? I took an offer like yours once in my life and still have the scars from the experience."

Da Wyz let out a boisterous laugh and pointed his forefinger. "I like you Joseph. I didn't expect you to take my offer, but wanted to see what kind of a man you are. You're both a healer and a wise man. You're more impressive in person than I anticipated. Like I said, I saw you the other night at the church meeting. You speak with wisdom and presence, but not much grace. Do you think those wealthy ones up the hill are gonna embrace the poor folks we send to them with rent subsidies? You think they gonna embrace us poor folks in their shiny schools and churches? You think they gonna build affordable housing instead of big churches? C'mon man."

"If they'll listen to the Master, they'll do it. He must transform their hearts. He has done it already in many of them. They're just blind to the need. They haven't been paying attention. All that running to chase the gold, they forget why we're here. He can transform any life, if we will but seek him." He paused for effect and said, "He can even transform you."

Da Wyz paused to think about that. Then he smiled a very wide smile and picked up his cigar. After taking a long draw he said, "What's he gonna do with an old sinner like me? I've broken lots of commandments, all of 'em I think. Plenty of times too. Even proud of it most of the time. Been doing that since I was a kid. What's he got to offer me? I got it all man, money, women, drugs, respect. What's God gonna do for me?"

This was a speech he'd rehearsed before. Something is wrong here. Something off . . . Now the words came to Joseph. "He can give you what you seek deep in your soul. He gives joy, peace, and eternal life. You don't have these at the moment. The way you're going you won't get them, either."

Da Wyz wet his lips. He put down his cigar. He started to speak but stopped.

Joseph prayed silently and continued. He felt the power of the Spirit move in him, unsure of what would happen next. "Jeremiah, that is the name your mother gave you, correct?"

Da Wyz sat back in his chair and resting his elbows on the chair arms he pressed his fingertips together. "Yes. I don't use it much. How do you know it? Why do you bring that up?"

"I serve the Master who knows all. Sometimes he tells me things that matter in the moment. He also told me to tell you that he loves you and doesn't want this for you. He wants you to love him and care for others. He wants you to know him; know his peace, joy, self-control . . . "

He waved a hand and said, "Yeah, yeah, I hear all that from Reverend Tony. It doesn't move me."

"You've confessed to many evil deeds in your life. You've hurt many people. You've gained at their expense. You've killed. Committed adultery. Followed after idols. Shall I keep going?"

"No need. I already told you that stuff. It doesn't take a prophet to see that. Are you looking for confession? Are you for real or just a con man?"

"So why send for me? Something is moving you. You're seeking something."

Da Wyz stood up, ready for a fight. His chair skittered several feet behind him. "You're just an illegal Mayan cook without a home, no family, no nothin'! You come in here with high and mighty words about God gonna give me peace and joy. I don't need that stuff. I don't know what your game is, cook, but I'll tell you this, mess in the Wharf, you're messin' with power you don't understand. I'll come at you with everything. VM will burn! Are you tryin' to unite the Latin gangs? The word on the street is you meet with them each afternoon.

From what I can tell, you're working the gangs in VM, working with the Syrians, working up the hill too. Now I find you working my Wharf. What's your game, man?" He reached into his top drawer and pulled a pistol pointing it sideways at Joseph's face. "I should just kill you now."

"Is this why you sent for me? To kill me now? You could have tried that in the street any evening as I walk home. You know where I live. Why bring me here to kill me? You're seeking something else. Something you believe I can give you. Is that not so? Do you fear the answer?"

Da Wyz's hand began to shake like the gun was too heavy now. He lowered the weapon and placed it on his desk near him. Retrieving his chair, he sat back down. He started looking up at the ceiling while the chair swayed back and forth. Looking back at Joseph, he took off his glasses and folded them up. "You're different, I can feel something different about you. You know something no other preacher I've seen does. Never saw a blind woman healed. Heard about some of that stuff but never knew anyone it happened to. I can't get it out of my head. Why didn't you want credit for it? If I could do that, I would be Da Wyz indeed."

Adjusting in the chair now, Joseph said, "Jeremiah, may I tell you a story?"

Da Wyz nodded.

"There was a young man from the barrio who was smaller than the others. He was abused by the bigger kids all the time. Each beating added to his resolve and the bitterness deep in his soul. He nurtured it. Found strength in it. As he grew, he realized it gave him the fire he needed to remove any enemy who stood in his way. He did it out of fear and hatred. It worked really well. Over time he found others who wanted his protection. Nothing came for free with this one. You had to pay your dues with what you had, your body, your duty, your blood. It was the code he followed and any who followed had to accept it. The creature comforts came, money, power, along with many other vices. He was surprised to live a long life. Thought it was a reward for all he achieved. But the fuel of hatred, shame, and bitterness leaves a soul empty, hurting in the dark of the night. The demons of the past come back to haunt. The fear of losing all this is too much to bear but he knows that is the only way out. He seeks truth but has never known the love he must embrace to find it. Then he remembers, there was one in his life who loved like no other. His mama loved and cared for him. She nursed all those wounds from the beatings. She told him you could be more than the bullies. But this now middle-aged hombre realized he'd become the worst of the them. The shame of being beaten as a child is now replaced with the shame of knowing what he is. An evil sinner in need of grace. Listen or Don't."

Da Wyz looked down at his desk, the gun laying there. "Your story is as subtle as being hit by a truck, Joseph. I am that hombre as you call him." His shoulders dropped, sweat now dotted his white shirt. "My name is Jeremiah Michaels, I'm the most powerful man in the Wharf, possibly in the city, because I'll do things to get my way others won't. I've grown this business to be respected by lots of folk, even those up the hill. But you're right, Joseph, I don't have peace. I drink or drug myself to sleep at night. In the dark of the night, I still hear the cries of people I shot. I hear the screams of their mothers. A few weeks ago, I heard a mama crying for her teenager killed by my command. I wasn't there, but I heard it. That never bothered me before, but now I can't shut it off no more. I'm looking for healing. When I heard about Roberta, I thought maybe you could help calm my mind. I can't tell this to none of my brothers here. I got to have some relief."

Joseph now realized he knew a secret told to no one else. *He won't let me leave with what I know. He can't trust me to keep it quiet. Dear Lord, how do I get out of this? Greater is he who is in me . . .*

Da Wyz looked back at Joseph now. "I watched my mama die of cancer last year. It ate her up, slow. All my money and all the docs couldn't help her. She did the experimental treatments for a time. In the end, she got this peace about her. Said God showed her a better way. He was ready for her. Told the docs to stop it all. She was ready to go. I held her weak little body as she died. Her last words to me were, 'Be there Jeremiah. Be in heaven with me.' Ever since then I couldn't shut the door on my past. Something's gotta give. I want what she had. I didn't understand it, I still don't. I need what she had."

"Jeremiah, I don't have a touch that will calm your mind like I did with Ms. Roberta's eyes, but I know the giver of peace. I already said, he wants you to know peace and joy. All you have to do is believe he died for you and rose again."

Jeremiah looked at Joseph with fire in his eyes. "I've heard this before. Your words are just like Tony's. Man, I'm just too bad for this, too far gone. I can't change now. My role is set. I hoped you'd be different. I want a healing touch!"

"It won't be easy to change but the Master can transform you. He changed me many years ago and I've been his servant since. I know peace and joy and love and all the good things he wants for us. The good news is that you don't have to change yourself, he'll do it."

"You live in boarding house with nothin'. What about all this?" Jeremiah waived his hand around the room. "It's all I know. All I ever wanted until I saw there was something more in my mama's dying eyes. I knew I couldn't get there on the path I've chosen. But it's all I know. I'm too far gone."

"You didn't tell the truth Jeremiah about your mother a moment ago, she didn't say 'Be there Jeremiah.' She said, 'Be there Eze.'

"How would you know … Yeah, she called me Eze. It means 'king' in Igbo. Absolute monarch. That's what I am."

"It has a greater meaning, Eze means high servant of the people. Since you were a child your mother didn't challenge you to be king but a servant of your people."

Jeremiah looked up at Joseph and shook his head. "I'm too far gone."

Now Joseph stood and declared, "That is a lie from the enemy! Get away from here Satan! I rebuke you in the name of Jesus the Christ! No one is too far gone while they're still breathing! Listen to the word of the Lord. He loves you with a crazy love. He let you live this long because he wants you to know him and all his glory. Don't let Satan fill you with his lies! That will lead you to destruction. That is what he seeks for you. If you have to give this up, the Lord promises that he is sufficient for you. He promises life everlasting. Tell me what do you love most of all?"

"These days, it's my wife and two daughters. They're amazing. No idea why they put up with all the grief I give."

"Would you give them whatever you could."

"That and more."

"Yet you being evil can love so much. How much more does the Lord love us, since his love is pure and holy?"

Joseph paused to let the comment sink in and then said, "He loves you more than you can imagine."

Jeremiah said very quietly with his head in his hand, "I'm tired and ready to change. I just don't know how."

"Eze, that is a miracle I can help with." Joseph walked around the desk and placed his hands on Jeremiah's shoulders where he sat. He could feel his sweat through the silk shirt. "Pray with me. Repeat these words. They don't heal a hurting soul unless you mean them. He did the work; we just have to accept it.

"Father . . . I know I am a sinner . . . I need to be saved . . . I know it because of all the bad things I've done . . . all the selfish things in my life . . . I want to but . . . I know I cannot save myself . . . I have tried and failed so many times . . . I must rely on you. . . . Please change me now. . . . I believe Jesus died for me and rose again. Please send your Spirit now to comfort me and seal me in your kingdom. In His name, I pray."

Jeremiah repeated the prayer. His head still bowed. Joseph prayed over him further. "Father, please comfort this sinner's soul. Save him by your grace. Show him the mercy you give with abundance." He felt Jeremiah's guilt melt away under his hands. A burden lifted.

When he finished, Joseph now saw a man born from above. There was light in his eyes. Before he saw a prideful, painted on smile; now he saw the smile of a man at peace.

"What do I do now?"

"We need to get you baptized my brother, you must learn to follow the Lord now. You are to be a high servant of the people," Joseph smiled.

"This moment I pledge five million dollars to create an endowment to this housing plan you proposed. That's just the start my man. I will seek ways to help my brothers in every way I can."

He stood and gave Joseph a bear hug. "My life is new. I must be done with all this Biz and move to better things. This is amazing. I'm new! I'm new!" He appeared to almost float around the room.

Deion came back in the room after hearing the shouting to be sure all was well.

"Deion, this man is amazing. He is a holy one. He knows God like none I've met before. Get Julia, we need to call a news conference. I have announcements to make, and I won't wait long to make them," Jeremiah said.

As Deion left, Joseph took Jeremiah by the arm and looked deep into his eyes.

"The Master doesn't want me involved in publicity in this way. Please don't mention me to others. Let's get Reverend Tony over here for the conference. Sunday, he can baptize you in the worship service. I'll be there."

Jeremiah knew how to keep a secret. He grinned at Joseph and said, "Got it."

As Deion came back with Julia, Jeremiah said, "Deion, take my very good friend Joseph back home. Listen to him, if you will. He speaks true things about God."

Jeremiah gave Joseph another bear hug and smiled again. "I'll call you later. There are so many other things I wish to know, but what you've shown me has changed me for good. I can hardly wait to learn more."

The assistant began scribbling notes on a pad as they left.

Da Wyz moved into full Biz mode, "Julia, call Reverend Tony, and tell him I'm sending a car for him so he can come here right now. Deion, take Joseph away and swing by and collect Reverend Tony like you did earlier. I want the newspaper and TV coverage, this afternoon. We have big announcements. I'll write a speech. Tony must come now; did I say that? Get my wife to join me. I need her to bring the kids over. Tell her to dress for the press. Wow, what a morning this is!"

Deion took Joseph back to Restaurant Tapas and dropped him off. They didn't speak much. Joseph closed his eyes and praised the Master for what happened and what was about to. A psalm of thanksgiving came to him. He loved being a part of changed choices.

As José walked in, Ramone said, "It's about time; we got customers!"

A PSALM OF THANKSGIVING

Lord you are moving mightily in this place
I never tire watching you remove each vile trace
As you make a stone-cold heart live anew
By the power of your spirit that you imbue

Bless you loving Master for working through me
I never grow weary of new life you let me see
I get angry, impatient sometimes with your pace
You always bring joy for those remade by your grace

I rejoice that you move among men to this day
You continue to amaze as you show the way
There's no greater joy than to see you transform
 A heart in prison that refused to conform

We miss such blessings that we should observe
You don't give us the justice that we deserve
Instead you bring peace by your grace alone
From our catastrophe you bring shalom

CHAPTER 27

Jackie arrived at Restaurant Tapas Monday night about 9:15. She was intrigued by this guy who seemed unsure of himself but so sure of his mission and message. It'd been a long day already, and she longed for a nice warm bath and glass of pinot after this interview.

She covered many newsworthy events of late. The most recent being Da Wyz's out-of-the-blue press conference a couple days ago. Jeremiah Michaels' conversion and endorsing the plan José espoused was enough to get her to the door. She also liked the idea of getting to know this man better at long last. They crossed paths in odd places, the Syrian camp and Villa Maya. Not to mention the near miss at the Church of Carlisle. *He has such a welcoming smile and intense gaze and he looked good in a pea coat too.*

She entered while the last customers were finishing up dessert. It looked like flan to her, but she couldn't be sure from across the room. The restaurant, adorned with hearts, cupids, and other Valentine themed decorations, even had a bowl of candy hearts on the end of the bar. She just had to find an orange *Be Mine. Those are my favorites.*

Ramone greeted her with a smile and double handshake. Smelling wonderful as always. "José is cleaning up. Will you take a table in the dining room to wait?" He directed her to a booth near the window. "Would you like a glass of white wine after a long day?"

"Not yet, but a cup of coffee would be nice. Milk, no sugar please."

"Lucinda, por favor, café con leche para Señorita Hyatt."

After about ten minutes José came out of the kitchen with his apron on and a food stain on his shirt. Looked like tomato sauce to her. "Well at least you dressed up for me."

José looked confused and gave an awkward smile. Then he looked down and noticed the apron. He untied it and took it off. "I guess our uniforms are quite different." With a glass of water in his hand, he sat down across the table.

Jackie slipped off her long charcoal gray coat and laid it on the chair next to her. She draped her red scarf on top. She wore a black dress with a solid red blazer. Her hair was down with a few curls framing her face.

"Ramone lets me cook at night after the restaurant closes to ex-periment with dishes. I can always use a fresh taste tester if you're willing. I guarantee you won't leave hungry, although you may have some heartburn to deal with. I work with ingredients left from to-day's meals. I only make small dishes to save money. It works well, though, because we're a tapas place. I warn you some of these are works in progress."

"I'm game for that, but you have to answer my questions while you work."

"I agree, Señorita Jacqueline."

"Jackie please, I use Jacqueline on the air and in court." *Not even a little reaction to that.*

They were off to the kitchen. He showed her to a tall stool near the counter so she'd be able to hear him over the fan and sizzling oil. Usually she would use the recorder on her cell phone but with all the background noise that wouldn't work here. So, she decided to use the stylus and screen.

He opened a beer, which he offered to Jackie.

"No beer for me, but the white wine Ramone offered me sure sounds good about now. The cameras add ten pounds, and I don't need the beer gut."

Ramone stopped by to say good night and tell them the rest of the staff had gone.

José went to the bar, and poured a glass from an open bottle in the cooler. He brought the wine in a long-stemmed wine glass. "It's not expensive, and Ramone allows me to use the opened bottles for cooking."

He raised his beer, and they clinked glasses in a toast.

"Happy almost Valentine's Day," Jackie said.

José paused.

"Don't you celebrate this day?" Jackie said, puzzled by the pause.

"No, I just remembered some of the lessons of St. Valentine. How he taught of the Father's love at a difficult time. Now, we just treat it so flippantly. It was a holy celebration once. But it's good to be with you near the day. Sorry, I have no flowers for the lovely lady." They both took a small drink.

The dinner and a show are about to begin, Jackie thought. He poured some olive oil in a saucepan, chopped and added some garlic and onion, tomato sauce, paprika, red pepper flakes and some other ingredients she couldn't keep up with. The speed of his knife work impressed her. *Quick hands.* Once the sauce boiled he turned it to simmer.

"This will be Patatas Bravas a la José. That will need to simmer a while. I have some sliced potatoes that have already been roasted; we'll add them to the sauce, when it's ready. That may be twenty or so minutes. Give me a moment to get a few other dishes started, and we can snack and answer questions while we wait for the Patatas. Do you eat meat?"

"Yes, I'm a lady carnivore. I don't eat very much though. Otherwise, I couldn't fit in these outfits."

"I should've asked sooner. Do you have any food allergies or things that you just don't like? I eat anything and am willing to try lots of foods. Sometimes I just presume everyone is like that."

"No, I eat about anything. I don't like liver or brussels sprouts much. Otherwise your options are wide open."

"Good, how about ham and cheese croquettes?"

"Sounds tasty."

He put another saucepan with olive oil and butter on the stovetop. He added onion, no garlic, but some salt and pepper. He added flour, waited a moment and stirred in some milk. Then he added some diced ham and cheese. He spread it all on a pan and said, "I need to let that cool." He paused. "Would you like to help?"

"I'll try, but my hands need washing."

"I never do that," he said with a wide grin and pointed her to the sink and the hand cleaner.

She returned, hands held up like a surgeon awaiting gloves. "Here, you can whisk these eggs together."

He added some breadcrumbs and they created croquettes. They lived up to expectations, hot, but very tasty. He didn't tell her he added jalapeño pepper until after the first bite. She missed it. *Quick hands strike again.*

"I believe like St. Augustine that food is medicine. It can help the body heal or make the body sick. If we overindulge in the wrong food, we get overweight and have joint pain, heart issues, etc. If we eat the right amount of the right food, we get full and avoid the bad effects. Do you know what I mean?"

"Yes, I can see that, but I'm never sure what the right stuff is these days. The studies keep changing the answers. Answer this, Señor Chef. Is milk good for you or bad for you?"

"What do you think?" He smiled that welcoming smile.

"No, Señor Chef, you don't get off that easy. I'm the one doing the interview here. I ask questions to lay a framework first. I test my subject to see if he'll tell the truth, or only part of it."

He locked onto her eyes and said, "Milk is good for children. It has wonderful nutrients they need for strong bones."

"Now you're being a commercial for the national milk foundation."

"Let me finish. For adults, dairy, and milk in particular, can be very hard to digest. Some are quite sensitive to it, so I would recommend alternative sources like nut milk, soy milk, and so forth." He paused. "How'd I do?"

"OK, you speak your mind, and you're well informed about milk." She grinned.

"What're we eating next?"

"This is a bean dip I made too much of earlier. It's served with tortilla chips. I can never make too much of in this restaurant."

The fresh and brittle chip splintered when she bit into it, the dip ended up on the counter top with a splat. She gave a nervous laugh.

"I did something wrong with this batch of chips, they're too brittle. Sorry for that. Here, take a larger plate."

She cleaned up her mess with a paper napkin and went for another one. This time she carefully broke the chip ahead of time and enjoyed the bean dip without the mess. "Once I got to taste it, I find it very soothing compared to the zip in the croquettes."

He went to check on the sauce, simmering on the stove. The intoxicating fragrance of the dishes began to fill the air. Both Jackie and José were hungry due to the late hour.

José got some salsa verde he made earlier in the day. "This will go well with the chips also."

With a break in the action while the sauce simmered, Jackie began the interview with more earnestness.

"Have you heard about Da Wyz's big announcement?"

"Yes, he has become a follower of the Master and now is going to give a lot of money to the poor for housing."

"Exactly. He's going to do what you suggested at the meeting back in January. How do you explain that?"

"He must've been there and thought it a good idea. I don't remember seeing him. I'm glad someone took the idea and went with it. Others from up the hill should do it too. Perhaps I should go speak to them. Or perhaps you can reach them with this story."

José handed her a house salad he made fresh out of the spinner. He dressed it with oil and vinegar and something she couldn't identify.

Jackie began to wonder if she was being set up to get this guy's message out. She didn't like to be used. "Wow, this salad's amazing. The pairing is excellent." As she swallowed her first bite and chased it down with a sip of wine. "What story should I tell them up the hill?"

"Would you like a refill on the wine? Something else, perhaps?"

"Same is fine." She nodded.

As he walked back to the cooler, he said, "You could repeat my suggestion and let them know that someone from the Wharf is doing it already."

"Might get their competitive juices flowing. See who can give the most for affordable housing," she said.

"I would prefer they did it because they cared for those less fortunate, not to beat Jeremiah. God loves a cheerful giver. From what I see that's what he's become. Others should follow his lead." He returned with a fresh glass.

"I see you're on a very informal basis with Da Wyz. Most people don't call him by his given name. Most people don't even know it. How well do you know Da Wyz, as he likes to call himself? Do you know what kind of a man he is? I'm not convinced this is just another stunt of his. But I confess I don't see his angle, if he's working one. He's a loathsome creature, who profits from hurting others. I hope no one follows his lead in that. Sorry for the editorial. Back to my question. Do you know him?"

"I've met him before."

"Didn't realize you worked the Wharf too? I haven't run into you there, yet."

"I'm not sure what you mean."

"Da Wyz works the Wharf. Didn't realize he came to Villa Maya for dinner. You and I have met here, with the refugees, and I even saw you up the hill at Carlisle Church the other night. You do get around. On top of that you seem to have Susan Hamilton wrapped around your finger. We all know that Mayor Hamilton is the head of our city, but Susan is the neck that turns it." She smiled hoping for a laugh.

He grinned back, "I'm sure Jeremiah gets around all over. He's hard to miss."

Her curiosity was now piqued. *This guy seems very guarded. He answers questions with brevity and not much precision. Perhaps he's illegal.* She decided to probe deeper.

They continued with the chips and dips.

"I need to know who I'm talking to. Tell me about yourself before I get any more of your message."

"Well, not a lot to say. I came to Carlisle a few months ago. Arrived right after the riot on the riverfront. I work with the church here to minister to the poor. We're all working to give the people a better life. Trying to keep families together, keep gangs to a minimum, heal the wounds life inflicts.

"I learned to cook over many years of traveling and watching what people eat. Don't think I would make it in a fine restaurant, though. Too stuffy for me. I want to be with the people and care for them. I teach them what I learned from the Master many years ago. I read a lot and pray a lot and listen to the Kol Yahweh."

"So, you're a Catholic lay priest who listens to God's voice. Didn't they burn Joan of Arc for that?"

He paused a moment at the Joan of Arc comment. Same faraway look as the St. Valentine reference. *What is he thinking about?*

"I was a priest a long time ago in another land, but now I don't identify with one denomination or another. I go where the Master leads. I've found there are many out there doing his work, regardless of the title we give them."

"How'd you get into this line of work? Where is Señora Chef and all the *chefettes*? I thought Catholics believed in big families."

"I don't have a wife and family. I enjoy the community I'm in. They're plenty of family for me. My travels and my lifestyle aren't very attractive to women who want to settle down and have stability in their lives. I used to work the farms but found cooking more to my gifts. People seem to like it, so when I go somewhere new, I try to find a place that appreciates my skills. Food is a great icebreaker. I use that place to make the whole community better. We become a mutual blessing. I've found the Master blesses it and often the powerful come to me in my restaurant."

"Sounds like you move around a lot."

"I go where the Master leads."

"Who is this Master you follow?"

"He goes by many names, I choose to call him Master since that is what his close friends did back in the day."

"So, God or Jesus, led you here to our city to bless us, correct?"

"Yes and no, he led me here for reasons that aren't entirely clear to me yet, but will become clear when he shows me more. I don't get all the plan at once. Enough to affirm I'm in the right place, and he's blessing my efforts. Like all the rest of us, I'm called each day to follow what he says."

"Does he, like, send you texts and stuff?"

"Now you're toying with me. He speaks when I am still, meditating, and praying. Seldom is it verbal; often it's a feeling that is affirmed as I go. He never sent me a tweet."

"You're a very trusting soul. I don't listen to my boss half the time, and he yells orders at me. What's clear to you so far?"

He brought out another dish. This time, vegan enchiladas. "These were left over from a dish I made too much of earlier, and I've been keeping them warm." He took one and placed the other three with a spin in front of Jackie.

He took another draw from his beer, "I'm to work here and help those in this area. I'll venture out to other areas to help them also. I must challenge the comfortable and comfort those who are troubled. If you look at it, that was his message from long ago. I'll speak the truth of his love and his desire that we care for each other. He also told me that I would meet with you and share this information."

The last statement stung over the wine and the amazing food. *Whoa Jackie, this is a little creepy now. Just when I was starting to like this guy. Keep your head lady.* She collected her thoughts but couldn't shake a very uneasy feeling. Like she'd been had. She began to wonder if anyone knew she was here other than Ramone.

"You knew I was coming to see you?"

"Yes, it had been shown to me."

"This is creepy."

"Don't be nervous, I serve the one who knows all. Sometimes he shows me things. I'll confess, I was very pleased when you did come by and when you agreed to this conversation. I'm also very glad about our conversation so far. You must be able to tell I mean you no harm."

That did comfort her, but she had journalistic ethics and didn't like the idea of being played. Her thoughts were swirling now. *Was it the wine, the food or this man who is like none I've met before?*

"Perhaps we should talk about you. It may set your mind at ease."

C'mon Jackie where's your poker face. Do I look that disturbed? How much do I want to tell him about me?

"So, what did the big guy have to say about me? What do you already know? I hate to repeat anything. Tell me what you know, and I'll fill in the blanks." She said with a playful smile.

He offered her another enchilada, as gesture of kindness to allay her concerns.

"The big guy, as you say, hasn't told me much, only that you were coming by, and I should speak with you and spend time with you. I've observed a few things, though, if I may say them."

Jackie nodded after deciding to eat some more of the enchilada, her guard relaxing.

"You're a very attractive woman in your early thirties. You work out and watch what you eat. You take very good care of your outward appearance. You're a bright lady with a sharp mind and a sharp tongue at times. Like all of us, you have a view of life which has been formed over time and don't like it when it's challenged. You don't believe in the Master or in a grand plan. You put forward a very strong presence but that masks some insecurity, which you often cover up with witty comments. You don't have a love in your life except your work. You wish there was more."

"OK, I like the attractive woman part. The early thirties comment was flattery; you know I'm older than that. But it was a kind thought." She was comforted by his charm and the food.

"I grew up in Charlotte. My mom still lives there, but she doesn't get around well now. My brother's in Chicago. My dad divorced my mom when I was thirteen. Too many other women. Went to college at the University of Georgia. I got married after my first internship at CNN. It was great for a while, but he got tired of being with only one woman, and I didn't need the aggravation in my life. Our careers came first. Thus, no children. They're not conducive to career."

She looked down at her phone for a moment and continued. "I started doing the weather on a local station near Atlanta but wanted to do investigative work. I enjoyed that and making a difference for *the little guy*. I left greater Atlanta a few years ago looking for a smaller city to work in. In the news biz one always wants the network job, but I prefer to do the local stories. I can do the anchor role, but like to do the interviews instead of just reading copy. Not a big fan of long flights, so the international assignments didn't much appeal to me. Because I have no family, it makes it easy for me to work the weekends, so they give me anchor at times but they know I'm a good reporter who can get to the truth." She said the last part with pride.

She looked around the room now. After a brief silence she smiled. "I'm starting to like the idea that God told you about me. Didn't realize they watched the WWNS News in heaven. I should tell the boss and ask for a raise."

She didn't want to get too close. *He's right I like to use sarcasm to throw people off. Is this guy a story or just a fascination?*

At long last he produced the Patatas Bravas. He plated it, and they enjoyed one last dish of tapas. *It was salty with a hint of spice. Not overpowering like the croquettes.*

"What do you think of it?"

"Wow, I'll come over every night for dinner now. Wait, that didn't come out right."

"I understand. I accept the compliment. Would you like some dessert to finish off the meal?"

She smiled at him, but held up one hand, "TV and ten pounds. As it is, I'm going to have to work out an extra hour tomorrow."

"How about some berries – no whipped cream?"

"OK, but just a small bowl. Give me a little whipped cream. Let's get back to the matter at hand. Endowments for affordable housing. Have you seen that work other places?"

"No."

"So how do you know it'll work here?"

"We must try something and that seemed to be the best chance we have. I believe it came from the Master. It allows us to get involved and doesn't require . . . what you'd call, an act of congress."

"Are you saying God wants us to do this? That sounds like socialism to some."

"Compassion often does, but my desire is not to rely on the government or business for this but on people; the church can help in so many ways. Remember the church is us, not those buildings. That's where it meets."

"Can the churches work together?"

"Let's call it the Church, not the churches. If we follow the same Master then yes, we can work together if we'll look for common ground. We shouldn't seek to argue over our differences. They can be acknowledged, but we should focus on what we have in common. What are the teachings we can all embrace, and what can we do to ease the pain of our neighbors in need?"

"This sounds very noble. How do you plan to get the message out?"

José began to clear the plates and put them in the sink.

"You can help me."

"I'm not a preacher. I don't even like church. All that liturgy and all those self-righteous hypocrites give me the creeps."

Jackie got up to help with the dishes.

José motioned her away, but she insisted.

"Look this is an interview not a date. You made all the food, the least I can do is help clean it up."

José agreed but only after he warned her that this wasn't like the dishwasher at home. She slipped off her jacket and hung it on a peg near the sink. The black dress was sleeveless. She knew she looked good in this style. She grabbed an apron and began filling a big sink with water. José continued to clear the counter.

She tested the spray nozzle, which was more like a fire hose than she was used to. *I got this.*

"Jackie, I must challenge your view of church. Is it a museum for the saints or a hospital for sinners? If a museum for saints, we fail miserably because we're fallen men and women who seek to know God. However, if your view is, the hospital for sinners; it's much more inviting. The church doesn't have it all together and often makes very large mistakes. We see that in the news and in movies. Interesting that's still how the Master chooses to get his message out. He's never given us another way. The church, for all its flaws, is still his bride. It's exciting to be a part of the plan to make us better. We must start with the church and see how it can help with this crisis. It's still the only group that promotes transformation in the hearts of people. That's our only hope to fix what's out there."

She began to wash raising her voice to be heard over the sprayer. "Many feel that the church is outdated, and we can do all it does with nonprofits and government agencies."

"What do you think of that, Jackie?"

"Remember, my interview. What do you say to that, José?

"I say you can't legislate this or make people want to help others without transformation of the heart. These other groups may be noble minded but are made up of flawed people. They'll fail without a changed heart. It all comes back to self-interest. *I'll do what's best for me and my friends unless I answer to a higher calling.* The church must answer to this higher calling."

While he approached with the last of the plates and glasses, Jackie hit the spray nozzle on the sink and the force of the water wrenched it away from her soapy hands. It blasted José in the chest. He backed away, stunned.

"I am so sorry. Are you hurt? I feel terrible."

The shock wore off; he grabbed a towel and began to dry off. "I'm fine. I'm wet, but fine. Is that your way of saying I'm all wet?"

"No, no! I was just trying to wash . . . I feel just terrible. What can I do?" She tried to help him get dry.

"Not to worry, I have more clothes in the back. Let me finish this. I'm sure you have notes to write up and other things to do. This is my realm, after all. You can hand me another towel though."

She gave him a hand towel and stepped away.

As he dried himself, she noticed that he looked good in that wet shirt. A very muscular build.

She grabbed her jacket, bag, and phone, and thanked him for a wonderful meal and good conversation. She wasn't sure how much of the interview she could use, but it did provide good background. Her embarrassment waning, she shook his damp hand and headed out through the dining room.

✤ ✤ ✤

José decided to change his shirt after she was gone. He took it off and wrung it out over the sink before heading back to the lockers.

✤ ✤ ✤

Jackie caught a glimpse of herself in the bar mirror while she put on her coat and realized she still had the apron on. She took it off quick and went back to the kitchen to give it to José.

He was clear across the room now with his back turned and no shirt, so she decided just to leave it on a hook by the door. She looked back to see if he saw her and noticed that his back was marked with long raised scars. They seemed old but she couldn't be sure from that distance. Quietly she hung the apron and left without José's notice. She checked her watch, headed to her car, and said, "Good, no monsters yet."

She was amazed at his naiveté, but also impressed by his savviness on matters of the heart. *How did this newcomer to our town know us so well, yet was so optimistic about what could be? Keep your head lady; this is all a lot to take in. Maybe you had more wine that you should have. Still not a bad Valentine's dinner. I forgot to ask about the Syrians and how he speaks Arabic. Perhaps I'll catch up with him again soon.*

José smiled while he finished the dishes. She was a beautiful soul in need of the Master's touch. *I'm sure we'll meet again. I would like that very much.*

CHAPTER 28

Pastor Rich called a special meeting of the church elders and leaders at 7 PM on Wednesday.

I'm sure many are wondering why. When pastors call special meetings, they are often to announce resignations.

They were all gathered in a well-lit, Sunday Bible Study room on the second floor. Many attended still in their work clothes; the bankers and insurance agents in jackets and ties. The others who made it home in time to change had on more casual attire. All were Caucasian.

"Ladies and gentlemen, I'm challenged by the Holy Spirit to do something about this affordable housing plan and systemic poverty in our city. With Jeremiah Michaels, Da Wyz, now funding so many housing subsidies, it's time for the church to act, too. Many I've heard are calling it blood money. Regardless, it's money put to good use now. We should be ashamed we have to be shown the way by a gangster. I'm going to change the sermon series from the current focus on the Book of Matthew to a focus on helping the poor and combating racism in the Christian community. It's only a side road in our series since the Lord, no doubt, had these type people in mind in much of Matthew anyway."

He could tell by the looks on some of the faces that some of the elders thought that the resignation may not have been so bad. *I wondered if that would be easier than confronting a wealthy, white, southern church with a reality they didn't want to face. Most are ig-norant of the matter, but Jesus didn't give a pass for such things. He told us to make disciples of the whole world, teaching them the whole message he spoke.*

Wes Meissner was the head of the elders. He'd been with Hart's stores for years and was now Senior Vice President of Purchasing. He traveled to Asia often for long trips to scout out the latest fashions and merchandise they could add to their product lines. He also supported a number of ministries there under the veil of being a business consultant. Despite his advanced age, he still seemed very fit. "What does this mean, Pastor?"

"It means, we need to think hard about how much we're going to spend on this gym and church building when so many in our community are lacking decent schooling, education, housing, and medical care. We, the church, shouldn't be so absorbed in our own busyness that we miss the needs of our neighbors. I confess, I've been guilty of that. It's a poor witness to the gospel. I wanted to build the big church and school and show off God's glory to our community. I don't think we'll give God glory in that way. We have needs, no doubt, and need to build the classroom space and the gym per the plan, but we can cut back on some of the amenities and create a fund for others to match. We could use it to build houses on vacant lots near the church or we could even use it to supplement Da Wyz's endowment."

"I don't think we should associate with Da Wyz. That seems like bad karma. As a member of the elder body, I'll never tell you what to preach, Pastor. But since I'm also a church member, who has labored to get this building approved and underway, I can't see back tracking on what was approved. We have the financing arranged and are well into construction," Paul Stanley spoke up.

"I know. That's why this is a special meeting. I didn't want to wait any longer. God put this on my heart right after Christmas, but I have tried to bargain my way out of it. He won't let me off the hook. The meeting we had here last month just convinced me further." Pastor Rich said.

He found it hard to swallow, and he was tight all over. He continued to confront the group with the conviction on his heart.

"I want us to appoint a subcommittee to find ways to make this less expensive so we can give money to help the poor in our city. I'll preach a couple of Sundays on this topic and we can bring it back to the church for a vote or at least let them know we're going to reduce costs and try to address some of the reasons for the riot last fall. My request to y'all is that you pray about this and speak of it in a positive way to the other members, so this doesn't get killed before it starts."

"Do you plan to build affordable housing around the church? That's a big step and we need to debate that. We have lots of members nearby whose property values could be hurt. Me for one . . . " Paul said.

Rich held up his hand and said, "Paul, I know you're speaking your heart, and I love you for it. But you're thinking in the way that got us here to start with. We must think in a new way. This Justus character who spoke last month at our housing meeting gave me an idea. I've spent time with him since. He has a power from the Spirit I've not felt before. He speaks wisdom. We must listen to what God tells us. Justus is the catalyst, not the guy with all the answers for us. We have the Holy Spirit here, we just haven't been asking the right questions or listening to the voice of God. I want us to start and start now."

"So, your mind's made up already. Are you announcing this or asking our opinion?"

"I'm asking you to pray about this and approach it with an open mind. We can't stand by and let gangsters do the work of God's church, while we pretend to reach out but in actuality are only a club for wealthy white folks who defend their privilege to keep everything like it is. Instead, we must see where we can make a difference in the lives of hurting people. I know this is not popular, and we'll have a fair amount of distrust, but the Holy Spirit is moving, and I want us to be responsive to him, not have him pass us by. Your spiritual shepherd can't let that happen."

"Do you want us to discuss it with you here?" Wes asked.

"I want you all to pray now and come together again Sunday after services to let me know your thoughts. I want a holy consensus not a majority rule."

"Wow pastor, you're asking for a lot. Four days?" said Paul.

"It's OK for us to take more time but we need to address this with urgency. I'm going to meet with some of the other pastors at our lunch this week to discuss it. Brothers and sisters, we have got to move. I'm convinced God is calling us to reach out to the impoverished in our community. Who knows, perhaps it is for such a time as this that we've been made wealthy, so that we can show God's love to the hurting nearby."

⁂ ⁂ ⁂

Sunday after lunch they gathered again. He could see the apprehension on many faces. *Several were open minded. Several opposed it with fervor.*

Thomas Spratt got up to speak on behalf of the dissenters. Thomas, a native of Carlisle, had lived there all of his fifty years. He owned his own insurance agency. "Pastor, I work hard and provide well for my family. You know I'm a constant presence at the church. I admit, I can be quick to anger at times, but I also pride myself on being a reasonable man.

"If we all agreed, there would be no debate. Pastor, you asked us to pray and do some soul searching. We've done that. We've not come to consensus. We've got some folks who are downright angry about this. They approved a building and all its funding from donations and loans. They want their kids to go there and for a safe place they can be proud of. The amenities we approved weren't upscale. We don't like being asked to reassess this now, two thirds of the way in, because the blacks on the Wharf can't keep the peace. Part of the reason for our school is that we don't want our kids in the public schools with all the violence and anti-Christian messages. Why should we be asked to sacrifice our kids' education for those who don't work hard enough to get off welfare? We already pay taxes to support schools our kids don't even use. You want us to do without, while we help them move to our neighborhoods and bring their crazy ways here. No, sir, you're out of line with this request. The more we give 'em, the more they want."

Pastor Rich looked at Tom. "Thank you, Tom, for your openness. Does anyone else wish to speak?"

Anne Comer, head of the finance committee, got up next. He knew she was very organized and articulate. She had been a member since moving to Carlisle ten years ago from up north. With two kids nearing high school age, the Christian school mattered a lot to her. With a slight Yankee accent in her voice, she said, "Pastor we believe in what you're trying to do. We have often gone across the world to reach out to those less fortunate and failed to do so in our own city. For that I'm ashamed and know we must do more. I don't think we can change the building program at this point, but I'm very willing to start a separate drive to help those on the Wharf or in Villa Maya. I'm open, but can't commit to changing the building program now. It's just too far along."

Lisa Sharp also stood to address the group. Pastor Rich knew Lisa was a homemaker; she home schooled her three boys up to high school. Her husband, a successful plumber, always spoke out for conservative causes. They told him they liked literal interpretations of scripture and lived their lives that way. She dressed very conservatively, with blouses up to her neck and long sleeves, no matter the time of year.

"Pastor, I respect what you say about the Spirit moving in you. What you have said is right. We're often so focused on our own world that we forget that people are hungry in our city. Our cupboards are full, and we take comfort in that. If the Lord is leading you to do this, I'm with you. It seems silly for us not to look for savings in our building project. We should look. If this is of God, he'll show us a way to save money on the building. I also favor Anne's idea of a separate campaign."

The pastor bowed his head, feeling the Spirit move in the room, but also sensing the tension from others who were resistant.

Wes stood to address the group. "Rich, you've done many different things since you arrived. I think that's part of what made you attractive to us and us to you. I'll listen and encourage and help in this process. The idea of rent subsidies seems like something that impacts faster than building around the church. I'm open to either one or both. In addition, we could add some scholarships to the school for the poor children. We can't ignore what's happened. Let's act."

Paul Stanley stood. "I think we're over reacting to a small issue from five months ago. We all know the riot was caused by a bunch of outside agitators that stirred things up to suit their agenda. Why are we doing anything? Let's give some money to the problem if we wish, but I say let it blow over."

Pastor Rich continued to poll the group as other variations on these arguments were made. At last, he said, "Brothers and sisters, God is moving in our city. I can sense it. I beseech you to address this with an open mind. I appreciate the additional suggestions. I must admit, we're not going to get much out of the building costs at this late phase, but we can, at least, do a review. I'll bring some of these ideas to the church body over the next few Sundays. Please be there and give this your support. Please ask God to show you why you are resisting this message of salvation and love, if you are."

As Paul and Thomas left the meeting. Paul said, "We can't have this. The pastor is wrong and this must be stopped. Do we want those people near us? With our kids? In our school? Think of what it'll do to the area. This has to stop. We need to find others who see this our way and stop this now."

CHAPTER 29

Hamsa, Stu, and Jimmy became hard to separate. Hamsa enjoyed his new friends and liked hanging out in the woods near the Lumber River Dam. Stu's step dad had a shack up there with fishing stuff in it, including an old beat up row boat that didn't even look like it would float.

Stu swore it would.

Hamsa hadn't been around guys his own age since the war.

Stu and Jimmy both had handguns that they showed Hamsa how to use. He enjoyed target practice and listening to his friends talk about things he didn't completely understand. The right to bear arms was new to him. He didn't know what the NRA was.

Hamsa still spent time on the dark websites listening to the radical Islamists. He thought hanging with Stu and Jimmy gave him some training if he ever needed it.

After a few weeks, things seemed to change. Hamsa and Stu were sitting on lawn chairs in the shack around a beat-up table. Jimmy stood nearby twirling his gun by the trigger guard around his finger like cowboys in the old westerns. Stu dreamed up a new idea.

"Hey man, I'm getting tired of doing the same old junk. I wish we had some money to buy fireworks. I love shooting them off over the lake. Man, I'd love to build a big firework and watch it blow the water way up in the air. No one around here for miles. They would never know what happened or who did it," Stu said.

"Yeah man that would be cool. We can't afford that kind of ordinance though. When you were around the rebels, what did they do for bombs?" Jimmy asked Hamsa.

"I'm not sure, most just tried to steal them from the army troops. We had some guys who knew how to make them, too. It was cool to watch them go off. It was also so sad to see what happened to people and pets," Hamsa said.

"What did they make them out of?" Stu asked leaning toward Hamsa.

"Mostly they got grenades and stuff from the army or from some other government storage. We made some, but most of the time, they were already made. We just had to learn to use them."

"I'll check online tonight to see how we can make a big explosive up here. I bet we don't need too much money, if we do it right. We just have to get the right amount of stuff and find something to detonate it. Can you talk to any of the guys back at home, Hammie, and see if they can help us? It would be real cool."

"My computer's real slow and I get limited time because a lot of people are applying for jobs and such. What if I came over to your house and sent some emails and did some searching. I'm good at it. I learned to do it quick."

"Sure, come over after school tomorrow, and we can do it. My mom and stepdad both work, so I'm home alone with my kid brother. I'll take care of him while you check."

"I'll send some emails tonight from my computer, and maybe we'll get some answers by tomorrow," said Hamsa.

⁑ ⁑ ⁑

The next day at Stu's house, once the younger brother was off doing his homework, Hamsa showed Stu a bomb-making guide from the dark web that he had emailed to himself the night before. *This may be good training if I need it. I'm sure we can't afford much of this stuff, but it would be cool to build one.*

"Wow, this is so cool. How much damage do you think it would do, Hammie?"

"I don't know. Depends on how big you build it, I guess. Should be big enough to make a big splash up on Bass Lake. Might even blow up the shack. This stuff 's dangerous though. We got to be careful with it. I've seen the damage bad bombs can do."

"Ya know, I bet if we all bought a little of this stuff, no one would know. We don't want the feds on us. Maybe we can do it over the next few weeks. Let's shop around."

Hamsa started sweating. "I-I'm not too sure about this Stu. These are very dangerous plans. We don't know what we're doing. What happens if we get caught?"

"C'mon Hammie, it'll be fun. No one gets hurt. Jimmy and I do bootleg fireworks with gunpowder every summer. You ain't scared are ya?

"No, I'm not scared but I know what this stuff can do. I'll help, but I got to see my mom this afternoon. She has a job for me. I might be able to make some money for the project."

"Cool. I'll get Jimmy up to speed once he gets here later."

⁂

Jimmy caught up with Stu late in the day. "This is goin' even better than I planned. Hammie is helping us and gave me the blueprint for a bomb today. It is a Syrian IED. We just have to build it according to the plans and set it off. It'll get traced to him and the Syrians are gone. We need to find the ingredients. Looks like we can get a bunch of this at a hardware store. Let's find some money and start buying this stuff. We should both start working part-time jobs. In a few weeks, we can have enough to make a test version. We'll blow that up in the lake. Then once we know how to do it, we can make the real thing," Stu said.

⁂

Hamsa hopped the bus down from Stu's house toward home. The Syrians decided to name the apartment complex New Rojava in honor of the place they were forced to leave—the place where thousands were slaughtered by the regime.

Rima and Dijlin were waiting on Hamsa in the kitchen when he got home. They didn't look happy. Rima had printouts spread out on the table in front of her. "Hamsa, what have you been doing on the computer?" she asked.

"I don't know what you mean." He pretended he didn't know what they were talking about.

"Dijlin set up the network and the computer. She knew enough to put some tracers on things to keep us all safe. Do you want to tell us what we found?"

Hamsa was in full denial now. "I still don't know. I did one of the naked girl sites a while back, but I don't do that anymore."

Rima looked down began shaking her head. She pointed to the papers in front of her and began to cry. "Oh Hamsa, how can you lie to your own mother like this? What am I going to do with you? We're the only ones left from our family. Remember we said no secrets, no lies when we were back in the camps in Jordan. We have to trust each other no matter what." She sniffed back tears now.

"Hamsa, I got word from some of the folks who got on after you that there was odd content. Radical Islam, weapons videos. I didn't want to believe it but the comments kept coming. I put a sniffer on the machine a couple of weeks ago and then followed up going to some of the sites that were visited during your time allotment. This is bad. This could be bad for all of us. You've got to stop this now. You know what it was like in Syria. If they found anything like this, we would all be rounded up and killed. You, right in front of your mother just before they raped her. Is that what you want?" Dijlin said.

"No! Of course not! You don't know how hard it's been. I . . . " He stopped, tears welling in his eyes. "Oh Mama, I'm sorry. I shouldn't have done it. I won't do it ever again. Please don't cry, Mama. I remember the soldiers, the killings. I just don't know how I fit in Allah's plans now. Why am I here? I won't do it anymore, I promise."

"That's not enough. We need to get you with more positive influences. You need to begin going to the cooking school Yosef runs each afternoon. If you have time to do this, you have time to get a job and help out around here. I wanted to give you time to settle and get your grades up. This is the sign of idleness and is best addressed with lots to do. I'll call Yosef and tell him you'll be there starting tomorrow. Once you graduate from that, I'm sure we can get you a job in a restaurant nearby," Rima said.

"Mama, why did Allah spare me? I was on those sites looking for answers. I still don't have any. At last, I found some guys who like me at school. They're fun to hang out with. Now I can't do that anymore because I have to go hang with the Mayans who'll beat me up when Yosef isn't looking. I'll do what you want mama, but this won't make it all better. I'm still struggling in my soul."

"I know my dear son. I'm still struggling too." She got up and and gave him a tearful hug.

Dijlin wheeled over to them both and joined them, sobbing for losses endured in a war they did not start and could not get over.

EVIL STIRS

Evil stirs when good moves.
Not all embrace the movement.
Some like it the way it is.
Some long for the way it was.
Some strain for what must be,
But love always works toward good.
Love blesses and shines
Though darkness seeks to shut it off.

Yes, evil will have its day too.
But evil and good are not evenly matched.
When light and darkness collide,
Justice and Mercy arise.

CHAPTER 30

Reverend Tony came into Restaurant Tapas after the lunch rush. Jeremiah told him where Joseph worked. He came with some apprehension, some jealousy, and some anticipation of meeting a mysterious man of God.

Ramone, always bubbling, greeted him. "Buenos tardis, señor, table for one?"

"Yes. Ah, si," said Tony.

"It's OK señor, I speak English. Are you here for lunch or are you looking for something else?"

"I'm happy to eat, but I really want to speak with Joseph. Is he available?"

"So many want to see José these days. It's slow now. I'll tell him you're here. What's your name señor?"

"I'm Reverend Anthony Hibbert of the AME Zion church in the Wharf."

"Have a seat at that booth over there. Lucinda, take this man's order, por favor."

After a moment, Ramone returned. "He'll be with you soon. If he wasn't so good, I'd tire of being his personal assistant."

Tony ordered a hamburger, medium well with lettuce, tomato and mayo with a side of tots, and a glass of iced tea. He didn't know what a lot of the items on the menu were, so he played it safe. The chips and salsa they brought while he waited tasted great.

José brought the burger and tater tots to the table.

"Thank you." He didn't look at the man bringing the food since he was rehearsing what he wanted to say one more time.

José waited a moment, then said, "You wanted to see me, señor?"

Tony stumbled to his feet not realizing this was Joseph in the dirty apron. He shoved out his hand and said, "Reverend Anthony Hibbert of Commonwealth AME Zion Church. I'm thrilled to meet you. Will you join me?"

"Si, señor, I'll be glad to. I know who you are. What may I do for you Reverend Hibbert?"

"Call me Reverend Tony or just Tony; that's what most people do these days."

"How may I help you, Tony?" José slid in the booth across from him.

"I'm not sure how to address you sir. Are you José or Joseph?"

"In Villa Maya, I'm José. It helps me blend in. My given name is Joseph. I used that when I met Jeremiah."

"And when you healed Roberta Saunders," Tony smiled.

"Yes, when I healed Ms. Roberta," Joseph smiled back.

"I'm glad we won't play cat and mouse on those two matters. I'm thrilled to meet you after all these months. I respected Ms. Roberta's request to keep this quiet, but it was tearing me up inside not meeting you. Someone with that kind of power is awesome indeed. I'm talking Apostolic power, man. You got to tell me what's going on? Roberta said you told her, 'God was moving in this place.' What does that mean? How can I help?"

"You want to be a follower?"

"Depends on who's leading. I want to know more about you. I want to help. I'm a minister of the gospel. I don't amaze easily but two miracles have occurred in Broken Wharf in the past couple of months, and you were involved in both. Are you an angel of the Lord?"

Joseph chuckled at that question. "Do I look like an angel to you, Tony? It's been a long time since I was mistaken for an angel. No, I'm just a man. Flawed like all the rest of us. I follow the Master, Jesus of Nazareth. I've followed him for a long time. I work with the youth at Saint Francis here in VM. I seek to serve the Master and glorify him. Sometimes he does wonderful things through me. Most of the time, I'm the same as anyone else."

"Are you a Catholic priest, then?"

"Once I was, but that was lifetimes ago. Now I follow the Master without embracing one sect or denomination. My theology is orthodox, if that is what you're asking. My focus is on the early church and how the Holy Spirit moved in those days. He still moves today if we ask, wait, and watch."

Lucinda stopped by to ask José if he wanted anything. He asked for water and some more chips and salsa.

"So, you healed Ms. Roberta by the power of the Holy Spirit? How'd you convince Da Wyz to follow the Lord? I've been trying for years. Never thought it would happen." *Who am I kidding; I wished I'd have been the one to witness that transformation.*

"I didn't convince him of anything. The Spirit moved him to where he was ready. I'm sure all the sermons and wise words you spoke over the years planted the seed. I was there for the harvest. For that I'm grateful to the Master and now to you for all the ground work you did." Joseph munched a chip full of salsa.

"I see you have the gift of encouragement too," Tony said while he took another bite of his burger, wiping some mayo off his mouth with his napkin.

"And you a gift of discernment, amigo."

Lucinda brought the water and chips. José thanked her for her work.

"Tony, you've been praying for this kind of revival in your community for years. You need not fear me or be envious of the Lord working through me. I'm a vessel; he's the sovereign Lord. I wanted to seek you out, but he told me you would come to me when the time was right. I couldn't resist leaving a few clues for you. I have great admiration for the work you do in the Wharf."

"You seem to know my thoughts."

"This isn't the first time the Lord has used me in this way. I desire to engage with the local ministers who seek God's will in their villages and towns. As I said, I'm just a man. I need all the help I can find from like-minded brothers in Christ."

"How can I help you, brother Joseph?"

"First, keep this to yourself. You may share but only with those you trust to keep it from getting out in public. I don't know what God is going to do in this place. I've been called here on his mission. I don't seek publicity. The Master worked best in anonymity at the start of his ministry, so do I. That's why I swore Roberta and Jeremiah to secrecy and directed them to you. The day will come when I must go public, but it's not now. It'll continue to promote my mission if I can stay out of the spotlight. As it is, people are beginning to come here to see me. While that's OK for now, if the volume picks up, it'll become a problem.

"The Master said I'd have a special visitor today. I'm happy to see it's a friend. I don't seek followers; I seek allies in the mission. They're hard to recruit. I've found a few so far. Will you be one with me in the Wharf?"

"Based on what I hear, I think I already am."

"I need you to stay close to Jeremiah now. The enemy doesn't take losing one so prominent lightly. He can do amazing good if he listens to the Master. I need you to help him there. He's going to lose his grip on the Biz now that he'll not take life anymore. He's still a brand-new life in Christ and will be faced with many challenges. Backsliding is a real temptation for him. He's smart and resourceful, but he'll need wise counsel. I'll help where I can, but I must work on many fronts, not just the Wharf. I work here, with the refugees, and with those up the hill."

Ramone stopped by. "Do you need anything, amigos? Remember your class will start soon José."

"Thanks for reminding me."

Tony waited until Ramone left. "I'll do whatever I can to help him and his family. His wife, Miranda, and two daughters seemed thrilled with the new man he's become. So am I. But let me backtrack a moment. Are you convinced his conversion is real? I've known him a long time, and he's a very crafty liar."

"Yes, I'm convinced. But, we must judge him the same way we are all judged—by the love in his heart revealed by the fruit of his labor. He'll need help setting up this affordable housing fund. That needs to succeed for the sake of so many. Please guide him to someone he can trust to do that well."

"I know just the young man for that. I just have to convince Reggie, Ms. Roberta's grandson, to do it."

"No, Tony, let the Master convince him. That way he gets the glory. Let's set up a regular meeting every two weeks to check on progress. Ramone gives me Wednesday afternoons off. Will you meet me at St. Francis Church? I'm sure they'll let us use a room."

"Let's meet in my office. It's just down from Ms. Roberta's and I'd love to have your presence in the Wharf more. I believe blessings follow you around."

"Not sure that's so, but thank you. OK, we'll meet next Wednesday and every other one thereafter. Might be good to have Jeremiah there next week."

"I'll do it. By the way, I meet once a month with a group of pastors here in town. It's headed up by Pastor Richard Taylor. I think you should come and speak to us. I'll talk to Rich about it. We'll meet in about three weeks. If he agrees, it'd be good to hear what's on your heart for Carlisle."

"Father Menendez asked me something similar a couple of months ago. I think it's time to attend. It's clear the Master is moving fast among us now. It would be good to have more allies."

He crunched one more chip and finished his water.

"Finish your tater tots, Tony, I have to get ready for my class this afternoon."

"Yes, I didn't understand what the maître 'd meant. What class is that? Do you teach the word?"

"I teach some of the local gang members to cook. Try and get them out of the gangs and into a better life. I do highlight a scripture at times to pique their interest."

"See you Wednesday, ally."

Tony was in awe of this man of God. He started the meeting with apprehension but now impressed by his humility, his wisdom, and his love of God and man, he knew God is indeed moving in our midst. This man was at the center of it. He finished his tater tots, wiped his hands with the paper napkin, and texted his friend Pastor Rich about this encounter. He wanted to share the exciting news.

CHAPTER 31

Jackie arrived at the first home sponsored by Da Wyz's rent subsidy program. She didn't want to miss this. The blessing fell on the Henrietta Johnson family. They moved into a three-bedroom, two-bath home in the Marietta Heights neighborhood. The neighbors greeted them with mild enthusiasm. This neighborhood kept to itself and didn't object to a black family of five moving into the cul-de-sac. There were no protests or signs of hate.

Bradley took good shots of the house and yard. They'd formed a bond now, and he found ways to make her stories look even better. She found it good to be able to trust her co-worker with the details, so she could concentrate on the story.

Da Wyz apparently knew better than to make too high a profile of himself with this program, so his wife, Miranda, helped Henrietta move in. Miranda had been a fashion model earlier in life. Her long blonde hair, blue eyes, and pale white skin photographed well. The contours of her chin and cheeks caused many a teenage boy to yearn for her and many a teenage girl to desire to look like her. Although, too diminutive to make the big-time model circuit, not leggy enough, she otherwise looked the part. She had caught Da Wyz's eye a few years earlier and had retired from photo shoots. She took to this new role well, showing that she had a brain behind that alluring face and figure. She and Reggie Saunders, fresh from the Bank of the New

South, were heading up the Carlisle Affordable Homes project; Carafe Homes for short. *How do I know that Saunders name?*

Miranda dressed in a sweatshirt and jeans but you couldn't help but notice her. She and a small crew of movers got the family loaded and unloaded in a day. Henrietta didn't have enough furniture to fill the house. She only had one car for the two-car garage. Jackie made sure to get her on camera with that beaming smile thanking Miranda. Henrietta wept and smiled at the same time. They cut away to show the children ranging in age from three to fifteen running around the yard and exploring the new territory.

Miranda, on camera now said, "Welcome to your new home on behalf of Carafe Homes. We're proud of you as our first recipient of this service. May God bless you and your family in this new place. Thank you for being willing to leave the place you were to make a better life here."

Jackie resolved to cover more of these moves over the next few weeks while Carafe Homes continued to move families out of the Wharf. In an earlier interview, she learned that Reggie planned to resign from his role as a VP at Bank of the New South. But when his boss got wind of it, they decided on the idea of Reggie being an Executive on Loan to Carafe for a year. He continued to get paid by the bank, and he worked full time on the project. It saved the endowment from having to pick up his salary.

With Reggie's experience and enthusiasm, the fund prospered. Showing off his eye for detail he told Jackie how he invested the excess and made certain all the trust documents were executed well. He opened the accounts with BNS as part of the Exec on Loan deal. The bank welcomed the free publicity for a good cause. *He gave too much information but I let him since he was so enthusiastic.*

He and Miranda kept in touch with Jackie in case the program ran into issues. They could turn publicity into positive public persuasion if needed. Jackie didn't mind this since she supported the idea and it kept her close to the project. She expected trouble. She just didn't know from where.

It didn't hit any resistance until the program showed signs of success. After the fifth family moved up the hill from the Wharf, people began to see a trend. The opposition couldn't tell how many families Carafe could afford to move but Reggie heard several homeowners' associations started getting nervous. Opposition showed as indifference at first. People didn't greet the new arrivals with open arms. There weren't any hateful notes or comments either.

Paul Stanley hoped this would go away on its own. As president of the chamber, he couldn't be against the program but he didn't like Da Wyz getting positive publicity either. He knew Carafe would keep the rents subsidy program to the less expensive neighborhoods up the hill to preserve their cash. His friends started to talk, though. Paul, always the competitor, didn't like this mostly because it wasn't his idea. He also disliked the success it enjoyed. He decided not to directly confront it in his role, but he began to make comments to various HOA presidents getting them more concerned about who was moving into their neighborhoods.

HOA meetings in many of the neighborhoods added agenda items aimed at amending bylaws and declarations. It seemed a matter of economics more than race. These new families didn't fit in. They didn't have all the cars and toys their neighbors did. The primary complaint centered on fairness.

"No one helps pay my house payment. I work hard for my family. It took a lot for me to get enough to live in River Hills. These people come in here with someone paying their rent. They aren't like the neighbors. They don't keep the grass mowed like we do. They walk around the neighborhood with their pants hung low. I don't like it at all. I moved here to get away from thugs and gangs, and now they're moving next to us," said a pudgy Tobias Martin during the River Hills HOA meeting, late in the month.

Renters weren't welcome at Home Owners Association meetings but could come for information. Reggie decided to attend this one on behalf of the Mashburn family, who had moved into a rental home in River Hills a couple of weeks earlier. He took notes to share with Miranda and Jackie when the time was right.

After many other comments, the issue never came to a vote. Most realized the owners of rental homes in the neighborhoods could do with them what they wanted to. The HOA could not, under fair housing rules, keep someone out who could afford the rent whether by subsidy or on their own.

Reggie stopped by the Mashburn home after the meeting. Tom Mashburn welcomed him into their new split-foyer, four-bedroom, vinyl-sided home.

"Can we talk for a sec?"

"Sure Reg, what's up?"

"I just came from the HOA meeting. The don't like having subsidized renters here. Please let me know if you have any issues with upkeep on the place. Our opponents are looking for a reason to stop this. You live here and have every right to, but if you get in trouble for any reason, let me know pronto. Carafe needs a good report to keep this service working."

"Hey bro, why you tellin' me this. You told me before. I know this stuff."

"Sorry Tom, I'm just a nervous kind of guy. This is making me crazy."

"Bro, you can count on me and my family. We're thrilled to be away from the Wharf gangs and thank you very much for gettin' us here. We won't let you down."

"How're the kids fitting in?"

"Derek, my fourteen-year-old, likes these pretty ladies up here. They seem to like him to. He has packs of them buzzin' around. I bet the local boys don't know what to make of a boy from the hood up here. The girls seem to like the change. He's not gettin' into trouble with them though."

"Any fights or things like that?"

"No bro, all is cool right now."

"Sorry to be paranoid on this; I just want all the families to get settled."

Derek came up to his dad with a slender girl on his arm. He wore a Raiders ball cap, black jeans, and a red t-shirt. She had braided blonde hair with blue tips and dark brown eyebrows, and was sporting a gray t-shirt with skull and crossbones on it. It was too long for Reggie to see what else she was wearing.

"Yo, Dad. We want to go down the street to the store for a drink." He leaned closer to Tom and said, "Can you float me five bucks? Got to impress the lady."

Tom gave him five dollars and asked, "You gonna walk?"

"No," Derek said, "Tabitha's sister gonna drive us."

"Derek this is Mr. Saunders. He heads up Carafe Homes," Tom said.

"I know who he is. He the big man working for Da Wyz. This is Tabitha Martin. She's my new, sweet friend."

"You're Tobias Martin's daughter?" Reggie asked.

"Yessir," she said. "Do you know my dad?"

"I met him earlier tonight. I work for the bank, not Da Wyz by the way."

"It's cool," said Derek.

They headed off down the street.

Derek with his pants hanging low around his hips. This has trouble written all over it. I better keep an eye on this group and the other groups, too, for that matter.

"Tom, thanks for chatting with me. Please let me know if there's any trouble."

"We cool, Reg. You worry too much, man."

Reggie headed back to his car.

Later, he told Miranda and Jackie, "We need to slow this down. I want to see how they integrate before we put too many more families in this situation. Five or six is a good start. I think I'll slow it down for a few weeks."

They all agreed long-term success was better than fast failure, so after moving five families in month one, they decided to revise their plans and only move two families a month for a time.

Jackie stayed close but believed this was working. Not thousands of people at a time but counting the children, they moved two dozen people out of poverty into better performing schools and meeting higher profile people. The success would come over the next few years. *It's a marathon. But we've started well. I need to report this back to José. It would warm his heart to know. Or am I just looking for a reason to see those eyes again? What would be so wrong with that, anyway?*

CHAPTER 32

Pastor Rich took the stage. He hadn't been this convicted about a sermon series, or this nervous, in many years. Preaching to the wealthy about the poor made him feel quite shaky. This required him to challenge the stereotypes he had of the poor, also. No question, he was going to be stepping on toes—wealthy powerful toes.

He saw Justus in the back of the congregation at the first Sunday service. He had to take time off and come across town on a Sunday bus schedule to be here. Rich knew he would be here. Justus told him so when they spoke by phone. Pastor Rich texted him in late February what God placed on his heart. Then there were the phone calls of encouragement. Justus always said, "Listen or Don't" when he finished. "I'm listening," he texted Justus. "Pray that others will too."

Now was the time. He prayed, "May God use this for his glory," while he moved to the pulpit.

"Church of Carlisle. Brother and sisters. Please open your Bibles or turn them on to Matthew chapter nineteen. We'll be reading verses sixteen to twenty-six. This story is repeated in Mark ten and Luke eighteen. You know it well if you've spent much time in church."

He read them the story of the rich man who asked Jesus what good he must do to be saved.

"Folks, Jesus took him through the normal Jewish teaching of the day. Keep the commandments. Jesus even recites a partial list of them. The rich man responds that he's done that since his youth.

"What's left for me to do? What's the formula I must follow?

"We're so used to this world, such that if I follow the steps, the outcome is certain. If I build the bicycle for my kiddo late at night on Christmas Eve following the instructions meticulously, before I go to bed, I'll have a working bicycle on Christmas morning. If I follow the recipe just right, the food will turn out just as expected.

"The rich man thought salvation worked like the world. Give me the steps, and I'll follow them. I know how the world works. How else did I get and keep my wealth? How did I become a ruler? God made the world and me. We must work the same way, right? But the world is a fallen place.

"So many of the world religions are works based. If my good deeds outweigh the bad, I'll enter Heaven. If not, I'm sent to suffer. You'll find that Islam and Hinduism have very similar answers here. In Islam, you're sent to suffer in hell. In Hinduism, you're sent back via reincarnation. Got to go back and do it again until you get it right. Just like that old movie.

"Even Buddhism seeks good fortune from the Buddha. If I follow the right path, I'll be blessed. It's the formula. I do and a god delivers my just reward. That is justice. The ones that set the rules always love justice.

"I know these belief systems are far more complicated than I have time to address here but my point is that the rich man wanted a formulaic answer. In the partial list given earlier, Jesus mentions the commandments he knows the man has kept. He is God so he knew that. You can see in his response that the man gets his confidence up. 'Yeah, I did all that.' You can almost hear him say, 'Tell me the last step. What's next? I can take it.'

"Jesus told him that is not the way God works. He asked him, who is good? The answer. Only God.

"So, if my works are not good or good enough, how can I earn the way in?

"The answer, you can't. Jesus said, 'Sell all you have and give it to the poor and come and follow me.' That's a tremendous thing to ask, to strip ourselves of all our hard-earned goods, not to mention all our earthly security.

"When I preached this before, I emphasize that Jesus is speaking to the man's idolatry. In the story as Jesus recited the commandments, he left two out. The first two commandments are to have no other gods before me and not to make idols of the things of the world. Now he exposes the man's inner weakness. Dependence on self and wealth. Not God. The man goes away sorrowful because he had great possessions. He couldn't do as Jesus asked. This was a formula that didn't make sense. Hard work would not produce the benefit desired. That's not justice.

"Does this apply to us now?

"After he leaves, Jesus speaks to his disciples and says it's impossible for a rich man to enter heaven. This astounds them. The teaching of their day was that God blesses the wealthy, because he's pleased with them. If they can't get in based on that blessing, who can?"

Pastor Rich paused to look at the congregation. He always preached with a bottle of water nearby. He unscrewed the cap and took a drink. He put the cap back with deliberation. He was building his nerve gathering his thoughts. When he looked out he realized his unintended drama built tension in the flock.

"We, in Carlisle, in this church, are all rich by the world's standards. We're proud of what we've accomplished. God has blessed us. There's no doubt. We're as lost as the rich man in this story if we think our wealth is God's blessing on us to express how well pleased he is with us.

"Like the rich man, we want wealth in this world and the world to come.

"The rich can't get into heaven. They can't buy their way in. They can't give enough to earn a spot. They can't do enough good. This is the point of the camel and needle. The largest living thing people saw in those days was a camel. The smallest thing they saw was the eye of a needle. The largest thing can't go through the smallest thing. That's impossible. That was his point.

"We're blessed to live in the US, the wealthiest nation in history. We're in one of the most blessed cities in this country. But we're not blessed to enjoy it all ourselves. We're blessed to help others. Not out of seeking good fortune from God, but out of love for our neighbors. Once he transforms our hearts, we need to be wise with our gifts, to share that blessing with those who do not have that gift. If you're wealthy, you have a gift many others don't. How will you let God use this for his glory?

"Church leaders from poor countries look at us as the wealthy Christians and can't understand why we don't help others more. Do we not know? Do we not see? Are we too preoccupied by more wealth acquisition?

"I'm not saying we should sell all, but we are called to sacrifice. How many of you tithe? This isn't that sermon, but we must decide how we will give sacrificially to help our impoverished brothers and sisters in this community. That is part of the reason we are so blessed.

"If we are the wealthy, then who are the poor?

"Look at the civil war in Syria and all the refugees worldwide. Hear the leaders in Europe who say if we accept these Muslims into our country we will be less Christian. Is that true? It's how the world works, but not how God works. There are scores of other examples but this is one we see. Syrians are in our midst now. These are even from a Syrian group that fought alongside us. What are we doing to welcome them into our community? Are we more worried about Islam challenging us, than our own God convicting us that we haven't done enough to help them? We make them villains and thus we don't need to help them. It's inconvenient. They're different. They dress funny. Worship Allah. We're busy.

"They don't want to be here. They want to go home. Put yourself in their shoes. They're our neighbors, not way over there. But right here in Carlisle. God brought the mission field to us. They want to go home. I've heard people in our town say, 'Well, if you want to go home, I'll buy you a ticket.' Is this what Christ would have us do? They cannot go home. Home is destroyed. One of the greatest tragedies in modern history has been met with suspicion by the American church. One of the greatest opportunities to show Christ's love to the Islamic world has been forfeited.

"We say, 'there could be terrorists with those people.' I agree, we must be vigilant, but we must also show God's love to a hurting world. If we err on the side of giving the benefit of the doubt, will God not protect us?

"This isn't the first time. Look at the history. During the second world war, we didn't want to let the Jews in, out of fear. We interred the Japanese American citizens, out of fear.

"We have let fear dictate our actions because we love our lives and lifestyles more than our neighbors. You know we're called to love our neighbors as ourselves. But, do we?

"We let the fear mongers dupe the Church of Christ out of being his witness in word and deed. We're still doing it.

"I know you think I'm being extreme to make a point, but I'm speaking truth to you, my church, in love. We can't let fear be what the church of Jesus Christ stands for in this city or in this world. We're called to be better. To trust God more.

"If you think I'm being extreme with the Syrians, let's get even more uncomfortable.

He paused again and took another sip. He could see his audience fidgeting in their seats. Some were looking at their watches or their cell phones.

"What about the Latinos in Villa Maya? Are they not also a mission field God brought to us?

"We say, 'They're here illegally. They don't belong. They don't speak English. They're a strain on our resources. They're gang members and criminals.' Yet we trust them with our yards to care for, our homes to clean, our crops to harvest, even our children to nanny or be caregivers. They're not evil. They fled intense, unpleasant parts of the world and came here seeking a better life. Are they that different from the rest of this congregation but a generation or two removed. What would drive you from your birth land to a new shining place on a hill? This is the same thing that motivated them to come here. 'They've violated the law. They should be deported.' Is that showing Christ's love to these who flee a horrible situation?

"Thus, we're the rich young rulers who accuse them of not complying with laws we made. Laws designed to keep them out. Many didn't go through the immigration process we created to screen them out. We oppress them with insufficient housing and schools. Then we're surprised when they turn to illegal activities to live in this land. What are we doing to welcome them, to give them a chance at a better life? Not as Americans, but as Christians. Christ's representatives. Remember, those who make the rules, love to mete out justice.

"The majority of Latinos are Catholic. That's true. 'So, let's just leave it to the Catholic Church to deal with them,' I have heard it said. Really folks? What must I do to earn eternal life is what the rich man asked? Let us ask our Lord what we must do for these neighbors to show his glory to the world. That is the currency of heaven.

"What is the greatest commandment? In summary, love God with all you are and love your neighbor as yourself. Is it not so?

"Finally, and certainly not least, what are we doing with the poor black community? I have heard it said that some believe that blacks and Latinos are not as smart as whites. 'You can see that in school performance. It's obvious, right?'

"What can I do to earn it?

"I must give my kids a leg up in this world. That's how it works. That's the world's formula.

"Yet a poor, predominantly black school suffers from lack of parental involvement. We can say, 'It's because they don't value their kids as much.' I assure you that's not so.

"We can say, 'It's because they don't work as hard as we do.' Again, the pay is not often as good but the work is very hard. It's opportunity that's lacking.

"We want to give money to the working poor. They're trying to make a better life for themselves. 'If they'll make the effort to get out, society will reward it.' Is that true?

"We say, 'I'm not prejudiced. I have black friends. I just don't like the criminals. I don't like their music. Pastor, don't you listen to the words of their songs or see how the rich athletes behave? They don't value family. So many mothers have children from several men. So many men are in prison or in gangs.'

"Have any of you ever been stopped for driving while being white? No? It happens to our black Christian brothers often. I'm not here to pick on the police. It's just our own bias that keeps these stereotypes alive and gives us a reason to stay holed up in our wealthy enclaves with our comfortable sermons that don't challenge us to deal with the hate and indifference in our city.

"Do any of you have to tell your sons how to react to a traffic stop so they won't get shot? I'm being provocative, but these are not ex-aggerations. Ask any of your black friends about this talk they must have for any black young man.

"There is hate in our city. We saw it during the riot last fall. We saw it when our first response was about all those outside agitators that came in to create chaos. Interesting of all the ones arrested last fall, all were residents of Carlisle or its neighboring towns. But that conclusion fit our bias. It kept us comfortable. 'Those poor people are so easy to sway. They just want what we have without working hard for it.' We're deceiving ourselves because we're not listening to the Master. Jesus is trying to get our attention. We must listen to him.

"Yes, there are those who are lazy and good for little, but we know of those who are like that in our own families. It's not Latino or black or poor that makes it that way. It's human nature in some.

"We've created systems that benefit the majority and the result either hurts or ignores the minorities. That's the way the systems work. That's the way we designed them. That's the way of the world.

"But God isn't like the world we have created. He has called us to be more than like the world. He has called us to overcome it, to make it better in his name.

"I'm running long and my intention is not to leave everyone with a sick feeling of hopelessness. We have to be convicted in love before we can move out of complacency.

"The next few weeks we'll speak about our biases in dealing with those not like us—in skin color, language, religion, economic status. We'll speak about the systems we put in place to keep us apart. Systems that give ourselves as the majority a leg up. How can we help the poor get affordable housing? How can we keep the poor from being arrested and convicted of more crimes than the rest of us? How can we learn from others who are not like us? How can we be Jesus's example to the world? I'll propose some solutions, but this is a church-wide challenge. All suggestions are welcome while we unpack this over the next few weeks. Remaining complacent is not an option.

"The disciples said at the end of this passage, 'Who can be saved if not the wealthy?' By implication has God not already blessed them as a certification that they are worthy?

"Jesus said, while this astounds you, remember God is not like you. What is impossible for man is possible with God! Let's work as a church to see God move in our city.

"Let us pray.

"Dear Father, you love us beyond our ability to understand. Help us to show that love to a hurting world that needs to hear about it and see it demonstrated. As sinful and blemished as your church is here on earth, it's still the way you chose to show your love to those near it. May we be your love at this hour, in Jesus's name we pray. Amen."

Justus smiled and whispered, "Listen or Don't."

THE CRY OF THE POOR

I heard the cry of the poor in the dark of the night,
They were seeking shelter,
They were seeking a light.
They were seeking food without fear,
They were seeking love of those near.

I called to the privileged in the light of the day
They said we are busy
Please go away.
Don't you see we are tired from defending our gain?
We are too far away to hear the cries of pain.

I called to those that seek to govern with love.
They saw the want,
They saw the need from above.
They said we can help if we tax and spend,
They said the poor we will defend.

The privileged cried out at the end of the day,
It is unjust.
Why are we forced to give our money away?
Don't you see how we struggle to gain what we do?
The dependence gets worse when we just give it to you.

The governors cried out what is the resolution?
The problem so vast
We don't know the solution.
Who will change hearts to be attuned to listen?
For the cries of our neighbors that we have been missing.

The privileged and poor are all the same
In the sight of God.

Selfish, rigid and afraid of pain,
We seek love and safety for ourselves and family.
We chose to segregate from what should be.

God heard the cry of the poor in the night.
God heard the cry of the privileged too.
We all suffer; we fail to do what is right.
He calls us to help him to restore the broken
With kind deeds, truth and words that are spoken.

Please listen for the poor who cry in the night.
One night it will be you
Who sees no comfort in sight.
Let's be hands that knit, salve and love
For the hurt will be healed as we please our Father above.

CHAPTER 33

It took the Syrians of New Rojava six months to get on their feet. Yosef, Susan, and the others continued to help. But they needed less help as time went on. Yosef taught English and Spanish to the refugees' children, and they taught their parents. They were a group thrown together by war and necessity.

Amena attended the community college to get some medical certifications. After seeing strong women in this country, like Susan, she was inspired. In Syria, she worked triage and knew she'd seen more human devastation than anyone else in the emergency department, but she wasn't certified in the United States. She had to go back to school for a time. At last, she found work at University Hospital as a tech.

Dijlin continued to study computers through online courses. She continued to struggle with being poor and crippled.

Sami cared for her as best he could. He was too old to find regular employment. So, he worked in the large garden they planted. The seeds idea worked to some degree, but Susan's team procured a number of seedlings to give the garden a boost.

Rima was taking over more of the leadership since Amena went to school and now was working full time. Rima worked some in retail but still struggled with the language under pressure from customers. She longed to have lots of family around but they were all gone. When she tried to sleep the loneliness caught up to her as the memories flooded in. She longed for the touch of her husband, remembered the smiles and hugs of her other children. All she had left was Hamsa now and she was determined to make the world better through him.

The prayer niche became more like ones back home. On the holy day, each Friday, one of the men, usually Sami, led the prayers. He would try to give some insight from the Quran as well, but most of the time he just led the prayers.

The need for translation services was winding down, but Yosef continued to find ways to help the strangers in their new land. He enjoyed their company. They reminded him of a piece of his past, a part of his youth.

Over the past several weeks of encounters, Yosef began to notice that Susan paid him a lot of attention. She tried to get him alone or she would whisper things to him when she passed. Deliberately pressing against him.

Amena must've noticed this too, because she began to distance herself from him.

Susan would offer to drive Yosef back to VM. He tried to come up with reasons to linger with the refugees, until she would finally leave.

Susan was back on this rainy, but mild day, assessing the needs of the refugees. Did they need more clothing or foodstuffs? She was dressed in a tight, white sweater decorated with a gold zipper up the front, a long black rain jacket and black leather pants. She always smelled of a hint of lavender. Yosef tried to only be around her in a group.

Once more she offered to drive him back to VM when they finished, and he finally agreed due to the weather and his need to get back to work. He'd run out of excuses.

It'd been a long time since he'd been in such a nice car. It smelled of fine leather, and was dark blue with a beige interior. Susan took the long way around after explaining there was a lot of messy roadwork on the direct route. With all the rain, she preferred not to get her car too muddy. He got suspicious.

She pulled into a hotel parking lot on the outskirts of downtown. She parked the car and turned toward Yosef while putting her hand on his thigh. Her dark chocolate eyes promising bittersweet delights. Her sweater now unzipped to a distracting location.

"Yosef," she whispered, "I'm a woman who's used to getting what she wants. I've wanted to be alone with you for a long time now. I find you intensely attractive. Your kindness to others and selflessness is so refreshing. You've done such great things to help my cause with the refugees. I'd love to reward you in a very special way that we'll both enjoy."

Yosef didn't know how to respond. His mouth went dry. She was a powerful, beautiful woman who just propositioned him. He couldn't help but look her over. The temptation was powerful. *If I turn her down in a harsh way, it could have a lot of difficult repercussions for many. If I accept, I'll be committing adultery.* He looked into her eyes, reached down and tenderly took her hand in his, removing it from his leg.

"Mrs. Hamilton, you're a very attractive lady who does good for many in our city . . . "

"Call me Susan, please. You have very strong hands."

"Mrs. Hamilton, I cannot do this. I follow my Master who forbids me to be intimate with a married woman. Your offer is wow, quite tempting, but I cannot accept and be faithful to my calling. Please know that I don't wish to hurt you, but this is something I just cannot do. What about Mayor Hamilton?"

She withdrew her hand as her eyes narrowed. "Are you turning me down? I already told you I get what I want. You've teased me long enough."

"Please Mrs. Hamilton, I don't mean to offend. Your offer is very hard to turn down, but turn it down I must. In the name of my Master."

"Yosef, what did you think I meant? I'm a married woman. I would never."

Holding up his hand, "I'm sorry if I misunderstood your intention. I feel very foolish."

She smiled now. "Yosef, you didn't misunderstand. I thought, when you accepted the ride, you finally were willing to take this to a new level. I guess I misunderstood. I am hurt."

"I don't mean to hurt you but I've made vows long ago about such things."

"Well, I am hurt. I know a way you can make it up to me. You could kiss it and make it better." She gestured toward her heart as her eyes glistened.

Oh my, she is quite beautiful, and she doesn't give up. Father, please give me strength. Dear Lord help me now!

"You know, it could've been a lot of fun. My husband isn't the most loyal man either. We both know how to have fun with others. Think of all those young political wannabes. He's just a man after all. I could even teach you a thing or two."

"I'm sure you know that what you're asking is wrong, growing up with your mother in the Orthodox church."

"How did you know my mother was Greek?"

Swallowing hard Yosef said, "Susan, I said you're very attractive. You have classic Greek facial features and some of the most beautiful women through time have descended from the Greek. I suspected these came from your mother."

"For a guy who is turning me down, you're doing a great job of turning me on. Yes, I grew up in the Orthodox church, but that stuff's so outdated. She took me for hours every Sunday as a child. Wait a minute, why are we talking about my mother?"

"I do need to get to work. Ramone is expecting me."

"Ramone will understand, if you're with me."

"Please Susan, don't ask this of me. I cannot no matter how much part of me may wish to. I made a vow. I must honor it. I must follow the teachings of my Master to honor him."

She started the car and backed out of the space, then smiled and winked at him, "I don't get turned down often. This is a first. The offer remains open in case you change your mind. Remember, I get what

I want; forbidden fruit will make me work harder now. We'll head to Ramone's. Thank you for your work. It's appreciated so very much. I hoped my gratitude could be expressed more tangibly. You're a man like few I've met before."

As she drove on through the light rain, José said, "Susan, I'm human, too, but I try to live by biblical principles in my dealings with others. It allows me to sleep well at night. It also gives me peace and keeps me from causing pain to others. I appreciate what you're doing for so many as well. I hope you see why I cannot pursue this. I must follow my Master's teaching no matter how hard it may be. You're offer, while quite enticing, reminds me I decided long ago the mission matters most. I won't speak of this to any other."

"I think I understand. And you better not speak to anyone about this. You can only imagine the story I could spin."

She dropped him at Ramone's a few minutes ahead of his cooking class without any further comment. He thanked her for the ride. She half smiled at him while he closed the door.

José took in a deep breath through his nose, then exhaled through his mouth. He thanked the Lord for saving him from that situation. He hadn't been with a woman for a long time, but he would not destroy lives in this way. He went to the back room to gather his thoughts and calm his mind. He ran some cold water on a hand towel and put it on the back of his neck.

✠ ✠ ✠

Hamsa came into Restaurant Tapas at 2:00. Ramone greeted him like he did everyone.

"I'm here for the cooking class with Yosef."

"Who?" Ramone said.

"Yosef."

"No one here by that name. José has a class for the Latino gang members. Which gang are you in?"

"I'm not in a gang. Yosef invited me to come to class. I'm from Syria."

Ramone figured it out from there. While he didn't like it, he sent him back to the kitchen.

José was already setting up and had a couple of Latino helpers. Still reeling from the encounter with Susan, he was happy to be back in familiar space.

He gave a large welcoming grin when Hamsa came in. "Welcome Hamsa. I've been looking forward to working with you. My other students are Luis and Hector. Amigos this is Hamsa."

Hector and Luis waved to him without emotion and both said, "Buenos Tardis," out of habit.

José could see Hamsa staying far away from the others. *Got to get him into the flow.*

"Luis show Hamsa how we set up the cooking space. We're going to practice on cactus paddles again."

Hamsa looked skeptical.

About thirty minutes later, Carlos arrived along with Diego. José had a full class today.

José liked the cactus paddles recipe since it forced them to practice knife skills and concentrate. There was little margin for error. They had to work together to cook them well and keep them from being slimy. Boys liked doing it too, because it seemed macho to be able to survive in the desert on what was available. It built confidence. *If I can make those taste good, imagine what I can do with real food.*

Carlos, one of the leaders of MX 60, still came to class often. He showed a knack for cooking and he got along well with José. His innate leadership abilities showing as he led the group when José got distracted by other matters. José knew Carlos's future would be very bleak if he didn't get a trade, and he used Carlos to fill in for him when he had to be about the Master's business. Ramone accommodated and appreciated having a backup plan.

As they were taking out the trash, Hector shoved Hamsa from behind and asked him why a Muslim was here. Hamsa turned to respond, dropping the trash on the ground. Before anything could start José stepped outside.

"Hector, this is your last class until you can show me you understand the rules of treating others like you want to be treated. Take your things and leave. I require all my students be treated with respect. You know that. No fighting."

Hector growled at Hamsa but backed down and left without further incident.

"Clean up the trash Hamsa, then come see me please."

Once back inside, Hamsa said. "You didn't have to stop it, I can fight now. Got tired of getting hit all the time in the Latino school. I don't win much, but I do fight."

"That's not the way of my Master and not what this class is about. If you wish to fight, you don't need to be here. If you wish to learn, as your mama wants, please stay. I'm happy to spend some time after class speaking about America and the teachings of Isa, as you call him."

"Thank you for taking up for me and for all the other things you do for us. I don't want to fight. I want to learn. I would like very much to spend some time learning about America. You can talk about Isa if you wish as well."

They both smiled and José put his arm around Hamsa and gave him a hug. "The time for fighting has past, now is the time for healing. Tell me about your friends, Stu and Jimmy . . . "

CHAPTER 34

Stu and Jimmy didn't take the news well. Hamsa told them he had to work and help provide for his mom. He couldn't hang out after school anymore. They rode him pretty hard for few days, but then they decided to let up. Stu wanted to be sure he could blame the bomb on the Syrians, and he needed a good rapport with Hamsa to avoid messing up the plan.

"We'll build the bomb anyway," Stu told Jimmy.

They spent several weeks gathering the materials—saltpeter, two empty fire extinguishers, ball bearings and ammonium nitrate, gunpowder from bullets and shotgun shells.

Despite being frustrated that the plan wouldn't work exactly as designed, they still ate lunch in the cafeteria together. They were the minority at Benson High and had to stay together.

"Hammie, I found a book about hunting in my dad's gun locker. I thought you might want to read it so I brought it with me today. Hand me your backpack and I'll slide it in. Don't want any teachers seeing it or we may get in trouble. Keep a look out," Stu said.

"That would be so cool," said Hamsa handing over the pack and looking over his shoulder. Stu pulled the book and a small bag of ball bearings and other bomb making material. He dumped it in as he put the book in the bag.

After lunch he told Jimmy, "I gave him the book and dumped the other stuff while he wasn't lookin'. He's such a dufus. Got no idea 'bout what's gonna happen. The book is full of gunpowder, too. When we turn him in, he'll have it all over his stuff." Jimmy laughed along with him.

Hamsa's time spent at the cooking class was useful. With José acting like father or big brother, he felt safe from the Latinos. He also saw that when they tried to hurt each other José was there to correct or send them away. Hamsa learned conversational Spanish from his classmates. These Latinos were tough and off putting at first but after a time, they accepted Hamsa and even listened to some of his stories about the war and the camps. They had stories of the journey to get here as well, which Hamsa had never appreciated before.

Hamsa stayed after class for an extra 30 minutes or so to speak with José, who kept his promise to give his perspective on America while also giving healthy doses of Isa's teachings. José continued to guide him in scripture reading from the Bible. He pointed Hamsa to the teachings of Jesus in Matthew and Mark.

"Yosef, why did Allah let this civil war happen? How can he allow so many to die?"

"Hamsa you ask good questions, but I must answer from my view of the world. I'm a follower of Jesus, Isa as you call him. He's a loving God but also a just God. We know from the story of creation, he puts tremendous value on free will. If we're to choose to follow him and enjoy that blessing, we must also be free to choose to reject him and endure the consequences. The fall of man in the Garden didn't just stop with man's relationship to God. It mangled our relationship to each other, the world and even to ourselves. This shows up in horrible ways in history. The Assad civil war is another manifestation of it."

"So how do we fix it?" Hamsa said.

"God didn't leave it like that. He provides ways to reconcile these broken relationships. The first and most obvious is between man and God. This required a sacrifice. A just God must be appeased. He needed holy blood to be shed to make the unholy, holy. Since none of us are holy, all have sinned. Who would intervene for us? That's what Christianity teaches. Jesus the only sinless one, died for us. I know that's hard to understand based on the teachings you've heard in the Quran about Jesus. Jesus restored all the broken relationships I mentioned earlier. We're transformed by his Spirit within us. It happens all at once but then it happens in a gradual way too. We're restored in an instant, but then we must become more like him in how we live. We have many habits that we developed before we accepted Christ. These need to be changed for good. They can be, but it takes a lifetime. We fail at times. I know that I still do, even after all these years as a follower." *Boy, did I almost make a mess of things that day with Susan.*

"Christianity is a relationship reconciliation belief system. That's why you see so many Christian mercy-based missions all over."

"Why then don't the Christians reach out to the Syrian refugees more? Some seem to hate us and want to get rid of us. Others just seem to ignore us. Only a few like you and Mrs. Hamilton seem to want us and care for us."

"Not all who call themselves Christian know Jesus at all. They're near others who are followers, but haven't accepted and believed that he sacrificed himself for them. Or they stopped once they accepted that he did sacrifice himself for them. Instead of continuing to grow in the knowledge of Christ and changing their lives to conform to his teachings. Thus, they have a repaired relationship with God, but don't repair the ones with others, the world or even themselves. Unlike Islam, many Christians don't follow the disciplines of prayer, giving, and so on. Islam teaches that those are the way to Allah and thus are vital to salvation. Christianity teaches these disciplines are the manifestation of our love for God after salvation. Finally, many Christians don't act on their beliefs due to lack of focus, many get too busy to listen to God's voice anymore. They've let the things of life distract them from what's important. My Master told a story about a seed sower and the types of ground the seeds fell upon. I'll tell you that another day. You can find it in Matthew chapter thirteen if you want to look it up on your own."

"Before I go, I want to thank you for following your Master. It means a lot to my family and the other people of New Rojava."

"It means a lot to me as well, Hamsa. It's my pleasure to be used by my Master and to see such a great group of people who've been through so much, begin to flourish. Have a good night."

✠ ✠ ✠

Stu and Jimmie spent several afternoons following the instruction for the bombs. They made them in Jimmy's garage. They finished the first on a Sunday afternoon. They loaded it into the van and took it up to the shack for detonation.

"We don't want a lot of people around when we try this so if folks are fishing up there, we'll have to wait. I hope no one's around 'cause I want to see this baby blow," Stu said.

"Tell me again how this is going to work," said Jimmy.

Stu shook his head in disbelief and said, "OK, pay attention this time. We have the timer set for ten minutes. See. I'll time it on my phone too so we know when it's gonna go. We'll keep the boat on a line, so we can pull it back if we need to. Once it goes, we can know for sure how far the ball bearings will travel so we know how close to get it to the buildings on the Wharf. If it don't go off, we know we did somethin' wrong and can fix it the next time. That's why we keep the boat on the line so we can pull it back in and fix what's wrong."

"Got it, I think."

As they drove across the Lumber River Dam toward the shack, Stu said, "Man, there're too many folks on the lake now. We gonna have to wait until they all head home." He looked out the window, at the sky full of gathering clouds. "Looks like we may get a storm later. Hope that sends all these folks runnin' to their cars soon."

It took a couple of hours and the continued gathering rain clouds before the Sunday boaters decided to call it a day. Around dusk, Stu drove back to the parking area for the boat ramp and saw it was empty.

They already had the old rowboat on the water near the shack. A gentle breeze kicked up and the boat pitched in the water. The bomb was under some old rags so no one would see it. Jimmy pulled it back to shore and Stu got in and set the timer.

"Wow the water's cold today. Go wade out there and give it a big push. We want it way out there in the cove before it blows," Stu said.

Jimmy pulled it in close then he pushed hard and the current caught the boat and it moved away fast.

"Yeah man, that's it!"

Jimmy scrambled back to shore and put his shoes back on. He still had hold of the rope to pull it back.

"OK we got about six minutes and then we're going to see some serious firepower," Stu said.

They both waited on the shore like kids with stolen firecrackers. Jimmy squinted into the distance, "Is that another boat coming toward us?"

Stu stared hard in the dusk and the wind. "I doubt it; the lot was empty. We got three minutes. We can't bring it back fast enough to stop it. Shoot your pistol over toward the trees. If anyone's out there, they'll steer away when they hear shots."

Jimmy picked up his pistol and got in his shooters stance, "I don't see nobody over there in the woods. I'll shoot that way." He fired off five quick shots.

"Even if they don't hear the shots they can see the muzzle flashes. That should keep 'em away. Now get back over here. We got less than a minute."

They both stood near the shack. They could still see their boat and didn't see any others on the lake. "Five, four, three, two, one . . . "

Nothing.

"Arrgh!" Jimmy growled in frustration.

"Let's give it another few minutes. Then I'll reset the timer. It's gonna blow, I know it. We did everything right. Had to."

They waited another ten minutes to be on the safe side. Then Stu saw something that scared him to death. "Man, the boat's sinking!

Look it's got water in it big time! Grab the rope! We got to get it close to shore or it's lost." He cursed and shouted. "Blasted thing musta sprung a leak in the shack over the winter. This really sucks man. All our hard work . . . "

"I gave you the rope when you sent me over there to shoot. What'd you do with it?"

They searched the shoreline but didn't find it. The boat had taken it out further and in the fast approaching darkness, they couldn't see it.

"Jimmy, you're a dufus! I told you to hold the rope. What's wrong with you? Now it's sinking, and we ain't got nothin'."

All they could do was watch it sink into the lake and into the darkness. They just stood and watched in silence.

Jimmy and Stu called each other names and cursed their luck all the way back to Carlisle. When Stu dropped Jimmy off, he said, "At least no one can find it. Including us. I guess we need to try again. Let's give it a few days. I need to think."

CHAPTER 35

Before long, the gangs of Villa Maya realized the Biz was in trouble. Biz enforcers still collected protection money but much of that money stayed with the enforcers now. It didn't go up the chain to the Biz.

Mario and Deion tried to maintain order but with Da Wyz unwilling to order the brutality he once did, the Biz disintegrated from lack of discipline.

Attacks from the VM gangs though not coordinated, happened with ever increasing regularity.

MX 60 got word the enforcers were keeping the protection money. The enforcers were known to many in the Wharf and without the Biz to bring all the heavy firepower, MX killed three in two weeks. They forced them to give a route list and charge rates through intimidation or torture. MX 60 then placed their own enforcers, who got all the money and undercut the protection prices the Biz charged in that area of the Wharf. The locals didn't like either group but opted for the cheaper one.

Without protection money, and with a depleting group of Biz enforcers, the VM gangs began to take over the drug trade in some areas also. The Biz experienced a cash crunch.

❖ ❖ ❖

Jackie concerned about the impending crisis scheduled an interview with Sheriff Ward. She came with phone recorder and stylus in hand.

She wore a tight white button up blouse with black pants and black shoes. She kept her jacket handy since there was still a chill in the air. Ward was in uniform, like always. They met in a typical conference room at city hall. Old wooden table, old cloth chairs.

"How many murders have we had in the Wharf since Da Wyz got religion and started focusing on affordable housing?"

"It started small, but now we're seeing one a day. Biz gang members. Most were shot with handguns at close range. Word on the street is VM gangs are tired of being oppressed and are rising up to take out the oppressors. While it's bad to have such killings, at least they're shooting each other and not innocents."

"What's the Carlisle police force doing about this?"

"We've increased our visibility. More feet on the beat so to speak. We've arrested the leaders we can find, but new ones seem to take their place just as fast. The new ones are younger and more violent than the more experienced ones now in jail. We're trying to contact the leaders of the rival gangs to find a more peaceful solution. They're fragmented and have ever changing leadership, so it's hard to communicate with them." He said almost under his breath, "I don't like the idea of this playing out, but sometimes it's necessary. Jackie, don't use that last statement."

"Where is Da Wyz these days? Anyone heard from him?" Jackie asked.

"Not sure. Guess he's holed up in his castle fortress he calls a house. Officer Jim may have a clue. I've not heard a word. Maybe he left. Wouldn't that be good news?"

No, I think I'll chat with Miranda at the next meeting I have with Carafe Homes.

Mario pulled together a small group of his team to assassinate members of the VM gangs.

"They think we vulnerable. Let's show 'em we not."

Later that night, four VM gang enforcers were gunned down in Villa Maya. Two were killed, along with their girlfriends. One's mother was killed in the crossfire. Two small children sustained serious gunshot wounds.

Juan and Carlos, the last two of the old guard leaders of the VM gangs still alive and on the street, met to plan a counter attack.

"Carlos, man, they must be getting desperate to be coming over here like this. They're shooting up more than the gang bangers now. We got to make 'em pay."

"What're you thinking?"

"Let do some drive-byes in the Wharf. Let 'em know if they gonna come in here and shoot up the barrio, we can play that game too."

"Got to be another way, man. If we start shooting up the Wharf, the cops'll be all over us. On top of that, we're the saviors at the moment, since we're charging less for services. They paying for protection. We can't be the ones killing bystanders there."

"What if we go after Da Wyz? Cut the head off the Rats."

"I like the idea, but I wonder if we won't be doing them a favor," Carlos said.

"No, man, they'll be too busy fighting over who takes his place. In the meantime, we can take some more of the Wharf for our own."

"How we gonna do it. He lives in a fort and works in a fort. No way to get too him. We would've taken him out years ago, if we could've. We need to get with the Salvadorans and the PRs to coordinate our next move," Carlos said. "We could use their help in this. With the Biz gone, there's reams of money to go around. Maybe it's time to unite."

"I like the way you think, man. You call Rico and set up a meeting. I'll get Sanchez to come from the Salvadorans. We need a place to meet that's neutral. No one's turf."

"We can't use the church. How 'bout Restaurant Tapas? It's in the middle. José and Ramone won't mind, if we do it after closing."

When Carlos talked to Ramone about it, Ramone's usual smile disappeared. "No amigo! We won't be neutral ground for a gang meeting. Too much chance for things to go wrong. I'll be out of business and lots of people could die."

"People're going to die anyway, señor. We trying to stop this. You know how the Biz has hurt us for years. Now's our time to make them pay. We can't do it in pieces. We got to be united," Carlos said.

"What happens if the police or the Biz hear about this? I get shut down or people die in my place. I won't allow it amigo. Get out!"

Carlos stormed out and ran into José as he left Ramone.

José stopped Carlos and shouted to Ramone. "What's happening, amigos?"

"Carlos wants me to host a gang leaders' meeting to unite the gangs of Villa Maya against the Biz. There'll be blood and bodies everywhere if they get found out," Ramone said.

"Wait outside Carlos," José said.

He stepped in and closed the door. Carlos listened through the door.

"Ramone, we have a chance to see all the leaders and even hear their strategy. We can help unite VM and become a force for good with this meeting. They'll bring protection, so I wouldn't worry about being attacked. The cops won't show, if the past is any indication. I see your concerns, but there can be good that happens here. The meeting's going to happen anyway. Let me be here, you can join if you like. Good will come from this, I'm convinced."

"Amigo, you're a man of God. I've seen this and accept it. I think you're playing with fire. If you're saying God will be with this, I'll agree. I'll stay away though. It gives me the chance to deny it if the cops show. I'm no hero, José. If this falls apart I'll swear you did this behind my back. Go ahead and set it up. No food or drinks though."

Carlos scurried away from the door as he heard Ramone say, "I think this is loco, amigo."

CHAPTER 36

Early spring arrived in splendor with Easter fast approaching. Life began waking after the long winter chill. Carlisle seldom got the severe winter weather remembered by so many that migrated from the north, but it still had its share of cold and ice.

The trees started blooming in mid-March and now the dogwoods and azaleas were painting the city with pinks, whites, reds and oranges. People seemed to breathe easier this time of year despite the pollen count. The whole city loosened up after the winter when the flowers bloomed and coats were exchanged for jackets.

Pastor Rich reviewed the emails and notes from the congregation while he started the new week. The mix of messages encouraged and discouraged. Convicted by the Spirit to do the messages on poverty and how to help, he read the messages of encouragement with joy.

The discouraging messages often had hateful overtones and were anonymous.

Cowards. If you have so strong an opinion, why not say who you are.

He found one set of notes very disturbing. Signed by a group that called themselves United for Jesus. These picked a point in each sermon and disputed it with great venom. It seemed like an anti-apologetic. *How can they claim to follow Jesus and spout this twisted version of his teachings? It would be good to find them to have a private debate.*

To see if they are hate filled or just ignorant on some of the points of doctrine they spew.

He checked his calendar. Today he had an interview with Jacqueline Hyatt, WWNS news. She wanted to speak about the sermon series. It got social media coverage, and she wanted to do a brief exposé for an excerpt on how Carlisle responded to the unrest last fall. She was due at 10:00 AM.

After that he had a 1:00 meeting with Paul Stanley. *Not sure what he wants to talk about, but if the last few weeks are any indication, he'll thank me for finishing the sermon series and getting back to my job now.*

He always opened his day in prayer. He got a cup of strong aromatic coffee from the break area and reviewed his sermons from the last few weeks to prepare for Ms. Hyatt. He gazed out his second floor window at the flowering pink and white cherry trees.

Jackie came in dressed in spring colors with a pastel pink shrug on her shoulders due to the early morning chill. He greeted her with a handshake and a smile. He sat with his door open at the small conference table in his office.

"Good morning, Pastor Rich. I believe that's how you like to be addressed."

"Your research is correct, ma'am."

"Please call me Jackie. I use formality in reporting but not in interviews."

"OK, Jackie."

"Do you mind if I record this? I'll use excerpts in my report. If I can get the station to air this segment, I may come back with my cameraman to ask this in a setting with proper lighting."

"That'll be fine."

She got set up and leaned toward Rich to start the questioning. "Pastor, what prompted you to start this series?"

"As you know, we had the unrest last fall. A group of pastors got together to see what the church could do to help. During those conversations, I saw that the wealthy congregations in our city didn't address the issues of poverty. After I did some soul searching, over the Christmas holidays, it became apparent to me that God wanted us to see the plight of the impoverished right before our eyes."

"How did God show you this?"

"I have a circle of counselors I consult. In addition, I just prayed, meditated, and listened to God's voice. We call it the Kol Yahweh."

"I have a friend who talks about that at times. I'm familiar. So, God told you to preach about poverty in Carlisle. I didn't hear all your sermons yet. I did listen to a couple online. Sounded like you didn't pull any punches. How were they received?"

"Well, as you can imagine, this series would agitate the complacent in our flock. It did just that."

As Pastor Rich went on Jackie remembered the wonderful dinner interview with José. He told her then, "I must challenge the comfortable and comfort those who are troubled."

Pastor Rich was still talking, but Jackie was distracted. *This is José's mission. Pastor Rich is helping him.*

"I received mixed reviews. Some thanked me for speaking God's word and leading with courage. Others think I've lost my mind. I'm glad I did it. I have a peace about it that I didn't think would come. For the detractors, I pray they'll see God moving here. For the encouragers, I pray they'll listen to God and do something now."

She shook off the memory and changed direction. "Do you know a man in Villa Maya named José Sabio? Let me read back something he told me when I interviewed him a few weeks back."

"I know a Justus Sabbas." After racking his brain, he remembered. "He told me his name in VM was Sabio."

"Here it is." She tapped the app on the screen to find her notes from the earlier interview with José. She read them back aloud.

"I must challenge the comfortable and comfort those who are troubled. If you look at it, that was his message from long ago. I will speak the truth of his love and his desire that we care for each other."

"Yes Jackie, that sounds like Justus to me. He's a powerful man of God, I've found. He speaks wisdom. I'm a word nerd, as many know, and after a few conversations with Justus, I looked his Hispanic name up. I found that Sabio in Spanish can be translated—wisdom."

"So, he's José the Wise? Really?"

"Or perhaps Wise Justice? You'll have to interview him again to figure that out. From your smile, it appears that idea appeals to you, correct?"

"My interview, pastor." Jackie came back to the topic at hand. "One of your points was that the church building campaign would look for ways to save money and give that to a fund like the one set up by Da Wyz. How's that going?"

Pastor Rich leaned back in his chair and crossed his arms. "We did a final review. Our campaign and building were very far along, so we couldn't find much. Most of the funds were committed and would cost more to undo than the savings would be. I did reveal to the church yesterday that we saved one hundred thousand dollars to help create rent subsidies. We're planning an additional campaign to raise more money in the fall, when everyone is back from summer break."

"Where did you get these ideas?"

"They came to us during our meeting here on affordable housing a couple of months ago. Did you make it to that?"

Jackie nodded.

"People made suggestions to only use half the funds raised in a capital campaign on church building and the other half on affordable housing. That didn't work for us since we were so far along. I did challenge the church to cut where we could."

"That was Justus' idea too, was it not?"

"Some of it was his idea at the meeting. We came up with our own idea to raise funds after meeting as a leadership team."

"What was the total budget for the building?"

"Over ten million dollars."

"And you are giving one hundred thousand to the poor?"

"That's in addition to the other ministries we support here in Carlisle to aid various impoverished groups. The one hundred thousand is specific to affordable housing." He noticed how quick he defended his flock. *Like a good shepherd should.* He could feel her gaze change. *She could see this was a small offering. It seemed like a guilt offering. I know it's not enough.*

"You say your church will do another offering in the fall. Isn't that a long time after the sermon series though?"

He began to fidget in his chair. *Is God using this interview to tell me something? Did I allow others to persuade me out of what God called us to?*

He settled back in his chair and said, "Yes with all the other programs and activities the church and Christian school has going on before the end of May, we needed to push the campaign to the fall. Raising money like this over the summer will be very hard due to declines in church attendance."

"OK, I think I understand. Please don't think me disrespectful, but it seems like you're missing an opportunity to put your words into action now. Da Wyz's program is underway. He got it up and running within weeks, not months, sir. Families are moving out of deprived areas to more prosperous ones, even now. I know this is the only church up the hill having such a sermon series this spring. What are all the others doing in your circle of pastors? Are you all alone in this?"

A cold chill hit him. For the first time, he felt alone in this. He knew it would be hard but he knew he had to preach on poverty. *Am I the only one listening to God or am I nuts? Is Justus of God or just a con man?*

"I'm not alone, Jackie. I'm a pioneer. That's a dangerous place at times, but it's also a remarkable place too. Thank you for your comments. They've made me think. Please don't talk about the campaign this fall. I'm convinced from this that we must do it sooner."

He could see Jackie was surprised and pleased by his comment. *She must like the fact that she can change people's minds.*

The interview proceeded for another twenty minutes rehearsing some of the sermon quotes and diving into deeper meanings of the topics of systemic racism, white privilege, and inherent biases. But Rich couldn't get his mind off of a campaign now.

"Thank you, Pastor Rich, for your time. Like I said, I plan to use this as part of a greater story to be aired later in the month, I hope, a follow up to the riot. Kind of a six months' later deal. I'll want to come back in to get you on camera. This is really good information you've given. Quite a bold step, as I see it."

"I'm happy to be used of God to a part of our community healing. May you have a blessed day."

He called Sondra his assistant, "Let's get a note out to the staff. I want to have a meeting this afternoon. We need to start a fundraising campaign for the impoverished of Carlisle this month. Let's plan on a time from three to five today."

The one o'clock meeting with Paul was scheduled for the church conference room. Rich thought that strange but headed there after a quick lunch at a local deli.

As he entered, he was greeted by a group of six. Two elders, Paul, vice chairman of the elder body, and Thomas Spratt. In addition, associate pastor Randall Pendergraph, and three other prominent long-time members.

"Close the door, Pastor," Paul said as he entered.

"What's this about?"

"As you know Wes is traveling in Asia now, so as vice chair, I speak for the elder body. Pastor, I'll be direct since there is no easy way to say this. We don't think you're preaching God's word to us anymore. We've grown tired of these sermons on the Wharf and Villa Maya. You're even encouraging us to help the Syrians. They're Muslim. We don't know if this is part of a grand plan for them to infiltrate the US. No siree, we don't see you leading us well."

Paul turned to one side in his chair and continued. "Now I understand you're calling a meeting to discuss a fund for affordable housing sooner than the fall, like we'd agreed earlier."

How does he know that?

"Paul, why didn't you come to me alone instead of with a committee? Randall, what are you doing here?"

"Randall is here at the request of those of us United for Jesus. He wrote a rebuttal of each of your sermons and sent it to you each week. You ignored his comments and kept on preaching this stuff anyway. We had to find other channels to get it to others in the church. We've found a large group that is thinking of moving membership elsewhere as a result. You won't even listen to your own staff when they point out your errors. You've lost touch with our church. We think you've even lost touch with God."

The last point stung hard. To see friends in the room devastated him. He sunk into his chair and looked up at the ceiling.

"So, what do you propose?"

"Pastor, we told you not to go here, yet you insisted. I hoped we could salvage you. We hoped this would pass over, but instead Randall tells us you did an interview with the news today. You even called a meeting today to create a campaign to fund this affordable housing deal working with Da Wyz. Therefore, we're here to ask for your resignation. We'll have Randall serve as interim pastor, until you're replaced."

He looked Paul in the eye now. "And if I refuse?"

"We'll have no choice but to let folks know about those extra payments we made to cover additional costs for your family adoptions and other matters. We'll make sure people know you like to counsel young ladies in your office alone. There'll be hints of improprieties that will tarnish your reputation. You won't be able to find another pastorate on this side of the Mississippi."

"You know those payments were approved by the personnel committee. You know the other charges are just outright lies. I can't believe men who say they're United for Jesus would make these statements. Do you really think this glorifies God? Do you really think I wasn't doing what I felt God led me to do in these sermons? Do you really think I'll resign over this?"

"Pastor, remember what the Bible you say you read says about church unity. We aren't a church united. You've divided us. We're evidence of that. We do this for the greater good if we have to. Sometimes the end is justified by the means."

"Men, this is wrong. You know that in your hearts, if they've been filled with the Holy Spirit. This is wrong. Randall, you're a minister of the gospel, how can you be a part of this?"

"Pastor, we know this is a shock. We know you need time to think about it. Go home and speak to your wife. Pray over this. You'll see we're right. It must be that God had you do this to prepare you for your next job. We're just encouraging you along the way," Paul said.

Pastor Rich got up to leave. He looked in the eyes of each man around the table. He started to speak and thought better of it. He made his way back to his office. Shocked and dumbfounded. When he walked by Sondra's desk he said, 'This afternoon's meeting is off." He closed his office door. Then he wept and prayed over his flock.

After a time, he called Tony and Justus and asked them to meet with him after work today.

"I prefer to do four if we can. I have to deal with the dinner rush," Justus said.

"Fine, let's meet at Tony's office," Rich said.

✠ ✠ ✠

Justus arrived at 3:30, based on bus schedules, and began a conversation with Tony.

"Rich has been betrayed. I know it. I don't know by who. I could tell it in his voice. Why else meet after work in the Wharf?"

"You know it because the Master told you, don't you?"

"Yes."

"Who do you think it is?"

"I don't know his congregation that well, but let's wait and not speculate," Justus said.

Rich arrived ahead of time too. He entered the office a deflated man. The men embraced. Then he recounted the story to Tony and Justus around the coffee table in Tony's office.

"I don't know who I can trust at my church right now. What should I do? If I don't resign, they'll start a rumor campaign to smear my reputation. I know the series unnerved people, but we knew it would. How can God allow this? I did what he asked me to? Where's the blessing? I was going to start a campaign to help with affordable housing this afternoon before this happened. Now I'm a toothless tiger."

"There is always opposition to the truth, when it's declared. You're challenging long held beliefs. They were deceptive and unkind, but still they were convenient and comfortable. They fit the biases well. You had to expect some struggle here," Justus said placing a hand on Rich's arm.

"Yes, but not like this. These were close friends. I've been to their homes for dinner. It's even one of the associate pastors, and who knows who else."

"As the Father told Joshua back in the day, 'Be strong and courageous . . . for the Lord God goes with you wherever you go.' You're not the first to be betrayed by a friend. I know it stings. Some of them may still come around to the truth," Justus said.

"What do I do? Do I resign? Do I let them win?"

"While they may see it as a competition with church unity at stake, I see it as a matter of truth. If the options are a church united in deception compared to one divided in truth, then I say division is needed for greater unity in time. That is the same question that has been asked through the ages. Go back and read Martin Luther, if you doubt me," Justus said.

"Rich what Justus says is right, but this must take time to develop. I suggest you let someone else preach for you this Sunday. Take a week off to pray and think about this. God will show us a way out of this dark night." Tony now spoke to his fellow pastor.

"Tony speaks wisdom. Let's spend time in prayer together," Justus said.

They prayed for what seemed like an hour and then Rich got up to go. "May I give you a ride?" he asked Justus.

"Yes, that would be much appreciated. I'm late for my shift."

In the car, Rich just kept coming back to suffering for doing what's right. Justus listened and let him talk. It disturbed him to his core, but he didn't want to show that to Rich.

As he got out he said, "The world can be a dark place but take heart, the Master overcame the world."

Evil made a run at me and lost now it's going after those I care for— my allies.

He could feel the darkness coming in the dawn of spring.

CHAPTER 37

Carlos, Juan, Rico and Santiago came into Restaurant Tapas after hours to meet. José closed the restaurant blinds, curtains and arranged some of the tables in the back room that had limited windows for onlookers.

No one would expect people were there. No late-night drinkers looking for a place to sober up would mistake it for open.

They all arrived in different vehicles. Santiago was the last to come.

"Where are the Columbians?" Rico asked.

"They're not a factor anymore, the leadership's gone, no one to talk to these days," Juan said.

"So why is he here, amigos?" Santiago motioned his head toward José.

"He's our mediator," Carlos said.

"So how we gonna do this? Who starts?" Santiago asked while he stepped his leg over the back of his chair to sit.

Santiago had a large grayish tattoo covering the left side of his face. In the light, José couldn't make out the words artistically inscribed on this palette of dark skin. He wore a black jacket with a gun holster visible underneath and a light blue t-shirt and jeans. His long black hair was pulled tight into a ponytail in the back. He was older than Carlos and Juan. Or perhaps just more aged by the life he lived.

Rico was clean cut. Short hair. Well groomed. Collared striped shirt and work pants. The pants were tight and a knife was visible in one pocket. *Gun must be tucked in the small of his back.* Tattoos of the cross on his hands. Biceps were much larger than a normal man. Obvious that he worked out often. You didn't want to get into hand-to-hand combat with this young man. He appeared to be the youngest of the group.

Carlos, now a wise old leader at nineteen was flanked by Juan. José perceived Juan as the meanest in the bunch. Juan knew strategy and made sure everyone recognized it. He was a field commander too. Both were excellent with handguns.

Carlos called the meeting to order. "We're here because of what's happening with VM and the Wharf. Da Wyz is done for at this point. No head on the snake anymore. He won't fight us head on. We can take what we want. But if we fight each other too, none of us gets what's due. The rats've been kicking us around since we got here. Now it's our time to kick them right where it counts. We already taking the protection money. We need to get the pimps paying us now. May have to take some out to persuade the rest to fall in line. Again, we can do more together than separate."

"Who leads this new united Mayan gang?" Santiago said.

"This group will. We pick one leader but we all lead our teams. Kinda like the Marines, Army, and Navy, you know. Each has a general, but there's one chief," Juan said.

"So, I guess I'm the new boss." Rico said. He folded his arms across his toned chest showing his biceps.

"Let's get to why I'm here. Santiago asked a good question. I'm here to help this happen for the greater good of Villa Maya and Carlisle. This will help to glorify my Master, that's what I have at stake. You can be a force for good, not evil in this place," José said.

Juan looked at him like he was loco. "Ha! I love you man. Always joking around. We're here to unite and conquer not start a children's camp. I say we take out Da Wyz. He's still the head. If we can cut that off, the rats'll scatter. Carlos has heard this before. It's still the best idea."

José rose to speak, but Santiago and Carlos started at the same time. Santiago out shouted Carlos, "Da Wyz is weak, while he's in place they'll struggle. We don't want to touch him. Besides how you gonna do it? His setup leaves no opening. We can't get to him."

Juan looked him in the eye and said, "I'm sure gonna try."

"I want no part of this now," said Santiago and he got up to leave.

"If I'm not the chief, I'm gone too," Rico said.

Carlos looked at José for wisdom. José just shook his head.

The meeting broke with no union. Perhaps even more division now the 60s looked fragmented.

Perhaps we try again later. At least no blood was shed.

CHAPTER 38

Stu figured out what they did wrong over the last couple of weeks. "It was the timer. We didn't have it set right. I wired it backwards. Instead of taking ten minutes, it was going to take fifty minutes. Then when the boat sank, everything got wet and ruined. So, nothing worked. Anyway, I got it now."

Now reenergized by his eureka moment, Stu and Jimmy rebuilt the remaining bomb to correct for the mistake. They completed it on a Monday in mid-April.

"Are you sure you got this. I don't want to drive back up to the lake and watch this sink again," Jimmy said.

"We ain't going back to the lake. The boat's gone. We'll plant this one in town and see if it goes off. We don't have to hurt too many folks. Just enough to get on the news. We can do it tonight. There's a bar on Riverside drive where a lot of the gangbangers hang. No loss if we kill a few of those, right? They kill each other anyway. If they get mad, they'll trace it to the Syrians and go solve that problem for us, too. If not, the cops'll trace it to the Syrians and ship 'em back to Syria where they belong."

"You sure you want to do this? Ain't it murder, Stu?"

"You ain't gettin' scared are you Jimmy? Gangbangers don't count as murder. They ain't like you and me. They like animals. Look how they act."

"Not sure man, but if you say so. You always was the smart one. You want to wait until the weekend when it's full?"

"Nah, let's do it tonight. I'm itchin' to see those Syrians gone. We waited long enough. It won't have a lot of brothers there, but it'll still be very effective. We won't get seen that way either. All we need is a loud pop and a few casualties to make the news. We could do it in Villa Maya but no one would notice. Ha!"

"Where you want to put it?"

"Since it looks like an old extinguisher, we can just leave it in the doorway near the street. If they have a planter or something like that out front, we can leave it there or behind it. No need to go in. No one'll mess with it. There's a good spot to watch nearby. But I say we drop it and run. I'll put it on a short timer. That way, even if somebody sees it, they won't have time to do anything. I wiped it all down for fingerprints. We handle with gloves from here on."

"Course someone could steal it. Won't they get a big surprise on the way to the pawn shop?" Jimmy laughed. Stu laughed, too, but didn't understand why his mouth was so dry now.

They loaded it in the van around nine o'clock and headed to Club Eleven-Eleven on Riverside. Jimmy drove. Stu stayed in the back seat and kept the bomb steady. Reality finally kicked in, and he started to sweat. His hands got clammy. He couldn't swallow.

"Man, I should've got a bottle of water."

"I can go to the mini mart if you want."

"No man, we got a bomb in the back seat. Let's just do this and go."

They parked in a vacant lot behind an abandoned warehouse just off of Riverside. They planned to carry it down the alley and just leave it by the door. Stu thought the way the club was situated, they could drop it and not be seen. It was heavy, but Jimmy was big enough to carry it on his own—he just couldn't take it far.

"You sure you're ready to do this now, man?" Jimmy said.

"We've come this far, and it'll get rid of the Syrians and some of the gangbangers. It's a win-win." Stu was really sweating now. His hands started to shake when he reached for the timer.

"OK, I'm going to set the timer. You take it and put it down real gentle. Walk slow back across the street, and run like your tail is on fire when you get out of sight. I'll have the car running and waiting."

He moved the timer to ten minutes. They never got the bomb out of the car. It detonated as soon as Stu set it.

Officer Jim arrived first on the scene. He saw the flashes and heard two explosions while he was on patrol on Commonwealth. He worked his way through the small crowd that rushed to the scene from the nearby clubs and found two charred bodies near what was left of a van. There was the smell of smoke and burned flesh. He struggled to determine why there were two explosions instead of just the gas tank. *The van must've caught on fire, and when that hit the gas tank, it exploded.* There was not much left to be identified. *Why didn't the occupants run out before it hit the tank? Is this another hit by the rats trying to cover something up?*

When he surveyed the surrounding damage, the more ominous reality hit him. *There must've been a bomb, too.* Ball bearings hit the walls of the neighboring building like bullets, some dinged the brick and concrete; others pierced the wood and boarded up windows. He'd seen this before from his military service in Afghanistan. The blast zone emanating from one side of the vehicle and plenty of shrapnel damage in that direction. He called for backup and began moving the crowd away for fear there may be another bomb nearby.

"Nothing else to see here folks. CPD has it now." Into his chest mic he said, "Bring the bomb squad and the fire department."

It took all night, but once they determined the van belonged to William West, CPD traced the steps back. They entered the house and garage with great caution in case of booby traps. There was bomb-making residue in the Wests' garage. Anybody who knew Jimmy knew he and Stuart Powell were constant companions.

"They made friends with that Syrian kid named Hamsa. They were good buddies for a while. Not sure what happened to him," Stu's mom told the police while she struggled to contain her grief. "Oh, my boy is gone. He was a good boy. Loved his mama." She composed herself and came back to the question. With a breaking voice she said, "That Syrian kid was here a lot last month or so. Haven't seen him for a while."

Sheriff Ward's investigation turned up Stu's laptop fast. They found an email on bomb making from Hamsa. Stu had forwarded it to Jimmy with some comments about what they should do next. It was obvious from the blast radius and the materials they could find that they used that recipe to make the device.

Sheriff Ward called a news conference the next morning to describe what happened. "It appears that two males, James Harold West and Stuart Zachary Powell, were killed last night by a bomb in their vehicle. We have no motive for the attack at this time. We are pursuing all leads. We have a laptop of one of the victims that should shed light on the questions. We have an additional person of interest we are pursuing now."

"Do you know the intended target for the device?" Jackie asked.

"We cannot be certain but based on the proximity to the clubs on Riverside, it appears they planned to place the bomb in that area, causing carnage where it went off."

"So, you think the ones killed were actually the bomb makers?" Jackie followed up.

"It appears that way at this time. The other person of interest will help us piece this together once we have him in for questioning."

"What about the rumors on social media that this is a terrorist attack?"

"That would be pure conjecture at this time. We need more facts, which will come out over the next few hours. Now I must go to oversee the ongoing investigation." Ward left the dais.

Hamsa and Rima watched the news the next morning after Dijlin sent Sami over to bring everyone together. Rima knew what happened once the names were disclosed. She was sad for those boys and their families, but she also had greater fears. It wouldn't be hard to trace this back to New Rojava and Hamsa. All the Syrians stayed home today from school and work. They were expecting the worst. They'd seen this before from reports in Aleppo, Homs, and in the many other cities and towns where the authorities arrested people without discrimination and seized property just because they could. They took people away never to be seen again. They didn't need evidence. There were no trials.

The CPD raided New Rojava mid-morning. They found Hamsa and his backpack. Quick forensics indicated gunpowder present and they found two ball bearings. They arrested him and ransacked his home looking for evidence. It didn't take long to find the book on hunting and gunpowder in his room.

The rest of New Rojava didn't fare much better. CPD commandeered the computer used in the clubhouse and two others they had acquired over the last several weeks.

In the middle of the search, desperate, Amena called Susan to ask for help.

"I don't know how to help you now. You've betrayed us all. We were trying to help you and this is how we get repaid. I can't talk to you now." Susan hung up fast.

Amena called Yosef next.

"We need a representative with Hamsa. You could be his translator. I told him to pretend not to understand English very well. Perhaps they'll have some sympathy for him. He needs a friend. Please help us. Susan has abandoned us. No one will believe us. They think we blew up two white kids last night and are coming for the rest of the city today. This is like where we left. Are you still a friend or will you run too?"

"Amena, tell Rima I'll go to help Hamsa, if they'll let me see him. I'll pray for you all now. This is a sad day across Carlisle. So much death. So much hate." Yosef said shaking his head.

When he arrived at the jail, he saw Jackie Hyatt reporting from the front steps. There were protestors with signs covered with hateful slogans about the refugees. Yosef just shook his head in disgust. He knew people were scared, but why pick on a whole group of people when only one is implicated?

Jackie wore a pink dress with a bold black stripe down the front. The stripe went around her waist and down the sides. She had her hair off one ear, showing a gold earring and gold chain necklace. Even though he didn't have time to linger long on her, he couldn't help but notice. *I think that's the way she wants it.*

"Jackie, I need to get into see the boy, Hamsa."

"What's a Tapas chef doing here looking for a Syrian bomber?" Jackie asked.

"I don't believe he's a bomber. He's a confused teenager who has been through more than any of us should bear. He's been in my cooking class for the last few weeks. His mother was trying to keep him from these two boys that died last night. I'm not sure, but I think they had ugly plans. He wouldn't have had time to do this."

"Why would they let you in? Are you an attorney too?"

"No, I'm a translator. I speak Syrian. I've been doing that with Susan Hamilton's group since they arrived. I can help his attorney."

"I've been meaning to ask about that. Anyway, since he has no money, he'll get a court appointed defender. Let me see if I can find out who it is. They should have one by now."

She made a few calls and came back with a name and a phone number. "Erica Miller is with the public defender's office. Give me your number, and I'll text you her contact information. You'll never get her on the phone. Let me get you in."

"That would be very kind of you, I don't know how this system works. He's a very scared boy right now, and he needs a friend."

She, Bradley and Yosef went up the stairs and into the county jail. Once inside she asked reception to speak with Sheriff Ward.

The Receptionist looked at her amazed and said, "He's not taking calls or appointments right now. Give me your name . . . "

"I'm Jacqueline Hyatt with WWNS news. He'll see me."

"Ma'am I've been given very specific instructions, no visitors or phone calls right now."

"I've got a translator for the Syrian suspect. He needs to see Erica Miller, the suspect's PD."

The receptionist punched a few keys on her switchboard and said, "Someone will be here soon to take you back."

After about fifteen minutes, an officer came out looking for Ms. Hyatt. She stood up from the lobby chairs. "Right here, officer."

"Erica Miller sent me out here for the translator."

"I'm coming to."

"No ma'am, only the translator. No press now."

Jackie must've known it was a long shot. She bit her lip and told José, "Go ahead, let me know what you find out." She pointed a finger at him. "I get the exclusive story."

"I will, if I can."

He went back with the officer to a small, clinical interrogation room where he found Hamsa scared to death, along with Erica Miller. She didn't look much better. He was dressed in an orange jail outfit. She wore a brown, two-piece, pinstriped suit with a beige blouse and matching pocket square. She didn't look much older than Hamsa. This was going to be a long day.

CHAPTER 39

Thursday morning arrived and Da Wyz stepped outside on his walled patio to enjoy the morning air. His pledge to move families up the hill was in full swing now. *They moved five in March alone. Reggie tells me the fund is holding up well, and we can move at least two dozen out by the end of the summer if we wanted to. I agreed with him, though we should slow down some.*

He could now appreciate how good God was. He remembered the scripture "Peace I leave with you, my peace I give you."

The peace beyond understanding his mother knew in her last days, he now enjoyed. Sleep came at night now without all the self-medication, regardless of what happened in the Biz. Many didn't appreciate that the Biz was going legit now. They would emphasize the river freight business that, up to now, he just saw as a good front to dispose of bodies. Now it held the key to going straight. *It takes a while to remove the illegal, but I'm gonna do it. Not everyone wants to be legit. There was more money in drugs, protection, and prostitution.*

Jeremiah recalled a conversation he had with Tony and Joseph the day before.

> "Deion's a problem for me. He was my right hand for so much of the success we enjoyed. Now, he doesn't like this. He won't listen to me about the Lord either. I guess I can't

blame him, he had to change a lot. Nobody likes that. He's getting fed up with going legit. But Deion's a good soldier too. He'll stay in line."

"Are you sure? He's a dangerous man. If he's unhappy he can stir up a lot of trouble," Reverend Tony said.

"I believe in him Rev. He'll come around. Likes the money. If he gets his money he'll be fine. Keeps him in fine-looking women. I don't know how Deion attracts so many beautiful women."

"Mario's a different story altogether. He enjoys busting heads and could care less what for. He likes being feared. Not sure how Mario's gonna last. Not sure what I can do about Mario, if I want him to go. That one will be delicate."

"The Master will find a way for you. It's a long road back from where you were. You've made great strides, but many want to see you fail. I'm convinced you'll succeed and make Carlisle a better place now that you're working to restore it," Joseph said.

"Thank you, Joseph. That means a lot coming from you. I can't tell you how much our talks have changed me. You've been a great example to me. You've been a wise counselor, for the short time I've known you. I look forward to learning more from you. Carlisle is better because the Lord sent you here."

"Let's all continue to pray about it and see what happens next."

Da Wyz went back inside and kissed Miranda with an intentional passion he hadn't shown since they were newlyweds. He enjoyed being near his daughters and loved seeing them off to school these days. He would even take them if the school didn't get nervous about him and his entourage showing up. They were all beautiful. *Miranda still looks like she did when we met ten years ago. No, even better. The girls never knew what daddy did. Now I can tell them when they get older and I can tell them what God did in my life. Someday they'll understand.*

As Da Wyz stepped out of his house to head to the office, Deion was waiting. "Good morning Deion," he said with a smile.

Deion tipped his head in greeting and opened the rear door of the limo. Da Wyz slipped in, and Deion closed it behind him. He got in the front seat next to the driver. Deion answered the phone as they drove away.

The limo drove onto Commonwealth Avenue, and crossed Ninth Street, and a dump truck slammed into the front of the limo at full speed from the side street. Da Wyz watched it all in slow motion. He could see the front airbags deploy. He saw the side airbags deploy also. He didn't have his seatbelt on so he was held in place by the spinning of the limo for a moment while glass and other loose items swirled around the inside. He slammed to the floor when the spinning stopped, disoriented and stunned.

The impact killed the driver. Deion was unconscious or worse.

Da Wyz tried to shake the cobwebs from his brain, but he knew the truck hit them on purpose. *Surprised they hit the front of the limo instead of the side. More likely to get me in the first round that way.* After a fast prayer, he flipped down the armrest near him. He had a small handgun in there. It was still in place and loaded–he hoped.

He got back into the seat and saw them coming now. Three guys, wearing masks and descending around the now totaled limo. The windows were gone on the driver's side and Da Wyz was trying to get his door open when the first shot fired. It hit him just below his left shoulder blade while he tried to get out of the door. It passed through his torso and lodged in the door upholstery with a thud. The place of impact went numb, like it did the other times he'd been shot. The pain didn't get him, but the impact did. At last he got the door open when the second shot sailed by his ear.

He spun out of the car low toward the rear tire. He checked the gun. It was loaded and he waited to catch his breath. *Sucker must've caught me in the lung.* Still stunned from the impact of the truck and now the impact of the bullet, he couldn't point the gun with any accuracy.

He had them make his gun loud so that in the event it ever came to this, the shots would spook whoever approached. Wobbling to his feet, he wanted to just shoot in the direction, but now as a believer, he didn't want to hit bystanders. He continued to pray while he got up. He heard another shot and felt it hit him in the lower right side when he turned to shoot. He saw another shooter coming around the other side of the car, the situation now dire.

All of a sudden, Deion's door swung open and took the second shooter off his feet. He went down and his gun went sprawling up the street when he hit the ground. Deion came out shooting. He shot erratically due to the blood flowing from the head wounds. With one shooter down, Deion turned to fire on the first one, and the third shooter hit Deion from the front of the car. Three shots, only one caught him around the shoulders. He went backward and fell.

Da Wyz got one moment to square himself before he fired. He saw the third shooter, too far away for a good shot. He decided to find the first. He swung his body toward shooter number one, but not fast enough. The first shooter fired twice, hitting Da Wyz in the face. It shattered jaw and teeth. The impact made him lurch toward Deion now motionless on the pavement.

As he fell, he hit the street hard, but it seemed like he was being guided to rest by a gentle hand. The second shooter got back up and pulled a second pistol from his ankle holster. He shot Da Wyz too.

He didn't feel those last couple of shots, but he could see them while he seemed to drift away. "God forgive them," he heard himself say, although no one could hear him.

The sirens began to sound in the background, and the shooters scurried away. They knew Da Wyz was dead. Target accomplished.

As the cops arrived, emergency vehicles were called for the wounded. Various cadences of sirens were now heard rushing to the scene.

Jackie got the call from the newsroom, grabbed Bradley, and headed straight to Commonwealth and Ninth Street.

✠ ✠ ✠

Reverend Tony got a call from Miranda Michaels. "They killed him, Reverend. They killed Jeremiah today on Commonwealth Avenue. They shot him like a dog in the street," she said, whimpering then sobbing.

Tony scrambled to his car to go to Jeremiah's house and comfort the new widow.

※ ※ ※

Jackie, now on the scene with all the police, could see the limo, but couldn't get close.

She sought Officer Jim. He knew this beat better than any, and he had been a good source of information in the past.

"It's developing. Looks like two dead and one in critical condition. Looks like a professional hit," Jim said.

She recognized Da Wyz license tag and limo and put things together fast.

"Was this Da Wyz's limo?"

"I can't say anymore until the official news conference later. But you're a smart lady."

※ ※ ※

José watched the news at the restaurant after the morning rush because no one left a Carlisle Guardian behind, plus he liked to see Jackie in action. He sipped a cup of coffee thinking about Pastor Rich's ouster and now Hamsa's arrest. He saw Jackie on the scene reporting from a street corner. The banner beneath her said "Three shot in morning commute." Then a picture of Jeremiah on the screen with "Da Wyz" under his smiling face.

"Dear Lord, no, please not him too. He was doing such good; he could do so much more for this city, for your kingdom. Please not him."

He got closer to the TV and turned it up so all could hear.

Jackie held her earpiece to be sure she heard it right from the producer. "There were two killed. We have confirmation that one of the victim's is Jeremiah Michaels also known by many as Da Wyz. The other was Matthew Wilson, his driver. We can release these names now because the next of kin have been notified. The third man in the car was Deion Griffin who is in critical condition at University Hospital. It appears to be a well organized hit that was . . . "

José didn't want to hear any more. He felt sick. The room swirled around him. He looked for Ramone. He found him in the back doing some inventory counts. "I need to go for today."

"How long; who's going to cover for you?"

"I need to go, I'll not be back for a while. I need to go. Find Carlos or Diego to cover lunch and dinner. Numbers are on the board. I'll be in touch."

Ramone looked at him with his usual smile but didn't say anything else. José could see confusion on his face.

José grabbed his jacket and went out the door. He wasn't walking anywhere in particular but he had to walk. He had to think. He had to pray. *Do you want me to raise him is that why he died? Talk to me! Please!*

"Why God! Why him? Why now?"

He meandered the streets not paying much attention to the traffic when he crossed an intersection. He didn't see the oncoming large red pick up until it was almost on top of him. The driver, looking up from his phone, didn't see José until there were just a few feet separating them. José turned and held up his hand. Immediately, the engine stopped and the pickup lurched to a halt. José just kept walking.

The driver was shocked, and thanks to his seat belt, was uninjured. He tried to restart the truck, but the engine wouldn't turn over. José knew that it would never start again. He left with truck and driver in the middle of the intersection.

José walked on until he found himself at St. Francis Church. He stepped in to pray. The prayers wouldn't come. The pain of loss now was too searing and fresh. All he could think was how he watched a man be born again in front of him. He saw Jeremiah transform. He could feel the Spirit take him, on that cold day a couple of months ago. The power moved when people relocated up the hill out of poverty's grip. The man was trying to make a new name for himself for God's glory.

"How could you let this happen? It was all going so well? Aren't you in Rich's church? What about a poor scared young man? What's next? The plan is coming apart."

He kneeled in silence, defeated. Weeping for his friends. Knowing he brought this on them. Knowing he couldn't help them anymore. Knowing he must go, before more people are destroyed, while evil seeks those close to him. Convinced he caused the gang wars now and so many were being killed. Innocents and guilty. Knowing there is no mercy now.

Now, he spoke out loud to the Master, "I am done with this place, Lord. Please take me away from here. Take me anywhere else. They're beyond help. They won't listen to me. They won't listen to you. The prejudices are too set. The evil too rampant. Best to let them destroy each other and take me elsewhere. Please don't make we watch this. I can't bear to watch it again."

Father Menendez saw someone wringing his hands and weeping at the altar. He approached the man and, to his shock, saw José. "What's wrong my brother? What has brought you, of all people here in this state?"

Like so many others, José knew the good Father wouldn't understand all that was happening. He spoke in a simmering and deliberate tone. "Just leave me alone, Father. Let me be. I must wrestle with this demon alone. Nothing you can do."

"May I pray with you, my brother? I'll stay here until you're better."

José looked at the Father with great rage in his heart. He yelled, "I said leave me alone! I must do this alone! I am alone!"

The force of the outburst knocked the Father backward. He balanced himself and backed away. Two sisters nearby saw what happened and came to assist. The Father waved them over then walked toward them. He asked that they pray for José and for the expulsion of whatever demon now tormented him.

⁂

After fervent prayer on his part, the Father checked back about thirty minutes later and didn't see him at the altar any longer. He still repeated a prayer for José's rescue.

Father Menendez texted Pastor Rich and Reverend Tony to let them know: "Just left José. He's in a dark place. I don't know the reason, but José needs prayer. He wouldn't accept my help. Evil is on the attack."

"Where is he now?" Tony asked.

"I don't know," the Father replied. "He may be at his boarding house."

"Sounds like he needs some time. This must be about the murder today or maybe the bombing. I'll drop by his place later to check on him. I'm with Miranda Michaels now. Pray for her also. She lost her husband today in the violence on Commonwealth," Tony said.

Pastor Rich saw the text traffic and began to pray for his friends. He didn't know what would happen next in his own life. However, he could still pray for a friend in need. He texted back asking to stay informed.

José was now back in his room. "We've done this before. I know it. God, you don't owe me an explanation. You're always reaching out to us and teaching us lessons. Surely, I don't need to go through this after two thousand years . . . after all I've done for your glory.

"Are you in control? Are you good? How can a man who turned his life around be killed like this? He was your witness. Won't you even protect your witness? Why Lord? Where are you in this? Are you sleeping? Are you in control? Where are you? How can I follow you, if this is what happens when I do? I seek to bring your peace and comfort not killing and pain. How can I convince others to follow, if this is what happens? How do we go forward? Lord, don't make me watch this? I can't bear it again. I must leave this place."

José's blood pressure was so elevated now from this torment that his nose began to bleed. He didn't care. It just bled all over the rug in his room, while he knelt before the Master. He struggled for hours. The people in other rooms in the boarding house heard his cries as evening came. Some were scared at the noise and the volume.

Maria decided to offer him some dinner in his room. She knocked, but then felt she needed to leave. She put the tray by the door and said, "José, your dinner is here. Eat please, señor. Eat."

José didn't want to eat; he didn't want to be near anyone. He remembered times like this and each time seemed to relive itself again. The demons of the mind of his memories all crashed around him. Memories of ones who had passed away before Da Wyz on his missions . . . memories of friends betrayed for doing the right thing . . . memories of those falsely accused who would be convicted. They all seemed to flash in full color before him. Their faces still vivid in front of him, like he just saw them yesterday instead of so many years ago. He collapsed onto the bed from lack of nourishment and loss of blood.

In his dreams the torment continued.

By some miracle, Deion, while put out of action, did not die. Mario took over control of the Biz. He wasn't the executive that Da Wyz was, so operations continued to slip. He had new gang leaders because of the war with the VM gangs. The new gang leaders and their captains started to do whatever they wanted. The police began to crack down on the illegitimate Biz while it started to deteriorate from within. The Mayans also squeezed much of the profitable business over toward Villa Maya. New alliances had to be formed. New leaders had to emerge.

CHAPTER 40

José awoke with a start to the vibration of his mobile phone ringing. He shook the cobwebs from his head and made his way to the night table where the phone gyrated.

"Ola."

"José, this is Jackie. Is that you?"

"Si, ah yes, it's me."

"I tried to reach you at the restaurant this morning, but Ramone said you were out. He said you were in a bad place yesterday. I hope you're feeling better."

"Not much better yet. Unless you tell me all I heard yesterday was fake news."

"You know I don't do fake news, my friend."

"So, no, not much better. Any word on Hamsa?"

"He's still being held without bail, in solitary, for his protection. That's what I'm calling for. I want to hear what happened in the interrogation room earlier. I would've done it yesterday but with the whole Wyz deal happening, I didn't have time. Are you well enough to meet me for some lunch in an hour or so?"

José checked the clock and noticed it was after ten. *I must've been exhausted yesterday.* He looked out the window at the sunshine and thought about other sunny days in far more beautiful places.

"Hello, José, you still there? Look, I got you into see Hamsa, you owe me a story."

"I guess I do. Give me the place and the time and I'll be there. Not Restaurant Tapas please."

"I'll come by and pick you up. We can go someplace downtown."

He remembered the last woman who gave him a ride and thought about turning her down. *Maybe if I had accepted Susan's invitation back then, my friends would've been spared.*

He did want to see Jackie and he did need some information about what else was happening in town. "Come by around 11:30, so we can beat the crowds."

He gave his address and hung up. He noticed he had other missed calls too from Ramone, Tony, Father Menendez, Amena, and Erica Miller. He decided to get cleaned up before he had any further conversations. It took a while to clean things after all the blood. He did the best he could with what he had and made himself presentable. A shower and shave. A new man, he mocked himself in the mirror. *Perhaps it's time for some conversation and a different perspective.*

She picked him up in a late model white SUV. She was dressed for spring on camera. "You look very bright and refreshing this morning," he said, when he got in. He was in jeans and a burgundy striped shirt. The car smelled like Jackie's perfume. It had the scent of a friend.

"Thank you, Señor Chef. I wish I could say the same for you. You don't look so good my friend. Have you been sick? Too much spicy food?" She smiled trying to lighten his mood.

He looked into those delightful hazel eyes. They had a turquoise tone today. Even that didn't cheer him. "I'm in a dark place right now. Much I've worked these many months to achieve has come apart, in just a few short days."

"Wow, you weren't kidding. This is gonna be a barrel of laughs."

Sardonic Jackie. Please be kind. I need a tender ear now. "Where are we going for lunch?"

"It's on the station, but the budget is limited. There is an all-you-can-eat sushi place in the BNS building. Is that OK?"

"Yes, that sounds good."

She parked in the deck, and they walked over. "They validate, if you eat here."

They were seated opposite each other, in a quiet booth, with a dark tabletop and faux candle on one side. Bottles of soy sauce nearby. One each, regular and low sodium. They each ordered various types of sushi along with fried rice. Jackie pulled out her phone and stylus to signal the beginning of the interview.

"This is a question that has bugged me since our Valentine's dinner back in February. How does a chef from Villa Maya speak Syrian?"

"I grew up in the middle east. Semitic languages are similar, although dialects do vary."

"So, you're an Arab?"

"No, I'm the other one."

"You're a Jew."

"Yes, that's how I was born. I've been reborn a Christian and try to follow the Master now."

"I think I know this part. He leads you all over to help you do good, etc."

The plates of sushi rolls arrived, and each went through the required ritual of creating a custom soy sauce and wasabi bath to compliment the food.

As he finished with his sauce, he took a bite of his eel roll. He enjoyed the sensation of dining and paused to let it register. Then he continued his explanation. "The Master used to lead me. Now, I'm not so sure. I came here to help clear the hate and stop the killing. To show the Master's love to those who'll listen. Now, I find that nothing I've done has made any difference at all. In fact, I think I made it worse. Jeremiah's dead; who knows what will happen to Carafe Homes now. My young friend, Hamsa, is accused of terrorism. Two boys are dead who were full of hate. Gang members are being killed in a gang war the conversion of Da Wyz helped start. My friend Pastor Rich is being removed from his leadership role by a renegade group of haters, too. I've caused too much pain in this place. I need to go."

Jackie finished a piece of a tuna roll and pointed at him with her chopsticks.

"So, you're facing some resistance, and now you're going to run. You didn't strike me as the type to back down from a fight. I thought that's what you were picking all along."

"I don't run often, but I try to pick fights I can win. This one seems hopeless. Carlisle is lost to me."

At that comment, Jackie's tone changed in a marked way. She cocked her head to one side and moved from sympathetic friend to defender of her city. "Look José, or whatever name you're calling yourself today, this is the real world. If you push powerful people, they're going to push back. What's the old saying, *an eye for an eye*? If you're not ready to play in the adult version of this game, you're right, you should go. This place has ugliness no question, but it's not all evil. Right now, there's a boy in jail who needs a friend. His only one is planning on leaving town. There's an initiative that's working for affordable housing, that was your idea. It needs leadership now. Yet, you're planning on leaving town. The Pastor Rich thing is news to me, but if it is so, you have a friend who followed your instructions. Who is now in need. Yet you're leaving town. There's even a news lady who started to believe again in the goodness we all have in us, because of your message of hope." She swallowed hard. "Yet, you have no hope. I guess this was all a foolish dream. Now, it's time for the dreamer to wake up and face reality. Looks like you don't like the alarm call. Time to decide, José, Yosef, Joseph, Justus, are you going to play or run? I think you need to suck it up, buttercup."

At that, she took another bite of sushi.

José looked down at his plate, not very hungry. Her comments stung. He didn't speak.

"So, if you're leaving town, I want to know what happened in the interrogation room before you go."

José spoke about Hamsa's interview for a few minutes. Lunch went on in a distant, professional way for a time. After he could stand it no longer, he said, "I gave you what you asked for. Our business is complete. We're even now. I'll take the bus back to VM; I'm sure you have many stories to chase."

"José, I don't want us to end this way. I spoke harshly but . . . "

He raised his hand to stop her, "Jackie, thank you for lunch, but I must go now. There are no other words we need to speak."

On the journey back to Maria's boarding house, he thought about all she had said. He didn't have much fight left in him. His hope drained away. She spoke truth, perhaps not in love, but truth nonetheless. He realized that today was Good Friday. He didn't want to see any of his *allies*, so he made his way to a Tenebrae service at a Methodist Church up the hill. Tenebrae is Latin for *darkness*. That's just what he felt. The service progressed in silence with images of famous paintings of Christ's Passion displayed progressing through the stations of the cross. Paintings by Ciseri, El Greco, Rubens, Caravaggio, Raphael and Velazquez. José remembered when each was unveiled for the first time. The ever-increasing darkness of the service remembering the crucifixion suited his mood well. Remembering the crucifixion and all that led up to it, was just like watching it again. The betrayal, the arrest, the fleeing of friends into the night, the fake trials, the Roman governor washing his hands. And worst of all, the crowds shouting "Crucify him!" He wept for Jesus, his Master, for himself, for Carlisle, for so many consumed by the darkness of hate and fear he had known through the ages. A darkness that was tangible tonight.

He recalled what the Master said to Peter on that beach so long ago:

"If it is my will that he remain until I come, what is that to you?"

Now, two thousand years later, he heard the Master's voice speak to him again from the depth of his darkness. "Joseph, Joseph Barsabbas, feed my lambs . . . "

SUNDAY IS ON THE WAY

I watched as they made you carry your cross,
I know now you would never have put it down.
You provided the way back through your loss,
It was so sadistic to make you wear their crown.

I wept helpless as you struggled by
I didn't understand why it had to be this way.
You were the Christ not a criminal to try,
This showed the worst of us in the light of the day.

Dear Father why must he suffer so?
Surely another way can be found.
I watched as your blood dripped on the road,
Closed my eyes until I heard the cross hit the ground.

The soldiers cleared the path as you stumbled along.
They grabbed another to shoulder the load.
He tried to turn away get lost in the throng,
But with threats they dragged him back in the road.

To Golgotha they led all the long way.
They thought they would kill you but we both know now
You gave your life willingly this day.
Despite my despair, it would be better somehow.

The Darkness upon us
Despite the noon hour,
I could feel it engulf us
Dark ways seem to have so much power.

The crucifixion so cruel, so bloody, so brutal,
Yet your concern was for those nearby,
The ones who believed their hope now futile—
The soldiers, the thieves, your mother and I.

I wanted it to end long before it was finished
This darkest of days.
At the end it sounded like even your hope diminished
But Sunday is on the way.

ACKNOWLEDGMENTS ALONG THE JOURNEY

In 2016, I found myself asking God what to do from here. A man in his fifties looking for a new challenge. Looking for where God wanted to use me over the next many years. Being impatient by nature (God is still working on me here), I wanted to know exactly what it was as soon as possible. He made me successful in many endeavors, and I liked the comfort of knowing the complexities of my chosen profession. A word of warning to us all. Don't ask God that question unless you want to be challenged way outside of your own self-reliance.

After many hours spent in prayer over weeks and months, listening for the Spirit to guide, the message finally came. It sounded crazy to an independent man with no formal training and little experience.

"Write a Story." That was all He gave me to start with. I always enjoyed reading and did a lot of non-fiction writing for my business career. There is power in story to explain tough concepts to others. However, I wasn't qualified to write fiction. The Justus and Mercy journey began there.

Angela Haigler taught me creative writing in her classes at our local community college, and I began to write and have others critique me. God's pleasure coursed through me as my characters came to life in scenes and action. The learning had only begun. My prayers turned to the story the Spirit had in mind.

I live near uptown Charlotte and one night in September, helicopters hovered outside my window with spotlights on a riot in the heart of the city protesting the killing of a black man by local law enforcement.

The flash bangs were visible from my balcony, and the fear of so many nearby was palpable.

Looking back on novels I enjoyed over the years, the writings of Robert Parker, Lee Child and others that used a recurring character to tell their stories always interested me. I needed to create one of those myself. Not sure if it's okay to admit but, I also was an avid comic book fan growing up and loved the serial nature of so many of the stories.

During the previous few years, the Lord led me to spend a lot of time reading Christian non-fiction as well. Dating back to the early church writings of St. Augustine, St. Francis of Assisi, Brother Lawrence and St. John of the Cross. He continued to guide me through the Protestant writing of the early church by Martin Luther, John Calvin, John Wesley. The writings of modern-day authors are equally insightful, the wisdom shared by CS Lewis, Dietrich Bonhoeffer, RC Sproul, Richard Foster, Ravi Zacharias, Timothy Keller, Gregory Boyle and Richard Stearns. I hope that you see their influence throughout the story. I owe a special debt to Lewis, Bonhoeffer, Foster, and Boyle for the impact they had.

Kim Love Stump, a local author who wrote fantasy novels for young adults, met with me and gave me some of her wisdom. She also introduced me to Maureen Ryan Griffin, who reviewed my early work and gave me hard but much needed advice. Her review and critique of the poetry in this novel was invaluable.

My church family at Carmel Baptist Church also has impacted this project as well. Pastor Alex Kennedy's God-given messages inspire many concepts in the novel. The Spirit gifted me with teaching, so I taught Bible studies at Carmel for many years, shepherded by Jeremy Amick, a fellow writer who told me about the Blue Ridge Mountain Christian Writers Conference. The conference in May 2017 became my self-imposed deadline to finish the story. Several published authors reviewed some of the chapters and told me that it was a fascinating story but written badly. (They said it nicer than that.) Then, Davis Bunn told the group we needed to write for 10,000 hours before our work would be any good. I pitched the novel to many at the conference, and was told the same thing, "You're not ready yet." Discouragement set in. I was a writer, not a rewriter and shelved the project.

My lovely bride of 40 years, Janie, agreed to read the story and give me her thoughts. She has a great copy editor's eye and did her best to get through the very rough draft.

The novel sat for two years untouched. God told me to write a story and I did. He didn't tell me to publish it. But we all know, God doesn't leave us alone when he gives a charge. He empowers and will not be ignored.

At a church sacred assembly in October 2019, it became clear to me, I was going to become a rewriter after all. I took Janie's critique and reread and rewrote the entire book. Adding many details and plot twists not considered on the first pass.

I sent it to family who tried their best to get through it. Two of my brothers, Richard and Ray, finally did. Ray took it upon himself to be content editor, and we often spoke about improving it. He was recently released after many years in prison and gave me good insight into gang mentality. His enthusiasm for his life in Christ and new-found freedom was inspiring. He showed me the characters through his eyes.

Using connections and content from the Blue Ridge Conference and at Janie's continued advice, I found an editor, Karen Saari whose insights changed the story and made it read like a book. She challenged in ways no one had to that point and made the story so much better throughout 2020. She also showed me that this was two novels, not one.

There were others that gave insight along the way, missionary Jackson Landham gave invaluable insights into the Syrian Kurds sections. To be sure this was fair and balanced, I spent time with the Charlotte Chapter of Black Lives Matter who helped me see the world through their experiences. The healing the city tried to bring about through the churches after the 2016 riot, showed me my bias, but also gave me hope that the Bride of Christ must build the bridges to transform us.

Finally, after many rejected book proposals during 2021, it was time to look at partnership publishing. There were many options, but I felt led to EABooks Publishing, having enjoyed the lectures of Cheri Cowell from the Blue Ridge Conference. I appreciate Jim Watkins and his kind way as we began the process, and was blessed by the cover design and other work of Robin Black. Rebecca Ford shepherded and encouraged me throughout the EAB process.

In the end, it was God's prompting that led me to write this. If you enjoyed it give Him the honor; if not, it's all my fault.

To God, the Father

Jesus, the Son

and the Holy Spirit

three in one

be the glory for this.

I hope you enjoyed the story of the tragedy and triumph of Carlisle, Joseph, and Jackie. It's been a wonderful journey so far.

Please enjoy the conclusion of this story in my next novel:

Love One Another—Stories of Justus and Mercy Part 2

Made in the USA
Monee, IL
12 June 2023

35558906R00173